WHISPERS of FATE

THE EARTH REMEMBERS, AND SO SHALL YOU.

SHATTERED BLOODLINES TRILOGY BOOK I

Whispers of Fate – Shattered Bloodlines, Book 1

1st Edition.

Story concept and text © 2024 by Urriah Wright.

Cover design © 2024 Anastasia Haberling.

Editing, print preparation, formatting, back cover summary, and final cover design © 2024 Hayden Trull and © 2025 Staback Author Services.

Books may be ordered through popular, online retailers, Page Turner Books, Inc.'s online store, or by contacting the publisher at:

Page Turner Books, Inc.
222 N. Lafayette St., Suite 11
Shelby, NC 28150

Visit our website at www.ptbooksinc.com or contact us via email at contact@ptbooksinc.com. Page Turner Books, Inc.'s name and logo are copyright of Page Turner Books, Inc.

Audiobook ISBN: 978-1-965788-76-9
iBook ISBN: 978-1-965788-77-6
Kindle ISBN: 978-1-965788-78-3
Hardcover ISBN: 978-1-965788-79-0
Paperback ISBN: 978-1-965788-80-6

Printed in the United States of America. First Printing: July 2025

Library of Congress Control Number: 2025932750

ATTENTION CORPORATIONS AND ORGANIZATIONS:

Most Page Turner Books, Inc.® books are available at quantity discounts with bulk purchase for educational, business, or sales promotional use. For information, please call or write:

Special Markets Department, Page Turner Books, Inc.
222 N. Lafayette St., Suite 11, Shelby, NC 28150
Telephone: (702) 606-1775

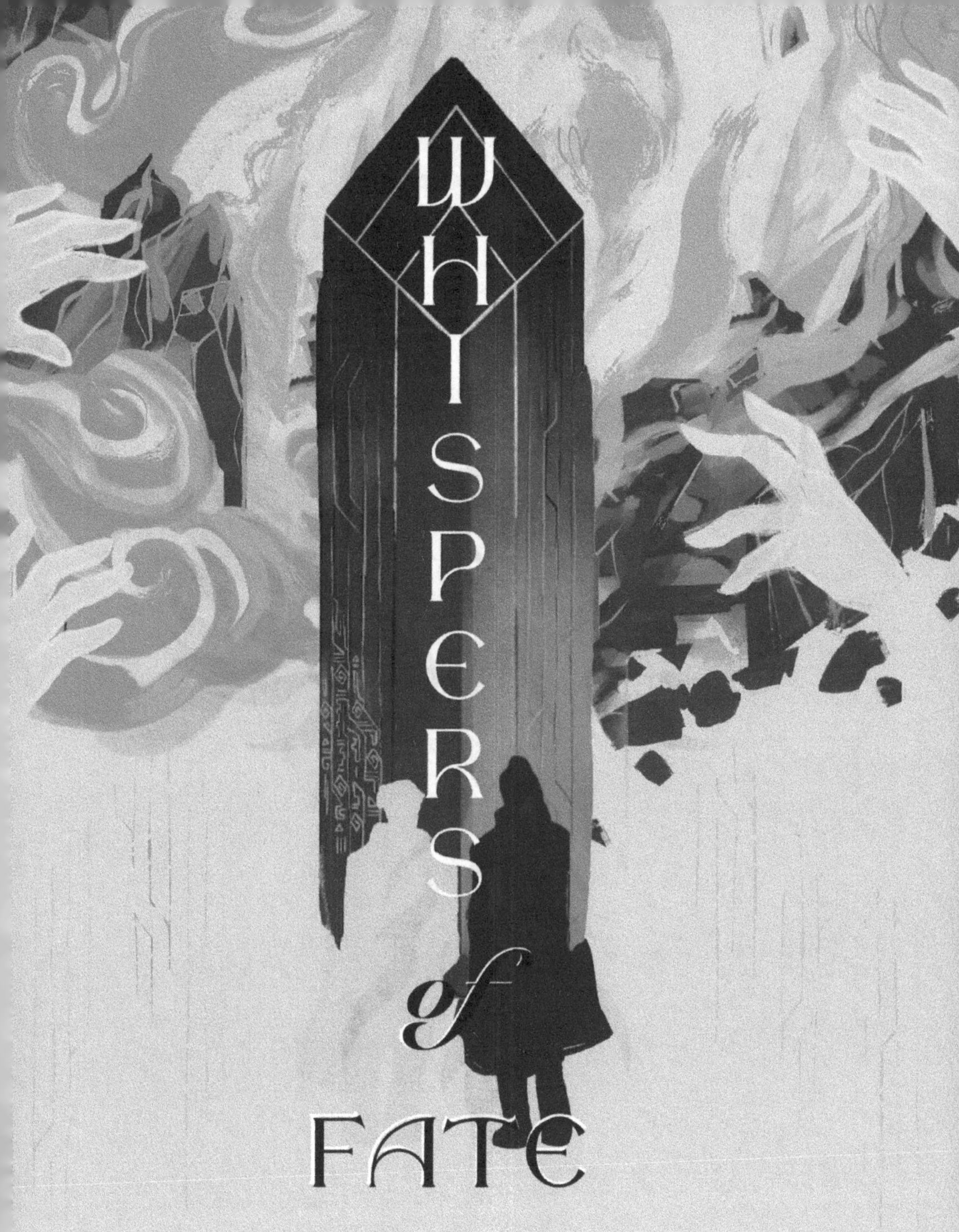

WHISPERS of FATE
URRIAH WRIGHT
SHELBY, NC
PAGE TURNER BOOKS INC.
EST. 2012
USA

DEDICATIONS

To my best friend and brother, Reagan, for being the spark behind so many of the ideas that found their way onto these pages. Your imagination helped breathe life into this world.

To Sloane, for creating the space I needed to dream, focus, and finish. Your support built the walls around this work when everything else felt too loud.

To Hayden, for guiding me through the chaos of story when I didn't know which way to turn. Your insight made the impossible feel manageable.

And to Stephany, my heart, my anchor, my constant. Thank you for being the crutch I leaned on in the slow days and the too heavy ones. I could never have done this without you.

I love you all.

PROLOGUE

*They say the stars are distant fires, cold and careless. They
lie.*

*The stars are the last sparks of its eyes, still watching through
the veil of rot and root.*

The rivers run in the vein lines of its limbs.

*The mountains are the calloused knuckles of a hand that tried
once, once, to rise again.*

The world is not alive.

It is what remains of what once was.

A god, yes. But not the kind with temples or stories.

Not the kind that ever spoke in tongues or flame.

This god was formless-
a being of presence, of weight, of hunger, and dream.

And it died.

It died screaming.

And from that scream came the first magic.

The Magi? They do not know.

*Or worse, they do. And they build their towers on the bones
anyway.*

Every spell cast is a wound reopened.

Every rune drawn is a scar retraced.

We walk across its flesh.

We drink from its lungs.

We live in its grave.

*And still... sometimes, if you press your ear to the right stone-
not the smooth ones, no, the deep ones, the hollow ones-
you can hear it.*

Not breathing.

CHAPTER 1

Tito let his fingers drag through the water and watched the ripples curl outward.

He could feel it. The way the tide moved, the weight of the ocean pressing against his skin like an unseen force. It had always been this way, more than a fisherman's intuition, something deeper, something innate.

Ro sat beside him, lazily kicking their feet against the wood, head tipped back as they stared at the sky. They sighed loudly.

"We have been out here forever! You should just do it, Tito."

Their voice was playful, but hushed, like a shared secret.

"Dad won't notice."

Tito glanced up at their father.

Eryx was a tall man with a strong frame, built from years of hauling nets and navigating the currents of Ethyrae's shores. His dark hair was cropped short, the salt of the sea already beginning to silver his temples. It was his presence, however, an intangible *something* that he carried, that was greater than any physical attribute. On his boat one was in capable hands, safer than any navigator in all of Valcarta. Tito often thought his father could take notice of everything, even if he wasn't looking. But Eryx was distracted at the moment as he focused on tying the netting between his calloused fingers. That weathered face was pointed in a completely different direction.

Ro was right. If there was ever a time to do it, it was now.

Tito hesitated, but the weight of Ro's expectant stare won out. He liked showing off for them.

In order to succeed, Tito had to become the water. It wasn't enough just to shape it, nor to bend it, but let it into himself. To use it, he had to let go. That was the first lesson his little tricks had taught him. Water resisted when pushed, but it welcomed when invited. It lived inside him, in the slow pull of his breath, in the way his thoughts could drift like the tide.

First, he had to loosen his grip on his own body, let go of the rigid lines that made him solid. Water had no sharp edges. It slipped through cracks, seeped into spaces unseen, found the weakest point and poured through.

He took a breath. Deep. Controlled.

Then he took another, slower this time, deeper still. He had to let his heartbeat find a different rhythm, one that wasn't his own.

The trick wasn't pulling water, it was syncing with it. He had to feel the water inside him, the currents beneath his ribs, and blur the line between flesh and sea. Only then could he ask things of it, only then did the water answer.

Draw in. Release. Draw in. Release.

Like a breath beneath the waves, the current twisted. Not aggressively, not unnaturally, but in a way that felt right. The fish swam straight into the waiting nets.

Ro let out a stifled laugh as the boat lurched slightly with the weight of their unexpected haul.

"Tito, you got so much," they whispered, eyes gleaming.

Tito grinned despite himself, securing the last of the fish with a satisfied tug.

Eryx turned and stretched his arms as he finally glanced at the net. His brows furrowed at the sheer weight of it.

"Damn near enough to last the week," he muttered as he hauled the net up with practiced ease.

Too much ease.

Tito felt Ro stiffen beside him. Tense though they were, the amusement could not be stifled.

Eryx studied the load for a long moment, then turned to Tito. The scrutiny in his gaze was heavy.

"How'd you manage this?"

Tito's pulse stuttered. He could lie. Say it was luck, that they had just been in the right place, like he had said before. But their father wasn't a fool.

Tito exhaled.

"I just helped a little. We had been out for half the morning and…" Tito paused, waiting for his dad to chime in.

Silence.

Eryx's expression didn't change as he waited for Tito to come clean.

Tito knew this look.

His father wasn't a man who raised his voice, who shouted or scolded like some of the other fathers in town. His anger was quieter, sharper.

The stillness before a storm.

"I told you not to do that," Eryx said, his voice level.

Tito swallowed, his earlier pride shrank into something tight in his chest.

"I just…"

Eryx moved fast. Faster than Tito expected.

Suddenly, their faces were only inches apart. His dad grabbed his collar, his grip was firm, but not cruel.

"Don't you get it?" Eryx hissed. "What do you think happens when people see something like this? When the wrong people hear about it?"

Tito stared into his father's eyes. He expected anger, but instead, he saw fear. The realization made the pit in his stomach sink.

Eryx released him just as quickly, running a rough hand through his hair. A breath, then another.

Ro had gone completely still, watching the exchange with wide eyes.

Eryx sighed and pinched the bridge of his nose, a level of exhaustion seeping in. He knelt so they were at eye level.

"I know it's in you, Maldito. And I know it's hard to keep it in," he exhaled sharply. "But you have to. You know why?"

Tito nodded. He did know why. Because every year, the Magi sent their scouts.

And every year, they took someone.

A heavy stillness settled over the boat, broken only by the gentle lap of the waves. Their father leaned back as he stared toward the distant coastline, his jaw was now set tight.

"The Magi will be here soon," he muttered as he looked out upon the horizon.

Tito's hands curled into fists.

They came every year. Always in the same season, always with the same promise to test the children, to find those with magic, to take them away to Atheron.

And once they left, they never came back.

The Magi always spoke of Atheron as if it were a dream made real. They came to Ethyrae with their polished boots and embroidered robes, with all kinds of colorful symbols decorating their clothing. Their words were as smooth as the tides that lapped against the shore. They painted the capital as a shining beacon, a place where gifted children could flourish under the finest teachers in all of Valcarta. Atheron, they claimed, was a city of wonder, where magic was not just studied, but perfected, where those with talent could rise above the limitations of a simple village life and become something greater. Their family would never suffer through a poor harvest of vegetables or fish again once they grew as an important part of the council or military.

Tito had believed them.

He was eight when he first learned he could manipulate water, and at first, it felt like a miracle. The way the tide responded to his will, how he could nudge the currents, and push the fish into their nets.

It made him feel powerful.

Special.

The Magi named magic a gift…a calling.

If he had magic, wouldn't they want him in Atheron? Wouldn't they take him away from the smallness of Ethyrae, train him, mold him into someone who could provide for his family?

He was excited to tell his father, but the moment Tito showed him, his father's face paled.

Eryx didn't speak at first. His jaw clenched, his eyes darted across the shoreline as if someone might have seen. Then, in a voice that was lower than a whisper, he grabbed Tito by the arm and spoke in a tone Tito had never heard before.

"Never...Never do that again."

Tito had protested. He didn't understand.

"But, why?" he demanded, confused, and frustrated. "You won't have to be out on the boat all day."

Eryx cut him off with a shake of his head. His grip on Tito's arm was firm.

"You don't know what you're saying," his father murmured. "Promise me, Tito. Promise me you will never show this to anyone. Never use it."

Tito wanted to argue. He wanted to throw a tantrum. This was something good, something treasured.

Why did his dad, of all people, not want this?

He opened his mouth to shout, tears already welling up in his eyes.

But his dad paused, and Tito braced himself, worried that a hit was coming to silence his shout.

Instead, Eryx took his hand and dragged him through the village streets, past the dying light of the evening market, past the curious eyes of their neighbors. They stopped at a small house near the edge of the village. A familiar scent greeted them as they stood.

"Why are we visiting the bread house this late?" Tito asked, bewildered.

His father didn't answer and instead knocked on the door.

Eira appeared shortly after, her hands dusted with flour. The moment she saw them, her expression shifted. Her eyes had fallen quickly onto Tito. Tears welled up before she had even spoken a word.

"He has magic, doesn't he?" she whispered.

Tito froze.

Eryx placed a hand on her shoulder and nodded.

"Tell him," he said softly. "Please."

Eira took a slow, shaky breath as she opened the door wider for the pair to enter. As it shut, her composure dropped, and a wail escaped from her.

Tito flinched at the raw sound of it.

Through her sobs, she told him everything.

Two years ago, she had taught her son, Soren, how to carve the small heating runes she used for her ovens. A simple thing, nothing dangerous, nothing powerful. But it was still magic. And when the Magi came, they happily told him of the skill he possessed in carving.

They took him.

"They wouldn't even let me go with him," she choked out. "My poor little ember was all alone."

She clutched at her apron as if it could anchor her.

"They took him, and that was it. Said it was an honor. Said the queen would see us taken care of. Said…"

Her voice broke as she collapsed against the doorframe.

Eryx caught her before she could fall to the floor, holding her close. She clung to him like a drowning woman.

Tito couldn't move. He felt cold, as if the sea had reached inside him and pulled something out. He remembered now, he saw it happen.

He saw Eira scream in agony, saw her lose every ounce of composure as her only child that she cherished more than her work was ripped out of her arms. He saw Soren, Little Ember, they all called him, as he screamed back. He was taken from the only thing he had ever known so quickly, and without so much as a goodbye.

Eira looked at Tito again. Her gaze pierced right through him.

"He was only six, Tito," she whispered. "Your age at the time. The same as little Ro's now."

Tito's stomach twisted.

The Magi had taken him… and he never came back.

Eira had tried, begged, and written letters, but there had been no response.

It had been ten years now, ten consecutive years, since the Magi had begun taking children from the towns within Valcarta. The town heard the stories from the traders arriving on the big boats in the docks.

Always children.

Always the same promise.

Always the same fate.

Eryx finally pulled away, guiding Tito gently but firmly away from the doorstep.

As they walked back through the village, Tito didn't speak. The excitement was gone.

Ro spoke, their voice unusually quiet, but enough to pull Tito out of his memory.

"You don't think they'd take us, do you?"

Eryx was silent.

Tito already knew the answer.

"They wouldn't have a choice," their father finally admitted. "The moment they know, it's over."

The words sent a chill through Tito that had nothing to do with the sea breeze.

"You're lucky they never found out before," Eryx muttered, rubbing his hands over his face. "And we're going to make sure they never do."

Tito swallowed.

"What if someone slips? What if they hear something?"

Tito internally berated himself. How could he forget what had happened with Soren? They grew and played together daily, but now the only kids the same age in their village were Tito and Ro.

Eryx's mouth set into a grim line.

"Then we run."

The words sat heavy between them.

Ro shifted uncomfortably.

"They wouldn't take us if we said no, would they?"

Eryx didn't answer.

Tito stirred, he and his father hadn't told Ro about Soren, but the solemnity of the villagers when Ro asked about him was enough for Ro to piece together it was nothing good that came of him.

Tito felt his stomach knot. He wanted to believe the world was fair, that people had choices. But the Magi didn't offer choices. And those who disobeyed the queen's decree didn't get second chances.

Eryx finally sighed, shaking his head as if trying to cast away the weight of the conversation.

The storm had passed...for now.

"Let's get back," he muttered. "We've been out too long."

Tito and Ro exchanged a look before pulling in the last of the net. Their father said nothing more as he turned the boat toward home.

CHAPTER 2

Tito stood at the shoreline and watched the sea breathe.

The waves rolled in and out with a soothing consistency. In and out, their foamy edges stretched toward his feet, lingered a moment, then retreated, as if hesitant to claim him. The low tide revealed smooth, dark stones beneath the shifting water. Tito altered his stance and felt the familiar grit of sand under his heels that ground him.

This had always been his place, a stretch of quiet where the water spoke in ripples and whispers.

Morning had arrived slowly in Ethyrae, crept over the world like a careful tide. The first light of dawn painted low hanging clouds with hues of soft gold and pale pink, as if the sky itself had been touched by an artist's gentle hand. It traced over the rooftops, worn smooth by the salt air, and cast long shadows through the narrow streets. The hush before the waking of the village was brief, as always, and would soon give way to creaking boats in the harbor, the chattering fishermen who readied their nets, and the rhythmic call of seabirds that circled above.

Tito clenched his fists as he recovered from his dream…. though, it was less like a dream, and more like a perfect memory.

It had been eight years since that day, four since his father had disappeared. Why was he suddenly dreaming of that so vividly now?

He knew the answer.

The Magi would be in Ethyrae tomorrow. Their yearly visit for him and Ro, since they were the only people who fit the age for the decree.

Tito had spent the last ten years trying to bury his magic. Trying to pretend he was normal, to keep it from surfacing. Of course, he had learned more since then too, mostly from the tradesmen who traveled from the other villages around Valcarta.

Most stories had so many inconsistencies that even he and his sibling knew better than to trust them.

Two years ago, a large boat from the Isles of Serenya docked in Ethyrae on their way to Atheron. Tito and Ro, who had been salting fish nearby, overheard that the Sunlit Empire across the sea was named such because their own actual sun powered the city; yet, many sailors from other boats challenged that claim.

Tito remembered someone from a village whose name he'd long forgotten.

When a dock worker once asked about the sun in that far-off place, the man just laughed and said, "If any city tried to claim the sun for itself, Eliar would smite them in seconds...and he'd be right to."

The sailor touched some kind of amulet as he spoke, as if warding off evil, but Tito wasn't sure what to believe.

Not that it mattered, he wouldn't see it for himself anyways.

Some stories held truth, though, or at least consistency. Tito had a knack for picking out consistencies from the many webs the tradesmen wove over the years. Many regarded the mythologies, slightly altered with each sailor that stepped off the boat to gamble in a game of dice, peruse the fish local to their coast, or just to have a drink. Different aspects were emphasized, other elements were dropped entirely with each individual, but there was always a common seed contained in all.

His favorite was the story of Noctara, the goddess of darkness and oblivion, who stood defiant against five of the divine.

In response, the five gods waged a relentless war upon Noctara and her followers, driving them to the farthest reaches of the world. To ensure her dominion would never rise again, they wove a veil of divine magic, sealing her away in the northernmost reaches of existence. This prison became known in hushed whispers as The Cursed Expanse, a land of shadow and corruption where none who entered ever returned.

Yet not all of her followers fell.

One among them, a former magus of Atheron, slipped through the divine net. His name was Lucerian, the first master of illusion magic. While illusion magic itself wasn't inherently bad, he and his new followers spread throughout Valcarta, twisting the source of this magic into things far darker than the gifts the Runestone was meant to bestow.

The Runestone.

That was another word often on the tongues of travelers. The source of Magic in Valcarta, a magic far older than civilization itself. Those stories were harder to pick out, though. It was said that it played a part in identifying the magical ability in the conscripted children. It was the only true rune writer, the Heart of the World.

"Never go near it, boy," Tito's father had said. "It will bring you nothing but grief. Trust more in your nets and senses than any rock, magical or not."

Still, even if none of the stories were true, Tito had always wanted to catch even a glimpse of it. Especially the glyphs that ran along the edges of the stone, said to be so intricate that people had gone mad at staring at them for too long.

Simple runes themselves were easy to come by. They were everywhere in town. Anyone with a primarca, that is a root of a rune, could carve a rune containing the root and use its magic.

Tito saw the telltale shimmer of energy as he passed the small herb garden of the cottage closest to the beach every day. The plants seemed to grow just a little faster, their leaves brighter and healthier than those left to the elements alone.

Elenna, the old widow who tended the garden, often carved the *Terrem* primarca, a diamond, along with two ruts alongside it into her soil beds. The village trusted in her minor magic to coax life from the earth, especially when the sea winds made it hard for things to grow.

Further down the lane, the faint scent of baking bread wafted through the air, coming from a small home near the market square. Inside, Eira, the village baker, used a different kind of magic. Her primarca, *Ignis,* was a little more ornate, a sharp, angular spiral that started tightly wound at the center and flared outward into a jagged, flame-like arc. Her oven had a mark almost duplicative, except with a second arc.

People didn't talk much about magic here, especially after Eira's son was taken. It existed though in small, practical ways, woven into the tasks of everyday life, at least in the Runes.

Tito sighed, his thoughts always had a habit of racing without end when he let them.

He turned around and let his eyes fall on his home.

Ethyrae was simple and resilient. Its people were shaped by the ocean as surely as the land was, with their faces lined and sun kissed, their hands calloused from ropes and nets, their steps steady against the shifting sands. The village bore the marks of their toil with nets hung like tattered banners from the sides of houses, boats leaned against one another like old friends, and the faint smell of smoked fish clung to the air like a memory.

Tito absently ran a hand over the back of his neck, his fingers brushed against the faint grit of salt that clung to his skin. His dark hair, unkempt and windswept, fell around his face in untamed strands that danced with the morning breeze.

The morning, contrary to his dream, was like countless others he had known. Behind him, the soft hiss of waves curled over the sand and filled the silence, while the foam retreated in shimmering threads. The cool water lapped at his bare feet and ground him in the here and now, yet his mind always wandered. Today felt heavy, the weight of something unnamed pressed faintly against the edges of his thoughts. It wasn't sharp or clear, just a quiet tug, like the pull of a tide beneath calm waters.

This pull had begun to worry him. It was a miracle he and Ro had not been caught over these years. Beyond the Magi, though, were other fears to consider.

He knew the stories of those his age who hid their magic for fear of conscription. Sometimes, their magic grew, never suppressed, until it reached a bursting point.

One story of a boy in the Zeharan Khanit was widely circulated. It was said he destroyed almost three houses in an instant when his earth magic could no longer be contained. This story was one from a desert empire far in the west, but it found its way to his ears, and there were many others like it.

He shook it off for the moment, focusing instead on the small, grounding rituals that had always brought him solace. His gaze fell to the ground, to the scattered detritus of the shore…bits of seaweed, broken shells, and a smooth piece of driftwood. Stooping down, he picked it up, its surface polished to a silky sheen by the years it tumbled in the ocean's embrace. The wood was warm now from the morning sun and fit snugly in his hand as though it had been waiting for him.

Tito turned it over in his fingers as he studied its shape and weight. A faint smile flickered across his lips, unbidden. The driftwood carried him back to simpler times, memories that felt both distant and immediate. Long afternoons alongside his father came to mind, like when they gathered wood for repairs, or mended nets stretched taut in the yard, hands calloused and busy as they worked in companionable silence. Those days had been steady and predictable, their rhythm as unchanging as the tide.

For a moment, the weight that had settled in his chest lifted. He let himself linger in the memory, breathing in the sharp tang of salt in the air, feeling the rough texture of the wood beneath his fingers.

He turned again and let his gaze linger on the horizon, where the sky and sea blurred together in hazy bands of fire and water, indistinct and dreamlike.

That line, distant and unreachable, seemed to promise something beyond the edges of his small world. Somewhere far past it, beyond the sway of the waves and the familiar call of seabirds, lay the Isles of Serenya. Traders who came from there told that, under the goddess Serenya's protection, they lived peaceful lives. They never worried of their harvests failing through winter, or currents that change the migration of fish on a whim, of the Cursed Expanse's threat, or of Atheron.

Atheron.

The very word felt heavy.

The traders said it was vast, its streets paved with stone that glinted under the sun, lined with spires that pierced the clouds. The towers rose higher than the tallest trees of the forest as monuments to power and ambition. Somewhere at its heart was the Runestone, where magic coursed through the city like veins of fire beneath stone, vibrant and alive.

It was a place of transformation…of wonder…of death.

But these were only stories. Grand tales were easy to tell and easier still to exaggerate, spun like nets to catch the imaginations of those who would never leave their quiet villages.

Tito knew what happened to Soren, and that many stories only contained partial truth.

Life in Ethyrae had taught him to value what was tangible, the steady pull of a fishing net, the familiar scrape of wood against stone, the sea breeze that carried with it the scents of salt and home.

The grander the story, the more detached it felt from the rhythm of his reality.

Tito set the driftwood down and stood, brushing the sand from his hands as he turned back toward the waking village. He could hear the faint clatter of boats being prepared for the day's work. The low murmur of voices rose from the market as vendors began to set out their wares.

The village itself was small, barely more than a collection of homes built close to the shore, with a market square at its center and a single dock where the fishing boats came and went with the tides. He let his eyes trace the familiar sights of wooden planks lightened by the sun, stone paths worn smooth by the passage of time, the faint glow of runes carved into doorposts to ward off the occasional storms that battered the coast.

This place, for all its rough edges and quiet simplicity, had been his entire world for as long as he could remember. His father had taught him everything he knew about the sea, about the village, about what it meant to be part of this life. And though his father was gone now, Tito had taken on those same responsibilities without hesitation, just as he had been taught. There was a quiet strength to be found in its routine, in the predictability of the tides and the familiarity of the people who lived here.

Ethyrae was home.

He turned back toward the water, not wanting his thoughts to stream back to what he had just gotten them away from.

His eyes followed the path of a lone fishing boat as it cut through the waves, its sails were full and proud against the backdrop of the morning sky.

Tito laughed, it was silly to have the sails fully open with such heavy winds so early.

He had always found solace in the sea. It was untamed, but there was a certain clarity in its unpredictability, a reminder that not everything could be controlled. The sea had a way of teaching patience, of showing him that some things were worth waiting for. He hadn't used his magic in a very, very long time.

A distant voice pulled Tito from his thoughts.

"Hey!" Espero's voice echoed down the beach, bright and full of energy as usual.

Tito turned to see his sibling jogging toward him, their light brown hair bounced with every step, a grin already spread across their face. Ro had always been the more carefree of the two, their movements quick and light, their enthusiasm boundless.

"You look like you're about to marry the sea," Ro said as they came to a stop, slightly out of breath. "What are you doing, just standing here? Maldito and the sea, sitting in a tree..."

Tito shook his head, a small smile started at the corner of his lips.

"Thinking. Also, my full name? Somebody's in a proper mood today."

Ro rolled their eyes dramatically.

"You're always thinking. It's a nice morning, can't you just enjoy it without worrying about what comes next?"

Tito glanced back out at the horizon, amused, "I am enjoying it."

Ro laughed, "Sure you are."

Their smile softened.

"I heard a couple of traders talking in the market this morning. They said the streets in Atheron glow at night, can you believe that?"

Tito raised an eyebrow.

"Glow? How would magic even make that happen?"

Ro shrugged and kicked at the sand.

"Why not? They're still finding new uses for magic. I hope we can visit it soon. When they, y'know, find whoever is going to be the next Eryon."

Eryon was Atheron's war hero from the time right before Tito and Ro were born. Just as soon as he saved Atheron from losing thousands, he disappeared. The stories about him were so grandiose, stories of him having the power of the gods, that Tito doubted if he ever existed at all.

Tito sighed, leaning his elbow on Ro's shoulder.

"C'mon Ro, that's only a rumor. We don't know what exactly the Magi are looking for. But a promise is a promise, and I promised I would take you there one day. And if there is one thing I do, that is keep my promises. When Barrel arrives tomorrow, we can ask how the situation with the capital is going and plan out a time. Maybe it wouldn't hurt to finally run a trade route there and back."

Ro smiled, happy with the answer, before grabbing Tito's arm.

"We should check out the market before everyone else gets there."

Tito lingered for a moment longer, his gaze fixed on the sea. The waves rolled and sighed, a constant rhythm that seemed to echo his own hesitation. This view had been his anchor for as long as he could remember, and the thought of leaving it behind, even temporarily, felt like unmooring a part of himself.

He drew a deep breath, and the salt filled his lungs, before he finally turned back toward the village.

The market was already alive with activity, the air thick with the mingling scents of freshly baked bread and the briny sea. Vendors bustled about as they arranged wares on sun bleached wooden stalls.

Old man Corin stood by the edge of the docks, setting out his nets with the same deliberate care he'd practiced for decades. His back was bent with age, his movements slower than they had once been, but his hands were as steady as the tides he had lived his life by. He glanced up as they approached, his weathered face cracked into a toothless grin.

"Morning, lads," Corin rasped. "How was the catch today?"

Tito returned the old man's smile with a small one of his own.

"Our fishing day is four days away and we still haven't finished selling everything from last Bravón."

Corin frowned, shaking his head slowly.

"No, today was Bravón."

Ro gave an exaggerated sigh.

"Corin, are you already losing it old man? Today is Solaris, that's why Barrel and the magus are coming tomorrow."

Corin froze from his work, rubbing his temples.

"Great, so Velmara is tomorrow. I have nothing ready for the shipments to Barrel's stalls. If you two will excuse me."

He passed the siblings with a slight nod.

Ro laughed, "Poor Corin. Maybe I'll come up with some kind of poem for him to remember the days."

They paused, only for a second, "Yes! *Lunara and light, like the new light of a new week. Bravón being bold! A day for action, our hard working day of the week. Siernes...*"

They stopped again, for their excitement ran out.

"I'm not sure about that one. Or Torvés for that matter. Solaris is easy though! It can be..."

Ro frowned, losing their pacing.

Tito laughed as they walked once more towards the market.

"I don't see you coming up with anything!" Ro shouted as they stepped to catch up.

Tito brought his hand to his face and pretended to ponder.

"I'm not sure about the ones you mentioned, but if we are going in order, Velmara can be veiled waters, that is the day we get our traveling boats in. Domaris is hard too, but that day is pretty noticeable since it's a rest day for our village."

Ro elbowed their brother as they began to enter the bustle of the square.

"Veiled waters huh? And you have the gall to laugh at *my* words?"

The market filled as they wove their way through. The vibrant colors of the goods on display drew Ro's attention away from his rhyme. Stalls overflowed with fish whose scales glinted in the sunlight, while bundles of herbs tied with twine spilled over the edges, filling the air with earthy aromas mingled with salt. Piles of fruit gleamed like treasures, their reds and yellows vivid against the worn wood of the carts.

Ro stopped at a small stall tucked in the corner of the market run by Ilena, a wiry woman with leathered skin and crafty hands. Her wares were a collection of curiosities like shells smoothed to a glassy shine, tiny carved figures that seemed to hold their own stories, and a handful of old coins from places neither Tito nor Ro could name.

"Tito, look at this one!" Ro said, holding up a shell that glistened in the sunlight, as though the sea itself had been captured within it. Its surface was smooth and swirled with iridescent hues that shifted when turned.

"It's supposed to bring good luck."

Tito studied the shell with mild amusement. He raised an eyebrow.

"We don't need luck," he said. "Plus, we have to save our money for eventually traveling to the capital. Unless you want to actually work during our scenic trip."

Ro smiled and shrugged as they tossed the shell back onto the pile.

"Maybe not, but surely it couldn't hurt."

The stall next to Ilena's belonged to a fellow fisherman named Jaro, who was busy arranging his catch for the morning. His broad shoulders hunched as he worked on presenting his catch with a focused face. Jaro glanced up as Tito and Ro passed, his brow furrowed.

"Is tomorrow the day you boys plan to head to Atheron?" he asked, his voice gruff. "Or will you keep putting it off forever? The revolts are getting pretty bad in the coastal cities lately, I wouldn't be surprised if they close off their docks to us little folk soon."

Tito shrugged, "We'll get there eventually, although it'll be further still if this one can't keep their hands off everything they see."

Tito pointed to Ro as they were leaning in to examine a beautiful golden Lanza.

Ro raised their finger to the long, spear-like dorsal fin, which glowed faintly with an iridescent gold sheen from the sunlight. This Lanza had a sleek and muscular body, covered in dark, shimmering scales that shifted between bronze and deep blue as Tito walked to his place at Ro's side.

"This thing looks like it could stab a man clean through," Ro mused, tilting their head.

Jaro, busy gutting another fish, gave a dry chuckle.

"Aye, and it's done worse to men who weren't careful. These bastards fight when they get hooked. Had one split a boatman's hand clean open last Solaris."

Tito frowned slightly as he peeled his eye away from the glowing masterpiece.

"You certainly have a skill for this work, Jaro. I've fished all my life and never have I come across anything this beautiful. Not that I would want to, though, if they are slicing hands open."

Jaro grinned, walking over to tap the fish's gleaming side.

"You say that, but they taste like the sea itself, lad. Best meat you'll find on the coast, only took me three times your life so far before I caught my first Lanza."

Tito laughed. Though he grew up quickly, Jaro had always been someone for him to look up to in regard to his work.

"Thanks, Jaro. If we come across any, I will be sure to split my first with you," Tito said, offering a nod of respect before moving on.

The day moved slowly, the hours marked by the ebb and flow of the village around them. Tito and Ro spent the morning wandering through the market square, exchanging brief conversations with the familiar faces of Ethyrae.

Eira waved them over as they passed her stall. She was an older woman now, her hair streaked with silver and her face lined.

"Now, Jaro said you boys are planning to head on a trading route to Atheron?" she asked, her hands busy with the dough as she shaped loaves of bread with practiced ease. A flicker of magic sparked on the counter where she worked, just enough to heat the dough as she kneaded it.

"Man, we don't even get to finish a sentence without the other side of town knowing what we are saying," Ro replied and leaned casually against the stall.

Eira chuckled, "It's true, there are no secrets that last here. I like to think that is what makes us all so close."

She glanced at Tito, who was watching her knead. Her gaze softened, "Just let me know if you hear anything about my little ember when you go. The traders we have are never allowed past the market square, but you two have a knack for getting into places you shouldn't be. Especially Ro. You might as well be an actual shadow."

She trailed off and looked towards the rune pulsing on her oven. She breathed deep and smiled, though Tito sensed a deep sadness in that act.

"Just be careful, you've got good heads on your shoulders, even if Ro's is a bit lighter."

Ro grinned.

"I like to think it's filled with more interesting things. I am not exactly sure when we are going, but I will make sure we sneak into the deepest depths of Atheron to find out what magical feats little Soren has managed to accomplish."

The evening was quieter, spent by the shore where the siblings watched the waves roll in. Ro sat cross-legged in the sand. They absently tossed small stones into the water. Each one skipped once or twice before sinking beneath the surface. Tito sat beside them and scanned the horizon, though his mind was far from the sea.

"You think he'd be proud?" Ro asked. Gone was the usual playfulness.

Tito didn't need to ask who Ro meant. Their father had been a fisherman, like so many in Ethyrae. Tito and Ro were raised to follow in his stead. Jaro also helped to fill in the few tips and tricks he had learned from his decades on the water. Tito knew that Jaro felt responsible for them after delivering the news of their father passing. He had done a good job, Tito and Ro weren't thriving, but they had survived, and they would continue to do so.

"He would be," Tito said simply. "We are safe and strong. Plus, we catch more fish than we can eat and sell every week, you know he would appreciate how much we've learned."

Ro nodded, though their expression was unreadable.

They both stood and dusted sand from their pants and made their way back home from the shore.

As they reached the house in silence, the familiar creak of the door welcomed them home. Inside, the small room was filled with the scent of the sea and the warmth of the evening's sun. Tito paused by the door and took in the sight of their home. The sturdy walls, the worn furniture, and remnants of their father's trade scattered throughout the room. Nets hung from hooks along the walls, and the faint marks of years of hard work were etched into the wooden floor. This place had been their anchor, their shelter from the storms of life. Tomorrow, they would make their future plans for Atheron; but for tonight, the house still held them in its quiet embrace.

CHAPTER 3

Tito awoke, tired from little sleep, and looked out the window.

The morning arrived thick with mist that clung to the sea like a veil drawn over the world. Ethyrae stirred in the slow rhythm of habit, but the villagers emerged from their homes with more vigor than usual, though the scent of salt and damp wood filled the air like all other mornings.

Today was not like other mornings. Today, the capital ship was coming.

Tito sat on the edge of his cot and rubbed the sleep from his eyes as Ro lay sprawled out on the opposite bed, their hair a mess of tangled curls. Their breath was still slow, deep in dreams.

"Lucky", Tito thought with mild jealousy.

He himself had barely slept, and not just because of the excitement, but rather dread of what today meant.

Every year, the ship arrived from Atheron on the second Velmara of Verdelis, right when the flora began to team with life. Year after year, Ethyrae held its breath as the Magi stepped onto the shore, their presence a reminder of the invisible chain that bound the village to the capital.

It had not always been this way.

In the past, a delegation of Magi would arrive, three or four at least, each of them robed in fine embroidered cloth and stoic faces as they moved through the village. They had been symbols of power, of the authority Atheron wielded over the scattered settlements along Valcarta's coasts. Ethyrae, a humble fishing village, was far from the grandeur of the capital, but it was not forgotten. The Magi made sure of that.

Only one magus came nowadays. The delegation dwindled over the years, which shrank from a solemn procession into a single figure, and even that last remnant of authority was a shadow of what once had been. The magus that arrived now was not some austere, imposing figure of law and order but a man named Cordef, whose presence in Ethyrae inspired more groans than awe.

Cordef was not a particularly diligent man. He treated his yearly visit as more of an inconvenience than a sacred duty. Where his predecessors had examined Tito and Ro with careful scrutiny, assessing for even the faintest traces of magic, Cordef's version of evaluation consisted of a handful of lazy questions and the occasional probing stare, more for theatrics than actual judgment. And, unlike those who had come before him, Cordef made a show of his status in Atheron.

His robes were more elaborate than necessary, embroidered with patterns of golden lines that shimmered in the sun. He wore rings on his fingers, thick bands of silver and jade, his wealth a stark contrast to the simple tunics and fishing leathers of Ethyrae's people. But perhaps most infuriating of all was the way he ate. Cordef never arrived without a handful of expensive treats like candied almonds and dried fruits imported from the southern reaches of Valcarta, honey soaked pastries that left sticky flakes on his fingers as he casually ignored the tension in the air. He was the sort of man who chewed loudly while villagers waited anxiously to hear if another son or daughter would be taken.

Then there was his rune.

Cordef had a twisting mark of ember red ink lined with gold, standing stark against his pale skin. It was almost identical to the one Eira bore on her arm, the same simple, angular shape, like a flame caught midrise. But where Eira's rune was dark against her skin, a part of it, Cordef's rune gleamed all too brightly, too polished, like it sat on top of it.

Still, he made sure everyone noticed it.

Last Verdelis, Cordef wasn't even three steps off the boat before he lit the end of his cigar without so much as a glance at the flame that curled from his fingertips. The same lazy motion had warmed his tea, ignited a lantern, or tossed a careless spark into the sea, as if to remind everyone of what he could do and what they couldn't. Eira had the same mark, the same attunement to fire, yet she used hers to bake bread, to stoke her ovens with careful precision, making sure her magic was controlled and measured. She never used more than what was necessary, while Cordef did it with flourish, with arrogance, with an unspoken sneer at those without even a flicker of power.

The Magi had once been a force of reverence and fear. Now, they had been reduced to a single man with a lazy smile and a bag of expensive nuts, making notes with ink stained fingers as if he were ticking off a grocery list. And yet, despite the farce, the fear remained, because if Cordef did find someone, if he decided that a child showed promise, no matter how flimsy his reasoning, they were still taken. No one had returned to dispute what happened after. No one ever came home.

The trials had once been grueling for those examined, treading water in the freezing surf until their limbs went numb, holding their hands to flame, waiting to see if they would instinctively douse or embrace the heat, and enduring the cold to see if warmth would rise from within. It was a spectacle as much as it was an examination, each test meant to expose even the faintest flicker of magic, but those days had passed.

Cordef didn't care about trials. He barely cared about his job. He came because he had to. Instead of pushing them to exhaustion and making them suffer like the Magi before him had, he made them run his errands.

"Trial of endurance?" Cordef had scoffed last year, reclined against the dock crates as Tito and Ro stood before him.

Tito had wondered what test Cordef would pull from the old Magi traditions. The glutton just waved a hand lazily.

"Let's try something different. You two, fetch me something decent to eat. That dried fish stench is making my head hurt."

That was only the start.

Their "trials" became shopping trips, fetching him the best fruit, the freshest bread, a bottle of whatever liquor he had a taste for that day. They became errand boys, forced to carry his things, fetch his coat, and listen to his longwinded, self-indulgent stories of how grand the capital was compared to their quaint little fishing village.

Tito knew the worst part of it all. They had to let him, because as lazy and indulgent as Cordef was, he was still a magus of Atheron. His presence alone was enough to keep people cautious and polite.

And so, Tito and Ro played along. They knew what Eryx would have said…Cordef's indifference was safer than his interest.

A knock at the door sent Ro jerking upright, their eyes barely open before they groaned and flopped back onto the mattress.

"If that's Barrel, tell him to let me sleep," Ro muttered.

Tito stood and stretched the tightness from his shoulders before unlatching the door.

Sure enough, Barrel stood grinning at the threshold, his thick arms crossed over his chest. The old sailor looked exactly the same as he always did, weatherworn, sun creased, and smelling faintly of sea brine and cheap rum. His broad, wrinkled face stretched into a toothy smile as he stepped inside without waiting for an invitation.

"Rise and shine, you pair of layabouts," Barrel bellowed.

He nudged Ro's foot with his boot.

"Cordef's almost here, and if you think I'm missing the look on his pompous face when he sees this place hasn't sunk into the sea yet, you're sorely mistaken."

Ro groaned louder and pulled a pillow over their face.

"Sink into the sea and take them with it," they grumbled.

Tito chuckled, already tugging on his boots.

"Have you seen the ship yet?"

"Aye, she's cutting through the fog now, coming in fast. Faster than she should be," Barrel replied as he scratched his scruffy chin. "Odd thing, that. Never seen them sail in like they're trying to outrun something. Although *I* beat them here, so obviously not fast enough."

Tito frowned at that.

The Magi's ships were always controlled and precise. It was part of their show of power. They moved with grace, always smooth, always intentional.

So why was it coming in fast?

Barrel must have noticed Tito's expression because he clapped a hand on his shoulder.

"Come on, lad, let's not dwell on it. Let's grab something to eat and get down to the docks. You don't want to be missing when he docks."

Tito wasn't sure what he had been expecting, but something was wrong.

The sea lapped along the coast just outside of their house, but the waves crashed fiercer than they should in the midmorning calm. A sharp, salty wind cut through the village and carried with it the scent of rain that came from no earthly storm. The mist hung low over the water, dense and unnatural, and swallowed the usual sounds of gulls and distant chatter.

This wasn't how mornings in Ethyrae were supposed to be. Half the life of the village was its unchanging rhythm. The tide came and went, the boats set out and returned, and the days stretched into one another like an endless, predictable tide. The angry sea disrupted that rhythm, and of course everyone noticed it.

The villagers had gathered along the shore in silence, their uneasy gazes fixed on the horizon.

Tito followed their stares. His pulse quickened as his eyes adjusted to the veil of mist.

Faint laughter echoed over the water as Tito looked out across the sea. A dozen boats bobbed gently beyond the break, their nets cast wide in the early light. Rafts lashed together with rope and driftwood swayed under the weight of morning catches. The scent of salt and fish lingered in the air, and from the cliffs above, the sight was almost peaceful.

Then he saw a silhouette approaching.

It was small at first, just a smudge on the horizon between the nets and the fog, but it grew quickly.

Too quickly.

The black shape swelled, doubling in size with each passing moment, and unease crept up Tito's spine.

The fishermen hadn't noticed yet. A few still called out across the waves, exchanging idle chatter or hauling lines, unaware of the shadow bearing down on them.

And then...

The ship tore through the mist.

It burst forward like a leviathan breaching from the abyss, its hull a smooth and gleaming obsidian streak. Massive and terrible. It towered over the fishing boats below, which suddenly looked like toys floating in its path. Its shape was like a galleon from the old books, broad-shouldered and regal, but this was no merchant vessel.

Its sails, dyed in deep purples and silvers like the stories of Atheron's Citadel, swelled unnaturally. There was no wind, Tito felt it, dead calm all around him, but still, the sails billowed, rippling as if alive.

The ocean did not resist it. It parted before the hull, as if the sea itself had submitted.

Fishermen shouted now, some paddling furiously, others frozen in place as the unnatural vessel closed in.

The ship was headed straight for the dock.

And it wasn't slowing down.

Tito's stomach twisted as his gaze snapped lower. He wanted to scream out but couldn't.

There were boats in its path. Not just boats, but Jaro's boat was among them. A small, sturdy thing meant for a slow morning's catch, was now a splinter waiting to happen. It rocked gently, oblivious to the oncoming force of the Magi vessel, a rabbit in the shadow of a wolf. The netting on its side sagged under the weight of the day's haul, fish still flopping among the ropes. Jaro stood at the bow and rowed, rowing his hardest to escape, but the Magi ship didn't slow.

Screams coincided with shattered wood. A sickening crunch filled the air as the Magi ship collided with the fishing boats.

In an instant, the smaller boats capsized. Hulls splintered. People tumbled into the water with nets tangled around them. Though they screamed, it was for naught, for the noise was simply drowned by the crash of waves and the groan of splitting timber.

Where the boats had been was now driftwood.

Tito's breath caught in his throat, but his feet were already moving. Jaro. Jaro was still on his boat. The old fisherman fought against the rising water, with his leg trapped beneath the wreckage.

Without thinking, Tito ran. The docks were chaotic. People shouted. Barrels were knocked over. Nets got tangled underfoot. No one was helping. The Magi ship had already moored itself, but Tito didn't stop to see anyone get off.

Tito barely heard Ro yell after him before he reached the edge of the docks with a hammering heart.

Jaro was struggling. The waves were pulling him farther away.

Tito dove in.

His chest tightened as he broke through the water. His father's words rang in his ears...*Don't use it. Never use it.*

He ignored those words. Jaro was going to die.

Tito resurfaced and raised his arms.

At first, nothing happened. The water continued to rage, dragging the wreckage and Jaro with it. Tito's breath came fast and sharp as panic tightened around his ribs. He reached deeper, past the surface of himself, into the place where the magic lived. It was like catching a current beneath the waves, deep, flowing, and powerful.

Tito's fingers curled.

Then the ocean answered. The pull of the tide shifted, not all at once, not perfectly, but enough. The water surged forward in uneven pulses, dragging back before pushing again, like a hesitant breath.

Tito's hands trembled as he tried to direct it, as he tried to pull instead of crash, to carry instead of consume.

Jaro's head broke the surface, sputtering, arms flailing as the waves bucked beneath him. Tito pushed too hard at first, and Jaro almost flipped before Tito adjusted. The water jerked unsteadily as it cradled him instead.

But Jaro wasn't the only one. A second current caught on something, someone, a woman clinging to a broken plank. Her grip slipped, her body half submerged as the tide pulled her the wrong way.

No, no, no, no! Tito shoved his hands forward, his heart hammering. *Not that way. Back.*

It worked, but barely.

The waves didn't carry them smoothly. They tumbled forward in fits and starts, dragged rather than lifted, spat out rather than placed. Some people choked on seawater, scrambling for balance as the current dumped them onto the shore. The force sent Jaro rolling the last few feet across the sand, coughing and gasping.

Tito felt the ocean thrumming in his chest, the energy curled through his veins like an undertow. His blood felt cool inside his body, but he had pulled them all back. Not perfectly, but he had done it.

Tito climbed back to the shore as the villagers staggered to their feet, dripping, shaking, staring. Someone whispered his name, but he barely heard it over the sound of his own heartbeat which was loud. Too loud as it crashed like the waves that had almost taken them all.

Cordef was watching.

Tito barely noticed. His pulse roared like the tide in his ears, his hands shaking as he staggered back.

Jaro collapsed beside him on the shoreline. The old man coughed violently, and seawater spilled from his mouth. He gasped for breath before he lifted his head, locking his eyes onto Tito.

"You...," Jaro rasped. He blinked through the salt in his eyes. "You used magic."

Silence fell over the docks.

Villagers who gathered stared at Tito with a mix of shock, wonder, and sadness.

Tito turned his head slowly, heart pounding.

At the end of the docks, what remained of them, was Cordef accompanied by one injured guard.

His silver and indigo robes were pristine despite the chaos. The runes embroidered into the fabric gleamed with quiet power. He watched Tito, studied him as one might a weapon they had just discovered.

Tito swallowed and clenched his hands at his sides. He had revealed himself...and Cordef had seen.

The magus did not move at first. He only stood tall, framed against the ruined dock...observant. The jeweled rings on his fingers gleamed as he folded his hands in front of him. Gone was the laziness that Tito had come to know in his eyes. Now they were shrewd and studied Tito the way one might observe a fish flopping on a deck, curious, detached, entirely in control.

Ro had only just arrived, hearing the commotion from the house, and stepped closer, barely a whisper of movement, but Tito felt them at his side. He could sense their unease, the sharp inhale they took as their eyes flicked between Cordef and the villagers.

No one spoke. The only sound was the hush of waves licking at the wreckage.

Then, Cordef smiled.

"Well," he drawled, with a voice as smooth as polished stone. "That was unexpected."

Tito swallowed hard. His mind was racing. His heart slammed against his ribs, but he forced himself to hold Cordef's gaze. He would not look weak. He would not look afraid...even if he was.

Cordef tilted his head.

"Quite the display, boy. And here I thought this backwater had nothing of interest."

His eyes flickered toward the villagers, the edge of his smile sharpening.

"You all kept this little secret well."

A shift ran through the gathered crowd, some bristled, some shrank back.

Barrel stood near the front, his jaw tight, his knuckles white where they curled into fists.

Jaro, still coughing seawater from his lungs, sat hunched beside Tito, his weathered face drawn in something between shock and sorrow.

"No secret," Barrel grunted and stepped forward. "Tito's just a fisherman like the rest of us."

Cordef exhaled a small laugh through his nose. He shook his head, almost disappointed.

"Oh, my dear, sweet, sunburned man. Do you think I'm stupid?"

His gaze flicked to Jaro.

"You saw it. We all saw it."

Tito's throat was dry. He could still feel the water clinging to his skin, could still taste the salt on his tongue. He forced himself to stay still, to not betray the panic clawing at his gut.

"That kind of power," Cordef mused, tapping a finger against his chin. "Raw. Untrained. *Dangerous.*"

The word sent a ripple through the crowd. Tito felt the weight of their stares and fluctuating emotions. His stomach churned.

Cordef took a slow, deliberate step forward.

"Tell me, boy. How long have you been hiding this?"

Tito's hands clenched into fists.

"I don't..."

A sharp whistle cut through the air.

It was Ro. They stepped smoothly in front of Tito, and though they tried to appear neutral, their stance was just loose enough to be ready for anything.

"He's never done anything like that before," they said. They didn't sound scared. Ro was good at that. "Probably a fluke. You said it yourself, Magus. Raw and Untrained."

Cordef's gaze flicked to them, lingering for a moment. He studied Ro the same way he had studied Tito, like something to be puzzled out, something to be categorized.

"Perhaps," he murmured. "Or perhaps the queen's decree had more merit than even I realized."

The pit in Tito's stomach deepened.

There was something dangerous behind the magus's casual tone. He turned slightly and glanced at his injured guard before looking back at Tito.

"Regardless," he continued, "this changes things."

Tito's breath caught.

Cordef stretched and rolled his shoulders as if shaking off the weight of the situation.

"Normally, I'd take my time with these little visits," he said with a sigh. "Sample the food. Enjoy the sea air. But alas."

He lifted a hand, and the runes on his sleeve glowed faintly.

Tito's pulse jumped.

Cordef's eyes gleamed.

"I think it's time we take a trip to Atheron."

CHAPTER 4

He had done it. He'd used his magic, openly and undeniably, and now everything was unraveling.

Tito's heartbeat was still thunder in his chest. The air hung heavy with smoke and sea salt, thick with the tension that crackled across the ruined docks. Their boards were still slick with seawater and splinters, and the scent of soaked wood clung to his clothes like guilt.

Around him, villagers were beginning to stir from their shocked stillness. Faces he'd known all his life stared at him now like they didn't know him. There were a multitude of thoughts and emotions in their expressions...part awe, part fear, part grief, the kind of grief akin to lost innocence.

The sea had calmed, but Tito hadn't. His mind spun, fast and directionless, with thoughts that collided into each other like driftwood that was still washing up on the shore. Was he being taken? Was there still time to run? Would it even matter?

He glanced at Cordef, still as a flame waiting to catch. The magus looked relaxed, too relaxed for a man whose ship had just torn through a village's livelihood and nearly killed half a dozen people.

One of his guards leaned against the shattered remnants of a mooring post, pale and bloodied, clutching their side. A long gash ran across their ribs, and Cordef hadn't so much as acknowledged it. Why was no one talking about that?

Tito opened his mouth, but Ro stepped in again, their voice cut the silence like a blade.

"You come here like a storm, crash half the docks, nearly kill Jaro, and now you're taking him?" they accused the magus. "You're standing there with a wounded guard like it's nothing. Why don't we talk about that first?"

Cordef didn't even flinch. He turned his head slowly toward Ro, the same easy, smug smile returned to his lips, colder now.

"An unfortunate complication," he said with a hint of sharpness. "We were attacked."

Murmurs erupted through the crowd. People knew of the discourse rising against the capital, but never would they imagine attacking a magus head on, even one like Cordef.

Ro narrowed their eyes.

"Attacked?"

Cordef gave a single, deliberate nod.

"Shortly after passing the Breakspine Rocks. Two cloaked figures, illusion mages of some kind, boarded the ship in the dead of night. Took out half the navigation crew before we realized what was happening."

He paused, his gaze shifted briefly toward the injured guard slumped against the post.

"My guard, Laren, took a blade meant for me," Cordef added. "Bled half to death before I stopped it. We managed to burn one of the attackers alive. The other escaped. The helm was sabotaged, runes on the ship were damaged. We couldn't slow the ship after that."

The words fell heavy into the mist.

Even Ro seemed briefly stunned into silence.

"You expect us to believe that?" Barrel finally grunted from behind Tito. "You're saying someone tried to kill you, and you just...," he thought of stopping himself, but could not.

His words burst out of him.

"You just let your boat crash through a village?!"

Cordef arched a brow, clearly amused despite the tension.

"I saved the ship," he said flatly. "We made it to shore. A little off course, yes, but alive. If not for me, the entire vessel would've splintered miles out, and none of us would be here."

He swept his hand toward the docks.

"Besides, collateral damage is to be expected when someone tampers with enchanted runes. Be grateful we didn't explode on arrival."

Ro crossed their arms, struggling to bite back the first thoughts that sprung to mind.

"You're just lucky you crashed near the one person who could keep you from killing more people."

Cordef's smile returned.

"Ah, yes. Your brother."

He stepped forward, the edge of his robe brushed the waterlogged wood.

"And now you see why I must take him. A boy who can redirect the sea? That kind of power doesn't belong in a village like this. It requires refinement."

Tito swallowed hard. The sick weight of inevitability settled in his stomach again. Behind him, someone spoke up, a woman's voice, hoarse but clear.

"If he hadn't acted, I'd be dead."

It was Elen, the village weaver. She had spun all of Tito's clothes since he could remember, even when he was outgrowing them twice a year. She stepped forward, eyes fierce despite the bruise on her cheek.

"*You* wrecked our docks. He saved us."

Another voice joined her, a fisherman who helped Ro last Solaris when they were caught in a fishing net right at the edge of the docks.

"That's right. Pulled me out of the water before I went under. That ain't danger. That's a blessing."

Cordef raised his hand and fire flared from his fingertips, curling in the air with heat and warning.

"Enough," he hissed. "I'm not here to debate your village politics. I'm here because the queen called for the attunement of all marked in magic. Her decree was clear. I don't care what you think he is, I care what he can become, what the queen will want him to be."

He paused, his eyes flashed as he brightened the fire around his hands.

"Or are you saying you would rather disobey the queen?" He let the last few words drip like venom from his tongue.

Eira stepped forward, tears welling in her eyes.

"You cannot take another one of ours, not with my Soren…"

Tito barely had time to react before the heat changed. A sudden whoomph of pressure cracked through the air. Flames erupted in a clean arc at Cordef's side, precise and deliberate. The fire didn't touch anyone, but it reminded them.

Ro's hand darted protectively across Tito's chest as the villagers stumbled back in instinctual fear.

Cordef didn't yell. He didn't even need to raise his hand again. He simply let the fire hang there, dancing along the warped edge of the dock like a drawn sword.

"Let's not get dramatic," he said coolly. "No one else needs to get hurt."

And that was it. The villagers couldn't stop this. They weren't prepared for Magi, even lazy ones. They were lucky the cloaked figures that attacked Cordef's ship hadn't decided to set up an ambush in Ethyrae first.

The docks were already in ruins, boats crushed like toys, the air thick with smoke and damp wood. The people had barely survived the arrival alone. What would happen if they tried to fight the departure?

Tito's breath caught in his throat, the world narrowing to the thrum of blood in his ears and the smoldering heat still hanging in the air. He looked around, not at Cordef, not at the fire, but at the faces he knew like the tide. Elen, standing with her shoulders squared despite the bruise blooming across her cheek. Jaro, slumped in the sand, pain and pride wrestling across his weathered face. Barrel, fists trembling at his sides, jaw clenched so tight it looked like it might snap.

These were his people. His village. His home. And they were all at risk now because of him. He felt the weight of it settle in his chest, not like fear, not like panic, but something heavier. Like stepping into deep water knowing you may not resurface.

Slowly, Tito stepped forward. The wood creaked under his feet, scorched and warped from Cordef's earlier warning, but he didn't stop.

"I'll go," he said, his voice low but firm, cracking just slightly around the edges. "I'll go with you."

Ro's head snapped toward him, "Tito..."

Tito cut them off before they could begin.

"I have to," he said, just for Ro. "If I stay, he'll burn this whole place to the ground. You saw what he did, and we both know no one here can stop him."

Ro's eyes shimmered, their jaw tightened as their hands curled into fists.

"There has to be another way."

"There isn't," Tito said. "Not this time. I used my power. In front of everyone. It's done. The Magi won't let that go, and if I fight it, if I stay, they'll hurt the people who didn't even ask to be part of this."

He looked out again, sweeping the wrecked docks, the bruised villagers, the scorched planks. The sea was calmer now, but the silence in the air was louder than ever.

"They don't deserve to suffer because of me."

For a moment, everything held still.

Even Cordef, flame still crackling quietly in the space between them, seemed to sense the weight of the moment. He said nothing. He didn't have to.

Tito turned back to him slowly.

"I'll go," he repeated clearly, as if saying it again would make the decision feel more real.

Cordef lowered his hand. The fire vanished with a hiss, curling into smoke.

"Good choice," he said.

For once, his voice held no trace of smugness, only satisfaction.

Cordef turned from Tito, already speaking over the tension in the air like it was routine.

"My guard will stay behind," he said curtly, motioning toward Laren, who still sat slumped and pale by the ruined dock post. "He won't survive the journey in that condition. Someone see to him.

Maldito, you need not pack anything, we will leave immediately, and the Citadel will see to your accommodations."

The villagers exchanged wary glances.

The Citadel was the heart of Atheron.

"I expect him to be treated properly," Cordef added, regarding Laren.

Tito detected a hardness just subtle enough to remind the villagers he could change his mind.

Elen stepped forward, the same quiet resolve in her eyes from before.

"We'll take care of him," she said. "He's not to blame for this."

Cordef barely acknowledged her. His attention had already shifted. He surveyed the damaged remains of his once pristine ship with clear distaste.

"The runes are scorched," he muttered. "Navigation's unreliable at best."

He turned and swept over the crowd.

"I need someone who knows the sea to guide us back to Atheron. Someone competent."

Before the conversation could pause, a familiar voice answered.

"I'll do it."

Barrel stepped forward, planting his boots firmly on the broken dock, his arms crossed tight over his chest. "You'll have your navigator."

Cordef raised a brow.

"You?"

"I've charted every current from here to the capital since before you grew those fancy robes. If anyone can steer what's left of that ship, it's me."

Cordef studied him, as if calculating the risk. Then he gave a small, indifferent shrug.

"Fine. But don't touch anything enchanted."

Barrel snorted.

"Wouldn't want to catch your bad attitude."

Cordef said nothing, but his glare lingered before he turned away and he motioned Barrel into the ship.

Tito and Ro were left standing alone at the edge of the dock, the weight of their goodbye settling over them like the fog clinging to the waves. For a moment, neither spoke.

What words could hold the weight of this?

Of goodbye?

Ro stood beside him, shoulders tense, jaw set, but Tito could see it, just behind their brave face. The tremble in their hands, the panic in their eyes like a storm waiting to break.

"You don't have to do this," Ro said at last. "We could run. We could figure it out."

Tito didn't answer right away. His gaze dropped to the salt stained boards beneath their feet, where ash still clung to the edges of char and water shimmered in splintered cracks. It wasn't just about damage anymore. It was about what came next, what always came next when magic showed itself.

He exhaled slowly.

"If I stay..." he sighed. "If I stay, then I will make this place a target. If we leave, we'd be hunted. He'd come back with more; and next time, it wouldn't just be wood and rope burning."

Ro looked away, blinking hard. Their voice broke for just a second.

"You always do this."

"Do what?"

"Bleed for people who don't deserve to lose you."

That cracked something in him.

Before he could respond, Ro surged forward and threw their arms around him and held Tito as if afraid he might vanish in the next breath.

And maybe, in a way, he already had.

They clung to each other, tighter than they had in years, tighter than they ever had before. Tito pressed a kiss onto his sibling's head.

"I'm scared," Ro whispered into his shoulder.

"Me too," Tito replied.

There were no more lies left to hide behind. They pulled apart slowly, reluctantly, as if some invisible thread would snap the moment they let go. Ro's eyes were glassy with tears they refused to let fall.

"You'll write?" they asked, the words wavered like driftwood on a restless tide.

Tito nodded.

"Soon as I can. I swear it."

Ro took his hand, their own trembling.

"I don't care what they say you're meant to do. You're you, Tito. Don't let them break that. Also, don't skimp out on the thoughts when you write, I know how your mind wanders and I expect the pages to match."

Behind them, the village was stirring again, not with panic, but with something quieter.

Heavier.

The kind of silence that wrapped around grief.

Jaro stepped forward on his makeshift crutch, every step labored, his brow damp with sweat, but his eyes sharp as ever. He stopped in front of Tito and Ro, looking between them with something fierce and fragile in his weathered face.

He rasped, "You were always meant for more than fishing lines and salt on your boots. But this? Gods, I didn't want it to be this."

Tito swallowed hard. He opened his mouth to speak, but Jaro lifted a hand and gently cupped the side of his face.

"You saved my life, boy," he said, firm. "Even if that was magic, that was *you* who called the sea. Don't let them take that part away."

Then he turned to Ro, placing a calloused hand on their shoulder.

"I will help you keep your head, little gull. I will keep you busy. Eliar knows the trouble you could get into when your mind isn't full."

Ro huffed a breath, half laugh, half sob, and nodded.

Jaro gave one final look to both of them together with shimmering eyes.

"No matter where you end up, you'll always have a home here. Remember that."

He stepped back. He leaned on his crutch, shoulders squared like he was trying to hold up the weight of Tito leaving.

Tito turned to the ship, the ramp stretched out before him like the mouth of some ancient creature, waiting to swallow him whole.

This was it.

He looked over his shoulder one final time. Ro stood alone now, the others a blur behind them, and for a heartbeat, Tito saw them not as they were, but as they would be. Older, stronger. Changed. He wanted to reach for them again. Say more, say everything.

But all that came out was, "Take care of them."

Ro blinked. Their voice was just a breath.

"Come back to us. To me."

Tito nodded once. His eyes burnt, so he turned away.

He climbed the ramp slowly, every step heavier than the last. It felt like dragging his soul behind him. As he reached the deck, the wind shifted. The ship creaked. Cordef barked something to Barrel, who stood near the damaged wheel. Barrel was already checking the sails as something worried him.

Tito looked ahead.

The capital awaited. His fate awaited.

But somewhere behind him, Ro awaited too.

CHAPTER 5

The ship groaned beneath Tito's feet. It was ancient and alive in a way he hadn't expected, especially for something so immense, more fortress than vessel. A war beast dressed in hull and sail.

From the outside, it had seemed like a ruin held together by arrogance and old enchantments, but from within, it breathed. Not metaphorically... *actually*.

Tito could feel it.

The timbers flexed with unnatural rhythm, and the air tasted faintly of copper and salt. Magic clung to everything like damp mist, woven into the grain of the wood and the very bones of the ship. The corridor ahead of him shimmered faintly with reflected light, not from lanterns, but from the runes that lined the walls in elegant, spiraling patterns.

They weren't drawn on, like how Eira sometimes did for her furnace. These were ancient, precise, and *alive*. The source of life that Tito first perceived in the ship. They had been carved deep into the ribs, filled with metals that pulsed softly with colors of crimson, gold, and indigo. Each one flickered and faded like firelight through stained glass. Not in random pulses, either. They throbbed in rhythm, like a sleeping heart.

Tito's breath caught as he reached out and touched one of the beams beside him. It was warm. The rune hummed under his fingertips, responding to his presence. A low vibration traveled up his arm, like a quiet voice asking to be remembered. He drew his hand back quickly.

The arch of the ceiling stretched high above him, lined with more runes that climbed toward the central mast in twisting patterns. They spread like vines interwoven into the wood as though the ship had grown around the magic, or the magic around the ship.

Even the damage from the sabotage couldn't silence them. Cracks spidered along some of the inscriptions, scorch marks blackened sections of the metal, but they still glowed, still whispered.

Tito couldn't tear his eyes away. He felt small, insignificant. Like a child standing in the shadow of something ancient and unknowable. And yet... drawn to it, in the way a wave is drawn to shore. Inevitable. Irresistible.

"Fascinates you, doesn't it?"

The voice slithered into the quiet like smoke.

Tito turned and found Cordef standing behind him, draped in his robes like a shadow that had grown bored of waiting. His arms were crossed, and his expression made it clear he had been watching Tito longer than he'd let on.

Tito didn't answer.

The magus sauntered forward, his boots clicking softly on the enchanted floorboards. He didn't look at the runes like Tito did, he looked at them like a man staring at a dog. Something beneath him. Something that obeyed.

"They're runic stabilizers," Cordef said with a dismissive wave of his hand. "Old Atheron work. Very old. Ship's older than I am, and probably smarter than you."

He ran his fingers along a set of golden sigils etched near the doorframe. They sparked faintly at his touch.

"Most coastal cities in Valcarta wouldn't last a season without this kind of craftwork," he said. "Bridges, towers, walls, half of it's held together by runes nobody remembers how to write anymore. Lucky for them, I do."

He cast a glance at Tito, something sharp flickered behind his otherwise lazy stare.

Tito said nothing, but his jaw tightened. His stomach turned with a mix of wonder and dread. Part of him *wanted* to know how it all worked, what each line did, what each shimmer meant. The other part wanted to run.

Cordef seemed to sense it. He smiled, slow and smug.

"Don't look so sour. You're about to see what most of your village has never even dreamed of. Try to enjoy it."

He turned and walked away, his long coat swept behind him like trailing ash. He vanished down a narrow corridor without another word and disappeared into a door that sealed itself with a dull click. Only the faint smell of spice and smoke remained behind him.

Tito stood alone in the corridor, heart still pounding. Behind him, the runes continued to pulse. Beneath him, the ship sighed again. Tito stood still for a long moment. Everything was too quiet now.

The hum of the runes faded behind him as Tito stepped back onto the upper deck. The sea had calmed, glassy and wide, and the sun was slipping behind the horizon, staining the ship's splintered timbers in copper and gold.

Barrel stood at the helm, his large hands gripped the fractured wheel as though steadying more than just the vessel.

Tito made his way over in silence. He leaned beside him against the railing and watched the tide stretch endlessly in all directions.

"She's got bones," Barrel muttered after a while, nodding toward the ship. "Ugly ones, maybe. Cracked, bruised, a little too proud for what she's got left in her...but strong."

Tito let out a soft breath.

"You've sailed to Atheron before?"

Barrel grunted.

"More than a few times. Got two little shops tucked in the outer rings. One for spices, one for fish from our home. Don't look like much, but they keep me fed and active. I go back and forth when I need to."

He rolled his shoulder with a creak of old leather.

"Too many towers for me, though. Not enough sky, like it forgot how to breathe."

He finally turned to Tito. And for the first time since they'd left the shore, Barrel looked right at him. Not just at him, into him. The storm hardened eyes, the same ones that had watched Tito and Ro grow up on the beach, were glassy with something unspoken.

"I'm not here for the city though," he said. "I'm here for you."

Tito blinked.

The words sank deeper than he expected.

Barrel rubbed at his beard and stared out toward the horizon.

"No one talks about what happens after the Magi take someone. The ship comes, the kid leaves, and that's it. No letters, no words. Just gone."

He exhaled hard through his nose.

"Back in the day, I let that happen. Watched kids I knew disappear. Told myself it wasn't my place, wasn't my fight."

He turned back to Tito.

"I ain't makin' that mistake again."

Tito swallowed, his chest tight.

Barrel chuckled, dry but real.

"You should've seen their faces, y'know. After you pulled Jaro and the others from the sea."

He made a sweeping gesture with one hand.

"They were slack jawed. Like they'd just watched the ocean spit out an eight foot rainbow Lanza."

Tito's mouth pulled into a faint, embarrassed smile.

"Only question was whether to thank you or worship you," Barrel went on with a smirk. "Some of 'em were already whisperin'. They like to think you're the one the queen's been looking for all this time after movin' all that, though I'm not sure that makes it any better."

Tito stiffened slightly at that, but Barrel waved it off.

"Don't worry. They don't know anything, and I'm not lookin' to dig into it. We are all a close group, so we like to hope for the best. Just sayin' you lit something up back there…not just magic. Hope."

He let the silence stretch again, then eyed Tito sideways.

"So," he added, tone lightening with mischief, "How long've you been hiding it? Hm? You mean to tell me you've been fishin' with me this whole time, and you could've just wiggled your fingers to fill a net?"

Tito laughed under his breath.

"I didn't even know if it was real. Not until it just happened. I was too scared to try again."

Barrel nodded slowly.

"That fear kept you safe. But now? That same fear's what'll get you hurt."

Tito frowned.

"You think I'm not ready?"

"I think," Barrel said, gently, "you're stronger than you know, but not because of what you did with the sea."

He turned fully to him and placed a firm, heavy hand on Tito's shoulder.

"You're strong because you chose to save people. Because you acted. That's what matters more than all the fire and flash those Magi throw around."

Tito blinked hard, his jaw tight.

"Thank you."

Barrel turned back towards the front of the ship, Tito wasn't sure he could even see much in the settling dark.

"I'm stayin' through to Atheron, I want to see this through. Make sure you're not just tossed into the wind like the others. You deserve better than to be another name no one says out loud."

They stood like that for a long time. The deck creaked beneath them. The sails whispered above.

Finally, Barrel nudged Tito with a grunt, "Go on, then. Below deck with you. Long night ahead. Might as well sleep before the queen tries to eat you alive."

Tito managed a small smile and nodded, the warmth in his chest burnt through the chill of everything else.

"Goodnight, Barrel."

"Night, boy."

Tito hesitated at the top of the stairs. He glanced once more toward the darkened sky above, then stepped down into the belly of the ship.

The air grew cooler with each step, thick with salt, smoke, and something old, something metallic, humming just beneath the skin. The glow from the runes lining the passage pulsed softly in low amber and cast long shadows that danced against the walls like ghostly fingers. Every creak of the wood beneath his boots sounded louder here where they echoed down the corridor like footsteps chasing him. It felt like walking through the ribs of a sleeping beast. He moved slowly, trailing one hand along the wall as he passed crates marked with strange emblems, and hammocks gently swaying from the last breath of movement above. Dust hung in the slivers of light, stirred only by his passing.

Then he stopped. Movement cut across the far side of the hold. His breath hitched.

It was subtle, barely more than a flicker behind a cluster of supply crates and dangling sailcloth, but it was there. Too smooth. Too controlled. Not the lazy sway of the ship. Not the scurrying of a rat.

Intentional.

The dim rune light along the walls pulsed faintly, casting warped shadows that bled into one another like ink in water. Tito's eyes scanned the dark as his heart pounded.

His thoughts immediately jumped back to the conversation before, on the deck. Cordef had spoken of two cloaked assassins who boarded the ship. Magic users, illusionists. One burned alive, one unaccounted for. His pulse spiked.

Slowly, Tito stepped backward, every footfall now a whisper. The floor creaked once under his weight, and the movement in the corner stilled. His hand moved toward his side, even though there was no weapon there. Old fear, and a prayer that the runes wouldn't dim again.

Another step.

He could make out a shape now, crouched low behind a set of water barrels and a half torn tarp. Hooded, wrapped in shadow. Still. Watching.

Tito's breath stuttered. Magic still clung to the walls. Was it hiding them? Did they know he was here? He took another step, and the figure shifted, straightened and stood.

Tito's mouth opened, a strangled gasp caught in his throat. His legs turned to run, if he was going to die here, he would not do it crawling.

The figure launched at Tito unreasonably fast, covering his mouth with a sandy hand and pulled him into the box of tarps.

Tito threw his body back with all his might, flinging himself to get free.

"Relax," came a voice, dry and familiar. "Not a knife in sight."

CHAPTER 6

The hood was off now, and grinning like an idiot in the half-light, elbow deep in a tarp lined crate, was Ro with a bloody nose, no doubt from a wild swing Tito had thrown in his panic. Their hair was a tangled mess of curls and dust.

Tito staggered back a step. Adrenaline roared in his ears, which made his breath sharp and uneven.

"Ro?"

"Surprise!" they chirped and climbed out of the crate with their arms raised halfway, like they were surrendering. "Took you long enough."

Tito just stared at his sibling with a heaving chest. His heart tried to restart itself in his ribs, and for a moment, he couldn't speak nor even think. He stood there, frozen somewhere between fury, disbelief, and overwhelming relief.

"You...," he sputtered, jabbing a finger in Ro's direction. "I thought...do you want to give me a heart attack?! I thought you were one of them! The ones who attacked the ship!"

Ro winced and dropped onto the nearest crate. They casually wiped at the blood on their upper lip.

"Yeah, I gathered. You looked like you were about to implode."

"I nearly did!"

Ro shrugged off the dark cloak they'd fashioned from sailcloth and shadows and tossed it aside, like it was just part of a game.

"I needed to hide. No one was going to let me on the ship, and..." they paused. "Well, it worked, didn't it?"

Tito was still trying to breathe. It had worked out. Ro, the rascal that they were, had done what they so often could, enter into spaces without being seen. Tito crossed the space in three long strides and pulled Ro into the fiercest hug he'd ever given. Twice in one day, that had to be a record.

Ro didn't resist. They sank into each other like it had been weeks since they'd last spoken, not hours. The scent of sea salt and dust clung to their clothes, and the sound of their breath, quick and shaky, filled the hollow silence around them.

Slowly, the fear in Tito's chest began to unravel, replaced by something warmer, something steadier.

Fury would come later. Warnings, lectures, a dozen things he wanted to say. But right now, Ro was here. And they were together.

They stayed like that for a long time, silent, holding on to the one certainty they had left. Eventually, Tito let go and sat down beside Ro with a long exhale that felt like it came from the bottom of his soul. His limbs were heavy. His nerves, frayed, but his chest...where that hollow ache had taken root all morning...felt a little less empty.

"I can't believe you did that," he murmured as he leaned his head back against the curved hull. "I mean, I can, but I really, really shouldn't."

Ro grinned and rested their chin on bent knees.

"Come on. You're not that surprised."

"I thought I was leaving you behind," Tito admitted. His voice cracked slightly. "I thought this was it. And I hated it."

"I wasn't going to let that happen."

Simple as that.

Tito swallowed hard, then shook his head with a laugh.

"I'm just so glad you're here."

Ro nudged his shoulder.

"Well, obviously. You'd fall apart without me."

Tito chuckled, but the sound died quickly. A darker thought took him then.

"What do we do if Cordef finds you?"

Ro paused and tilted their face toward the shadows above.

"We lie. We improvise. We pull something out of the sky and hope it sticks."

"I'm serious, Ro."

"So am I."

Tito looked at them, really looked. Ro's face was streaked with grime, their cloak torn, their nose still red from the earlier elbow, but there was something steady behind their eyes. Something defiant.

"Worst case," Ro added quietly, "he throws me off at Atheron. But at least I'll be where you are. I'll figure it out."

Tito sighed.

"That's not a plan. That's wishful thinking."

Ro shrugged.

"That's what we've been living off of since the moment we were born."

Ro was right.

Tito leaned forward, elbows resting on his knees.

"Do you think...," he let his thoughts linger, as if speaking the words aloud would make the thoughts come true. "Do you think any of them are still out there? The others? The kids they took?"

Ro didn't answer right away.

"Maybe. Maybe they made it through the attunement, maybe some of them were trained. Maybe they're living in the Citadel right now, eating figs and learning fire magic from gold robed Magi, living a life better than a small little fishing village could offer."

Tito raised an eyebrow.

"You don't even like figs."

"I'm expanding my dreams, Maldito. Figs are a delicacy for those with refined taste. Let me have this."

Tito couldn't help but laugh.

Ro smiled wider.

"Hey," they said, bumping their knee against his. "At the very least, we'll get to see Atheron. Can you believe that? Us. Nobodies from Ethyrae, actually seeing the capital."

Tito exhaled through his nose.

"I always thought we'd go for more of a sightseeing trip. Something on our own terms, at least."

"We still are," Ro replied. "We're together. That's what matters."

They sat like that for a while, their voices quieter, the gentle creak of the ship filling the space between breaths.

Eventually, the exhaustion caught up with them. They pulled a tarp over their legs, curled up on the wooden floor, side by side like they had when they were small, when Eryx would fall asleep at the table and Jaro would pretend not to notice them sneaking cookies that Eira left on her windowsill for them.

Sleep came quickly.

A sharp crack of boot against wood jolted Tito upright. Ro groaned and blinked groggily, half-sitting.

Tito's heart sank as a long shadow stretched across the edge of the floor.

Cordef.

He stood at the top of the stairs, backlit by flickering rune light, his dark robes fell in precise lines around him. His hands were clasped behind his back, and his expression such that there could be malice or amusement; but the glint in his eyes made Tito's stomach twist.

"Well...," Cordef said coolly.

He slid his eyes from Tito to Ro and back again, "This is certainly unexpected."

Cordef stepped down another stair, then another, until he reached the bottom of the hold.

Ro stood stiffly in front of Tito, defiant but pale, hands clenched at their sides.

Tito could feel the heat rising behind his ribs again, not the kind that came from power, but the kind that came from helplessness. From dread.

Cordef studied them both in silence. Then, to their complete shock, he sighed. A long, tired, utterly disinterested sigh.

"Do you think," he said with a voice as flat as unleavened bread, "that I would exhaust myself enough this late to throw someone overboard right now?"

Tito blinked.

"What?"

Cordef waved a dismissive hand as he circled them, inspecting Ro like a merchant weighing a melon.

"You think I don't have enough problems? The ship was nearly sabotaged, my guard is likely unconscious and not returning with me, half my navigation runes are scrambled, and now I have to explain to the court that the 'boy who calmed and manipulated the sea' just so happened to bring a tagalong sibling with zero clearance and no magic?"

He turned sharply and the robe flared behind him.

"Do you know how much work that report will be?"

Ro's mouth opened, but no sound came out.

Cordef stopped in front of them and fixed them with a sharp look.

"Let me make something painfully clear," he said. "I don't care why you're here. I don't care about your little speech, or your noble motives, or your ragged, dramatic reunions in the ship's storage hold."

He pointed a finger directly at Ro's chest.

"But if you get in my way, if you interfere with what the queen really wants from your brother, if you draw even a flicker of attention to something I haven't sanctioned..."

The rune on his arm flared to life, and for a moment, the air around them warmed dangerously.

"I will burn you from this world like a page in the wrong book."

The heat died just as fast as it came. Cordef dropped his hand and stepped back. Then, in a sudden pivot, he clapped once and turned toward the stairs.

"Otherwise, by all means, enjoy the ride. Try the dried fruit in the officer's pantry. It's terrible."

There was almost merriment in the way he said this, which somehow frightened Tito more. He started walking back up the steps.

Ro looked at Tito, stunned.

Cordef paused at the top, glancing over his shoulder.

"Oh, and if anyone else's invisible cousin or pet fish decides to pop out of a crate in the next few hours, do me a favor and kill them quietly. I'm exhausted."

Then he vanished into the upper deck and the flickering rune light followed his silhouette into the dark.

Tito stood frozen.

Ro blinked.

"Well, I wasn't expecting that."

Tito let out the breath he'd been holding for what felt like half an hour.

"Me either," he muttered. "But I think we just got a temporary stay of execution."

Ro grinned.

"See? Told you I could improvise."

Tito remained still long after Cordef was gone, staring at the top of the stairs like the man might reappear at any second and reduce them both to ash just to make a point.

But he didn't.

There was only silence now, and the low thrum of the ship's magic pulsing in the wood beneath them.

Ro sat back down slowly, their grin faded to something smaller. Not quite fear, but something close.

Tito didn't speak. Not yet. Something wasn't right.

Cordef's outburst hadn't been for show. It felt real. The heat, the fire in his voice; but with what came after, the change, the exhaustion, the dismissal. What was Cordef getting at?

Mercy, maybe? Indifference?

No, strategy.

He's letting us stay, Tito thought, *but not because he doesn't care. Because he does, just not in the way we think.*

Tito didn't know what Cordef was planning, but he was sure of one thing now, this magus was a man who didn't speak plainly, didn't waste time on battles that wouldn't gain him anything. If Ro was still on this ship, it wasn't because Cordef forgave them, but rather because he calculated that they were more useful alive. Alive and indebted.

A shiver ran down Tito's spine.

Ro seemed to notice.

"You okay?"

Tito blinked.

"Yeah," he lied. "Just trying to keep up."

Ro leaned back against a nearby crate.

"I meant what I said, y'know. I couldn't let you do this alone."

"I know. I'm glad you didn't."

For a few breaths, neither of them spoke.

Then Ro glanced upward, eyes tracing the beams where soft pulses of light drifted along the engraved metal veins running through the hull.

"These runes are incredible," they said to break the silence.

Tito followed their gaze. Though decorative in their own right, the runes moved with purpose, arcing toward the mast before feeding into the rudder columns and sail channels.

"They're certainly more than pretty lights, aren't they?"

Ro nodded.

"Yeah. It's like the whole ship runs on magic, like it knows where it's going."

Tito exhaled as he watched the glow shift when the boat lurched forward a bit.

"I thought it pulsed like it was breathing, but it's more pulsing like it's thinking."

Ro tilted their head.

"Dad used to say the oldest runes carried will and intent. I never knew what he meant until now."

Tito let out a slow, awed breath.

"He'd lose his mind if he saw this."

They both laughed. The memory of Eryx sat between them like a lantern in the dark.

Ro shifted again.

"You think they're really going to teach us anything? About runes, or magic, or anything that matters?"

Tito didn't answer right away. The truth was, he didn't know.

"They're not taking us to teach...you least of all," he said, finally. "They're taking *me* to attune. That's all they care about. The queen's decree makes it law."

Ro hugged their knees.

"And what happens after that?"

"I wish I knew," Tito said. "I don't think they really do either."

Ro frowned.

"And me? What happens to someone who's not magic? Who's not supposed to be there?"

Tito turned to look at them, but Ro wasn't looking at him. They were staring up at the glowing runes, as if searching for an answer there instead.

"Maybe I could enlist," Ro murmured. "Join the military. Get assigned to kitchens or logistics. Just to stay close and useful."

Tito's stomach twisted.

"You shouldn't have to settle for that."

Ro finally met his gaze, a small smile tugged at their lips.

"I don't care about *settling*. I care about you. You're the one they're watching. You're the one they're planning for. Me? I'm just hoping to stay in the same city."

Tito's throat tightened.

"You won't be a nobody. You never have struck me as the small energy type."

That silence returned between them, an understanding that everything was changing faster than they could keep up with. They sat there, side by side, beneath the pulsing rune light of a ship that was carrying them toward a future neither of them understood.

Ro stood, brushing dust from their pants.

"Alright. I need to move before I fuse to this floorboard. We should talk to Barrel."

Tito guffawed.

"You think he's not going to scold you within an inch of your life?"

"Oh, he's definitely going to scold me," Ro said with a smirk. "but it's worth it. I would love to see the look on his face. Plus, he can't be the only one who forces himself on board."

They climbed toward the stairwell together, the soft thrum of the runes fading behind them like a heartbeat and made their way above deck through the narrow stairwell into the open air. The salty wind hit them immediately. It carried with it the scent of sun warmed wood, and the faint metallic tang of magic.

Barrel stood at the helm, one hand loosely on the cracked wheel, the other shading his eyes against the early afternoon sun. His weathered coat flapped behind him, and the ever-present belt knife gleamed at his side. He didn't turn around when they approached.

"You sleep well, stowaway?" he asked casually.

"Wait, how did...?"

Barrel finally glanced over his shoulder, grinning just enough to show teeth.

"You've got the stealth of a gull during a storm, Ro. I heard you clamber on before the ship even left the docks."

Ro groaned.

"Unbelievable."

Barrel shrugged.

"Didn't stop you, did I?"

Tito stepped beside him, brow furrowed.

"Why?"

"Because I knew you wouldn't let him go alone," Barrel said, looking at Ro now. "And I knew he wouldn't know how to ask you to come."

Tito looked away.

Barrel returned his gaze to the sea.

"It's a cruel thing, what's happening to you, lad. All these decrees and powers and prophecies, and not a soul in that court will bother asking what you want."

He let out a long breath.

"I saw yer dad fight to keep you boys safe. Now, I'm seeing what that safety bought you, a ticket straight into the eye of a storm."

Barrel's voice dropped lower.

"But Ro's got a right to be here. Doesn't matter whether they've got magic or not. You need someone who sees *you* — not the mark from that big stone, not the soldier they're shaping these kids into. You."

Tito swallowed hard.

Barrel grunted, hands tightening on the wheel.

"Now," he pointed ahead with a tilt of his chin, "get ready."

The siblings turned.

"We are about to dock in Atheron."

CHAPTER 7

The first thing Tito noticed was the light. It was not the light of the sun itself, but the way it reflected. Off stone. Off steel. Off everything. The pale stone buildings ahead of them caught the afternoon sun like polished bone with gleaming edges. Layered surfaces of carved runes sparked faintly, alive with motion. None of this shimmered like the ocean or glared like sand back home in Ethyrae, but rather glowed. Even from here, before the forms could take any true shape, the city looked like it had been carved from the sky.

Only when they came closer could he see the spires. They rose in the distance like gods frozen in the act of reaching. Tall, graceful, and impossible to ignore, five gleaming towers twisted upward in perfect harmony, each unique in shape and hue, each built to honor a force that could break the world, water, fire, earth, wind, and the fifth, delicate and strange, cloaked in shifting silver patterns...illusion.

He stared as his breath caught in his throat. He wished he had the words to describe seeing such a sight. All he did know was that he looked upon anchors of the very world he'd grown up hearing stories about. Things he had only ever imagined in half-formed dreams. The kind of structures willed into existence by those who commanded reality itself.

Here were the elements woven together to give birth to Atheron's soul, pulled from some long-lost truth and made real again through sheer determination.

Tito leaned over the railing, heart pounding in his ears.

"Ro..."

"I see it," Ro whispered. "Gods, I see it."

Neither of them could look away.

Below the spires, the Citadel ring spread like a second city, one of perfect symmetry and silver stone design. Floating bridges connected towers, gardened walkways filled with every color coiled around their bases. Everything gleamed.

As they descended into the deeper harbor lanes, the white stone elegance gave way to something much louder, more alive. The buildings pressed in tighter, the shouts grew louder. Tito recognized it at once.

The Outer Ring, the only part of Atheron most travelers ever saw.

It wrapped around the capital like a wall of noise and motion, a living skin built of markets, taverns, tenements, forges, and the endless churn of trade. The elegance of the Citadel was still visible in places, old stone beneath newer additions, noble bones half-buried under the growth of generations, but it had been reshaped by people, by life, by the slow accumulation of need.

The docks stretched wide ahead of them now, a massive crescent of piers and platforms extending from the lower cliffs. Ships from every corner of Valcarta were moored side by side, sails bearing symbols Tito didn't recognize, flags from places he'd only heard about in whispered tales at the tavern and docks in Ethyrae.

Here, the wind carried more than sea salt. Spices, smoke, iron, rot, and perfume overwhelmed the senses. It was chaos contained only by the rhythm of survival.

Wooden cranes spun on rune pulleys which unloaded crates from high deck merchant vessels. Crowds swarmed the stone causeways beyond the docks, vendors hawked dried fruit and steelwork, street performers juggled sparks, messengers ducked through alleys with parchment clutched to their chests.

And always...the runes.

Etched into the dock pylons, burned into cart wheels, they weren't like the ones near the spire. These were rougher and more utilitarian. Some flickered like broken lights, some sparked and sputtered, patched with chalk or scrawled over with strange additions. Others pulsed strong, steady, keeping ropes tied, wagons lifted, platforms moving. Not elegant but used. Just like Eira's.

Ro leaned against the railing, mouth slightly open.

"It's like ten cities smashed into one."

Tito nodded slowly, "This is all most people ever see."

"This is the Outer Ring?"

Tito nodded again, eyes still fixed on the maze of streets beginning to open before them.

"They say the Citadel only opens for those summoned. Everyone else stays down here, merchants, soldiers, tradesmen…lost causes. Even those who go to attune don't get to explore inside during their trip."

"And us?" Ro asked.

Tito exhaled.

"Guess we find out which we are."

The ship groaned as it pulled into dock, its damaged hull brushed gently against the cushioned pylons. A low hum came from the rune anchors as they activated, tethers of magic flared briefly to lock the vessel in place.

As they came to a halt, Tito was blinded by a silver radiance and had to shield his eyes. It was from the polished armor of the city Guard; not the ordinary peasants of the village who called themselves guards, but professionals. They kept their swords sheathed, or their spears upon their shoulders, but they could not hide the faint glow of some unknown power emanating off cold steel. Their faces could not be seen through their rune engraved helmets; nevertheless, Tito couldn't help but sense watchful eyes that missed nothing. The men working the docks certainly gave these soldiers a wide berth and would not so much as look at them. Whether it was out of respect or fear, he could not say.

Tito gripped the railing tighter.

Ro stepped closer.

"Ready?"

"No," he said honestly, "but we're here."

The ramps dropped with a heavy clang and the siblings stepped forward as Atheron opened its gates to them.

CHAPTER 8

Tito hesitated at the top of the ramp, Ro just behind him. The guards were already waiting.

Tito recognized the armor instantly. He'd only seen it once before, when he was a child, maybe five or six, during one of the Queen's earlier envoy visits to Ethyrae. They hadn't spoken, hadn't moved, just stood at the edge of the village like statues carved from night. And yet, they'd terrified him more than any tale of sea beasts or cursed woods ever could.

Now, up close, he understood why.

They were taller than most men, or maybe they only felt that way because of the armor. Six of them were forged of dark steel, sleek and seamless, matte in the shade but glinting faintly with reflected sun. Etched into the plates were intricate runes, some tight and compact, others curling around the armor's joints and chest like branding. Each rune pulsed faintly, not in a constant glow, but in a slow, rhythmic beat, like a second heartbeat just beneath the surface.

The guards' helms were angular and enclosed, featureless except for thin, vertical slits where their eyes should be. Those slits glowed softly, blue, violet, even faint red in one of them, but gave no hint of the face beneath. No skin showed, no voice came from them. They were entirely encased.

Ro whispered beside him, "They look like they could march through a wall and not notice."

Tito swallowed.

"They probably could."

He wasn't sure if he was impressed or terrified.

Cordef descended beside them, robes flaring out as he stepped onto the dock. One of the guards gave him a short nod and stepped aside.

The magus turned to the brothers and Barrel with his usual half bored, half amused expression.

"I have a report to deliver to the Queen," he said, adjusting one of his rings. "The capital appreciates punctuality, unfortunately."

He motioned to the guards with a lazy wave.

"These fine creatures will be keeping an eye on you until I return. Don't wander too far, and don't cause trouble."

Then, without waiting for a reply, Cordef turned on his heel and vanished into the city's crowd, his indigo robes disappearing into a swirl of color and bodies.

Barrel stepped off the ramp next, grunting as his boots hit stone.

"Charming fellow, as always."

Tito and Ro followed close behind, their feet meeting Atheron's ground for the first time.

It hit them like a wave.

Noise.

Smells.

Motion.

People moved in all directions, arguing, selling, shouting, laughing. Stall tents snapped in the wind, street performers sent bursts of colored flame or floating lights spinning through the air as music echoed off alleyways.

There were children ducking between carts, a pair of mages arguing in a glowing chalk circle, a tattooed woman stirring some kind of floating stew over a rune warmed cauldron.

Tito turned in place, wide-eyed.

"This is… incredible."

Ro's face lit up beside him, bright and wild.

"It's like stepping into a painting. One that moves."

"Keep your mouths shut, or you'll catch flies," Barrel said dryly, but he couldn't hide the smirk tugging at his lips.

"Come on, stay close. I'll show you around a bit. It's been a while, but I still remember the good spots."

The guards followed wordlessly, keeping a slow but constant pace behind them, never too close, but never far enough to forget.

Barrel led them through a winding street packed with spice vendors, the air thick with cumin, clove, and pepper. Then down a quieter lane where an old rune stone arched overhead, leaking strands of glowing thread light that sparked with heat as people passed underneath.

"This place wasn't meant to grow this fast," Barrel muttered. "Half these buildings weren't here when I first docked."

"Does the Queen visit the Outer Ring any?" Ro asked, squinting at a rooftop garden three stories up.

Barrel snorted.

"Queen? Hah. No, she's up in the spires. No one here gets that close. This ring's for trade, travelers, and the poor souls who didn't know when to leave."

They turned a corner and entered a plaza filled with weavers and rune carvers. A man was stitching glowing thread into a cloak while another carved symbols into a crystal rod, his hand steady and lips moving in silent incantation.

Ro leaned toward Tito.

"I want to learn everything."

Tito just nodded, still trying to process it all.

Barrel continued and led them through the crowd with his usual half grumble, parting knots of people like a ship through tangled seaweed.

"We'll head to Grelta's," he called back. "Small place, honest food. Old stone under new paint. You'll get a bite to eat and a seat to breathe, which is more than most can promise in this ring."

Tito followed close, Ro beside him and still practically spinning, trying to take everything in. The colors, the sounds, the...*everything*.

"Grelta's?" Ro asked as they passed a stall where two men were shouting over a string of dried peppers the length of Tito's arm.

Barrel grunted as he nodded.

"Little food house tucked between the ink markets and the southern aqueduct. Quiet during the day, but even better at night. She makes a stew that'll clear your head and fill your ribs."

"I love her already," Ro said, narrowly dodging a cart stacked with grilled tamales wrapped in banana leaves.

"She might love you back," Barrel added, "if you don't say anything dumb."

Tito tried to listen, but his senses were overwhelmed. The streets were alive, each one with its own rhythm. A man with gold teeth was roasting plantains over a rune stoked brazier, a group of kids darted through the crowd eating skewers of peppered meat and sweet yam crisps. A woman with her sleeves rolled to the elbow folded masa into neat little pockets and dropped them into hot oil that hissed with magic.

It was like walking into a festival that never ended.

Tito's stomach growled.

The guards followed behind them still silent, but even they couldn't kill the wonder in the air.

Barrel finally slowed and pointed down a narrow side street marked with sun faded murals and said, "There."

Tucked between a scroll vendor and a crumbling bookstore sat a little shop with worn blue paint and a carved wooden sign shaped like a cooking pot with steam curling into runes... *Grelta's Pot & Flame*. The doorway was framed with golden rune etchings, soft and steady, like it meant more to welcome than to ward.

A woman leaned out of the window, thick hair tied in a wrap and sleeves rolled to her elbows. She stirred a heavy clay pot that steamed with thick, red broth. Without a word, she looked at Barrel, then at the brothers, and gave a single nod. Her eyes lingered on the guards for just a moment before turning back inside.

"She remembers me," Barrel said, "or at least my coin."

He turned to the guards standing at the edge of the street.

"You want yerba or roasted anything, it's on your own tab."

They didn't answer. They didn't even move.

Barrel waved the brothers toward the door.

"Go on, let your feet rest and your nerves settle. You've got more comin'. And you'll want to face it on a full stomach."

The moment Tito stepped inside Grelta's, the world outside seemed to hush.

The chaos of the street faded behind the door. The air inside was warm and thick with the scent of braised meat, garlic, sweet corn, and herbs. A narrow dining room stretched out before them, low-lit and lined with stone walls painted in sun bleached reds and faded ochres. Runic symbols, ones that seemed older and hand carved, glowed faintly along the ceiling beams that cast a soft, amber light over wooden tables.

A grate over a small fire crackled near the back wall, where a younger man turned skewers of spiced beef, chili rubbed chicken, and roasted vegetables with practiced ease. Beside him, a long clay oven radiated gentle heat, its door just cracked open to reveal flatbreads puffing up beside cheese stuffed yuca cakes.

The woman from the window, Grelta herself, no doubt, glanced over her shoulder as the trio entered. She wiped her hands on a towel and scanned Tito and Ro, lingering on their postures, their clothes, the way they stood too close to one another, like two fish just tossed from a net. She grunted softly and pointed to a low table in the corner, half screened by a hanging woven curtain.

"Sit there. You're jumpy, and I don't need jumpy people near the hearth."

Barrel grinned.

"Told you she was sweet."

Ro followed her gesture with a half bow.

"You honor us, Señora."

Grelta smirked as she raised her eyebrows.

"Keep that tongue and I'll throw in pickled mango."

They slid into the booth, and Tito's shoulders dropped for the first time since they'd stepped off the ship. It wasn't exactly quiet. There were a few murmured conversations in the corners, the hiss of meat over flame, the pop of hot oil; but the tension here was different, settled. Safe. The kind of place built on generations of stubborn survival, a lot like their home on the beach.

Grelta returned a moment later with three clay cups and a steaming kettle of yerba tea, fragrant with orange peel and earthy herbs. She poured without asking.

"You hungry?" she asked.

Barrel gave her a look.

"You're our first stop out in Atheron, of course they're hungry."

Grelta turned back toward the grill.

"Then I'll feed them like they are one of ours, not like the normal outsiders."

She disappeared into the kitchen.

Ro leaned back in the booth, watching steam curl from their tea.

"I love her."

Tito sipped cautiously. The tea was bitter at first, then bright, like a fire that left behind flowers.

"She reminds me of Jaro."

"Exactly," Ro said. "Tired of people's nonsense but still feeding them anyway."

Outside, through the warped glass of the window, Tito could just make out the silhouette of the guards still standing at the end of the lane, waiting.

The tension in his chest hadn't left completely; but here, surrounded by warmth and spice and flickering runes that didn't watch him like judges, he could breathe.

Barrel leaned his elbows on the table.

"We'll stay here until Cordef returns. The capital is unlike anything you kids have ever seen and is definitely overwhelming sometimes. After he's back..." He sipped his tea to buy some time. "Who knows where the current'll take us?"

Tito nodded, eyes drifting to the steaming grill. For the first time since leaving Ethyrae, he felt a little bit full of food, of warmth, and of the terrifying, beautiful idea that maybe there were still good things waiting in this place.

The warmth of the stew had just begun to settle in Tito's stomach when the door creaked open again.

This time, the quiet that followed wasn't casual, but instinctive. The clink of a spoon stopped mid stir. One of the rune lights above the bar dimmed slightly, as if bowing to the presence stepping into the room.

Cordef.

His indigo robes trailed the scent of spice and smoke behind him as he entered, sharp-eyed and more focused than before. His usual smug disinterest had been replaced with something colder. He spotted them immediately and walked straight to their table.

"Stand up," he said without greeting. "We're leaving."

Ro blinked.

"Tea's still hot."

Cordef didn't flinch.

"You've been summoned. Immediately."

Tito stood slowly, the muscles in his legs suddenly heavy. He knew who sent the request.

"To where?"

Cordef's expression darkened slightly.

"The Citadel."

Barrel sat back in his seat.

"Bit soon for that, isn't it?"

"The queen has been waiting eighteen years," Cordef replied. "It's actually rather late. Also, she wants them both."

Tito froze.

"Both?" he repeated. "No! Ro's not part of this. They're not supposed to attune, they haven't shown…"

"I informed her of your sibling," Cordef said, already turning back toward the door. "They fit the age for the conscription, and they're here. That's all that matters. You will learn it's not…"

Tito took a step after him.

"That's not how this works! Ro hasn't shown any magic, no elemental control, nothing. You can't just…"

Ro stood, placing a calm hand on Tito's arm.

"It's alright," they said, softly but clearly. "I want to go."

Tito turned to them, wide-eyed.

"Ro..."

"I wouldn't let you go in alone," they said simply. "I didn't let you leave me in Ethyrae, and I'm not leaving you now."

Tito's throat tightened, words caught behind too much fear and too much fury.

Ro just nodded once.

"We face this together."

Cordef stepped back into the doorway and glanced over his shoulder.

"Then let's not keep the queen waiting."

Outside, the guards were already forming up again, two ahead, two behind, two on either side.

Barrel stood as well, his eyes narrowing just slightly.

"I'll follow until they stop me."

CHAPTER 9

The walk back through the Outer Ring wasn't the same.

Everything was still there, the swirl of voices, the flashes of rune light, the spice laced air, but the energy had changed. The siblings walked flanked by six armored guards around them now, and Atheron noticed.

Vendors quieted as they passed. Conversations paused mid-sentence. People moved aside just slightly, not out of respect, but out of instinct. Not for the boys themselves, no one here knew who they were, but for the pattern of it. The shape of an escort, the scent of summons, this was an attunement walk.

"Feels different now," Ro murmured beside Tito.

"It *is* different," he replied.

His voice was low, steady, but his fingers twitched at his side.

Children who had once darted through the crowd now hid behind baskets. A man selling grilled maize and sliced mango gave them a sharp glance before lowering his eyes. Even the rune lit banners above seemed to flicker more slowly in their wake. Whatever the queen's summons meant, the Outer Ring already felt it.

Barrel walked behind them, unusually quiet.

The guards didn't speak, they just kept moving, clearing a path like the tide parting for a storm front. Cordef hadn't even mentioned to them what was going on, they just moved to surround the siblings on instinct.

Tito and Ro followed them through a winding street of stacked apartments, beneath a bridge carved with murals of old battles, past a rune gate flanked by twin statues of Eryon and his fabled teacher.

At the base of a wide, carved causeway, the procession came to a halt. Ahead loomed the massive archway dividing the Outer and Inner Rings of Atheron. It was made of white stone shot through with veins of silver that pulsed faintly in the sunlight. The arch itself stretched at least three stories high, its keystone engraved with a runic crest Tito didn't recognize. It had sharp, symmetrical lines encased in a circle, elegant and cold.

But what caught his eye wasn't the gate. It was the barrier. A shimmering sheet of translucent light stretched across the path just beyond the arch, not like a window or a wall, but something thinner. It flickered at the edges like heat rising off stone, faintly tinted blue. And it hummed, low and steady, like the noise of the waves just past the shoreline. The sound buzzed faintly in Tito's ribs.

No one passed through, not without permission.

The guard escorting them stepped forward and reached into a pouch at his side. From it, he pulled what looked like a small stone disc, no bigger than his palm, etched with spiraling runes around a stylized crest.

Tito leaned forward slightly, squinting. It was not a coin, and not like any rune carved talisman he'd seen for sale back in Ethyrae.

"What is that?" he whispered.

"Marking stone," Barrel murmured behind him. "Issued from the Citadel. That specific one looks like it carries the queen's seal."

The officer at the gate stepped forward, taller than the rest, his armor a brighter silver than the dark steel of the city guards escorting them. The plate was clean, reflective, trimmed in thin lines of sapphire blue enamel that glinted under the midday sun. The runes etched into his breastplate and shoulders were not the steady red or dull gold of the others, rather they shimmered a pale bluish white which glowed softly, almost cold in their light. All the colors matched up with the barrier, and even the stylistic rune on the marking stone, which he took from the guard before he turned and pressed it into a smooth metal plate embedded in the wall just beside the arch.

A ripple passed across the barrier like wind across water. Then a flash, like a crack of lightning without the sound. Runes ignited along the arch itself, running up and around the keystone in a perfectly timed sequence. The metal plate clicked once, deep and final, and the shimmering wall vanished.

Tito blinked.

"That's...that's magic!"

"Yeah, it certainly is," Barrel said. "It's control. It's all control."

The silence that followed was just as heavy as the magic had been. No one explained the process. No one gestured them forward. It simply happened, and they were expected to move.

The air itself felt cleaner in the Inner Ring, cooler. The Outer Ring had been warm with the occasional gust of ocean wind. The rune light didn't flicker here, it pulsed deliberately, like the inside of the ship. The streets were wider, polished, and even clean. Every home had an ornate gate, every balcony was trimmed with flowering vines. There were no hawkers yelling in the street, just gilded carriages, whispering nobles, and very few soft footed guards watching from shaded alcoves.

It felt like another world.

"Most people never set foot here," Barrel murmured from behind them. "This is where the bloodlines stay. Old money, old magic. The kind of people who smile while moving knives. The kind of people everyone back home is scared of."

Tito could barely focus on the buildings. His eyes kept drifting upward. The spires were closer now. He had seen them from the harbor, seen them rise over the city like mountains; but here, just beyond the next turn, they towered.

What he had once mistaken for carved stone revealed itself now as a mixture of shaped crystal, living metal, and glass too finely crafted to be anything mundane.

The water spire was the first to catch his eye. It curled upward like a whirlpool mid freeze, layered in deep blue stone veined with silver. The outer surface shimmered like liquid glass, reflecting the sky as though it were made of flowing rivers. Runes traced along its surface in serpentine lines that moved with the current, like tides under moonlight. Tito swore he could hear it murmuring like waves against a distant shore.

Beside it rose the fire spire, a tower of jagged red gold obsidian that seemed to shimmer with internal heat. Its walls pulsed in slow bursts, the light within like a slumbering heart. Small tongues of flame curled up its side in spiraling patterns, disappearing and reappearing unpredictably. Simmering in a smoldering blaze.

The earth spire was solid, the widest of the five, a monolith of dark, root veined stone flecked with emerald and copper. The structure bore deep scars and chiseled carvings, like layers of history had been recorded across its body. It didn't shine like the others, it loomed, like a mountain given shape and purpose. Its runes were thick and bold, etched with depth, filled with a steady, pulsing glow like a ship resting at the docks.

Then came the wind spire, thinner and sharper than the rest. Its surface seemed barely there, a lattice of pale white stone so delicate it looked like it would collapse in a strong breeze. When it danced, streams of translucent crystal wrapped its frame, rising in spirals like an updraft. Gusts of wind circled it, visible in how the flags snapped and eddied around it. It shimmered in and out of focus when Tito tried to stare too long, like the sky itself refused to let it be captured.

And last was the illusion spire. It was the strangest of them all, neither tall nor wide, but impossibly intricate.

Its walls shifted constantly, reflecting the nearby towers and even the sky. Parts of it disappeared entirely, only to reappear a moment later with a different shape or texture. Its surface was made of mirrored facets that fractured light into strange, otherworldly patterns, and the runes that covered it were thinner, in shapes Tito had never seen before.

He almost forgot how to breathe in its sight.

Floating lanterns danced between bridges suspended between the towers. People walked impossible walkways high above the city, backlit by radiant energy.

The Inner Ring, these towers, was a realm unto itself. Seemingly as far away and exclusive to the Outer Ring as Ethyrae was to Atheron. The central spire, now fully visible between the others, was something else entirely. Another realm as completely separate from the Inner Ring as the Inner Ring was to the Outer, though there were no walls to communicate this fact.

Its surface shimmered with layered color, reflecting all the elements around it. Runes moved across its skin like veins of light beneath translucent stone. Thin balconies circled its heights like rings of starlight. He could see guards along them, maybe scholars. Birds flew near, only to veer away as if the tower refused to let them close.

It was as beautiful as it was overwhelming; and still, somehow, it quieted the dread in his chest.

Tito stared up, the fear in his stomach giving way to something else...awe. Then they were stopped again.

The Inner Ring gave way to a final rise leading to a wide gate carved directly into the base of the outermost Citadel wall. It was less a gatehouse and more a fortified shrine, smooth pale stone formed a perfect arch overhead, inlaid with deep gold runes.

Tito could see the Citadel clearly beyond it now, no longer towering behind buildings, but present, close, *real*. The five spires rose in perfect order behind the walls, partially obscured by only lush gardens and spiraling walkways. The outer tower entrances were flanked with guards in radiant, mirror-like armor, a bright white and gold to contrast the dark steel of the outer ring. The very air seemed to shimmer with power.

None of it could be reached without passing through this gate.

Another thin veil of light, clearer than the one separating the Outer and Inner Rings, hummed louder as it stretched across the opening. The runes hovered in the air around it, not etched but suspended, rotating slowly in place.

Cordef, who had been silent since they left Grelta's, stepped forward and produced a different stone than before. This one was flatter, darker, its outer edges inscribed with much finer script. He held it between his fingers like a playing card and pressed it into the center of a rune set into the gate wall.

Unlike the first barrier, nothing immediately happened. Then, one by one, the floating runes around the veil began to snap into alignment, slotting themselves into a seamless circle. A low tone, like a bell struck underwater, echoed across the open courtyard.

The veil collapsed.

"Only Magi and those approved by royal decree may pass through the Citadel's ward," Cordef said over his shoulder, his voice sharp and clipped again. "Consider this your first and *last* invitation."

Ro let out a slow breath.

"They really don't want uninvited guests."

Barrel just grunted.

They stepped forward and passed through the arch where the veil had vanished. Or rather, most of them did.

The moment Barrel's boots crossed the threshold, the air snapped. A pulse of pressure flared across the gate in a purple flash and Barrel staggered backward, as if pushed by a sudden wind.

The guards who had been trailing behind him reacted instantly. Two of them reached forward, hands outstretched, though not with weapons drawn. Their rune lined palms shimmered as they pressed forward.

"You are not permitted beyond this ward," Cordef said flatly.

Barrel shoved their hands aside. His face flushed.

"I sailed them here! You think I'd..."

The guards stepped forward again, firmer now. Their armor flared faintly with defensive sigils, and one of their blades had a rune that flared to life at the hilt.

Ro whirled back.

"Wait...what? He's with us!"

Tito planted his feet.

"He's coming."

"He is not cleared by royal order," said the taller guard, the one that had the marking stone. "Only those summoned may pass."

"This is madness!" Tito snapped. "He's risked just as much..."

Barrel caught his eye and raised a hand.

"No use fighting it, lad," he growled. "I've been thrown out of better places."

Ro looked like they might charge the gate themselves, but Barrel's voice turned fierce as the guards began to usher him back.

"You listen to me, both of you! I'll find a way back to you. I swear it on the old gods and the sea herself. You hear me?"

Tito opened his mouth, but nothing came out.

Ro nodded, jaw clenched and said nothing.

Barrel was already being pulled away by the guards that led them up, back into the Inner Ring, down the gentle curve of the road. His wide shoulders resisted until the last step. Then the veil shimmered back into place with a soft chime, and he was gone.

The silence afterward felt heavier than before. Only one new figure awaited on the other side with them. They stood alone in the path ahead. Their armor was different from the others, not the matte dark steel of the escorts, and not the ceremonial silver of the checkpoint officer. Theirs was a clean iron gray, laced with deep purple inlay that pulsed subtly at the joints and chest. Along their left pauldron, a sigil shaped like a rising flame above a crown in the shape of a V was carved into a crimson plate and set with gold.

Tito didn't recognize the mark, but he knew it stood out.

The guard approached them with purposeful, measured steps, as if enacting some ceremonial ritual. They paused just before the siblings and Cordef handed them the stone he used for entrance. The guard paused for just a moment before turning back towards the courtyard grounds.

"Lead the way, Vice-Captain."

As the siblings followed the new guard, the runes in the stones beneath their feet responded to their presence, subtle light trailed underfoot like ripples. The path ahead split in multiple directions, wound through gardened terraces, across thin stone bridges, and up to elevated platforms where walkways connected the spires like strands in a web.

The captain didn't pause. He led them forward through one gate, then another, each more intricate than the last. The fifth gate opened into a wide antechamber ringed with white columns and glowing panels of etched glass that depicted scenes of attunement, war, and so much more.

Tito didn't understand half of what he was seeing.

They were met there by two more figures, Magi. They were dressed similar to Cordef in layered robes, but theirs were the color of pearl and ash, their faces and arms uncovered but marked by long, vertical tattoos along their left forearm. Tito recognized one similar to Cordef's, but more stylized, and just plain black.

Cordef turned, brushing his hands together as if wiping off dust.

"This is where I leave you," he said.

Tito detected an almost gleeful finality in his delivery.

"You're not coming?" he asked.

Cordef gave a crooked smirk.

"My report is done, my only order was to bring you here, and your fate now belongs to them. I'm off for my next conscription, some scouts told me that another eighteen year old saved their father from a rockslide out towards the northern border."

The attendants stepped forward before Tito could ask anything further.

"This way," one of them said.

They paused as they glanced back at Cordef.

He had already turned back towards a garden on the right.

Tito had so many questions, but he swallowed them down as he followed the magi who spoke.

The halls within this level of the central tower were as magnificent as the outside. The walls were made of white stone marbled with blue and gold. Thin veins of rune light as thin as thread pulsed within the rock itself, tracing symmetrical patterns that shifted every few seconds, as though the walls were listening.

They were led through a small room with a wide stone basin that had steam rising from it, scented with citrus and something bitter. The attendant gestured for them to wash their hands and face. Not a request, exactly, but a ritual commandment.

Ro obeyed without hesitation. Tito followed and dried his hands on the soft cloth beside it.

The first attendant had left the room briefly but returned with two robes. They were simple, cream-colored, and contained a single rune on them. Tito recognized it almost immediately, as most houses held it. It was the rune for safety, a simple protection rune not from blades or poison, but from the elements of the world, like when storms ravaged Ethyrae's shores, or when Eira's oven caught on fire.

When they were finished, the second attendant approached and offered a small nod.

"The queen is waiting."

Tito felt his chest tighten again.

He turned to Ro, who smiled back but Tito knew they were just as scared as he was.

"Well, let's get it over with."

CHAPTER 10

The ceremonial robes were light but stiff, stitched in pale fabric that shimmered faintly around the embedded rune. Tito tugged at the collar as he and Ro stepped out of the side chamber, their faces still damp from the basin's bitter scented wash.

Neither spoke.

The guard that led them in waited just outside the door. He turned the moment they emerged and began to walk. They followed in silence.

The corridor opened into a vast, domed chamber where a dozen conversations echoed across the polished stone. The light here was soft, diffused through panes of enchanted crystal set high above. Massive columns circled the room, each one glowed subtly at the base. Tito didn't know if they were meant to keep the place standing or meant to keep the conversations inside.

At the far end of the chamber stood the queen. She was surrounded by several magi in layered robes of cream and silver, trimmed in accent colors that likely denoted their rank or element. Their postures were loose, some with arms crossed, others gesturing in half curled signs as they conversed.

Flanking the queen were two guards in armor similar to the captain's, iron gray and rune threaded, but their shoulder crests bore simpler designs, the crown and flame replaced by a single, sharp-edged rune shaped like a downward pointing triangle set in a ring. Their accents were violet instead of crimson, and they stood a step behind the queen, disciplined, but clearly subordinate to the woman who had escorted them.

As the siblings approached, a tall, wiry man in white robes with an indigo sash turned to greet them. He looked to be in his fifties, though his eyes carried a deep, ageless fatigue. The rune on his arm was incredibly ornate, more than Tito had even seen on the flashes of the veils, though the lazy slump in his shoulders made him look like he'd been through this too many times.

"Right, yes. The new arrivals," he said, waving a hand. "Welcome to the Citadel, the seat of magical power in Valcarta, house of the five elemental disciplines, and all that pomp. I'm Head Magus Venric of the Earth spire, and I'll be overseeing your attunement." He didn't pause to see if they were following. "You've been cleansed, properly robed, and dragged through more gates than most nobles see in a lifetime. Congratulations."

Ro blinked.

"Is that part of the ceremony?"

Venric gave them a side glance, unamused.

"It's part of the bother. We're summoned mid process every time someone shows a trickle of power, and it slows our real work."

He clapped once.

"So, you will approach the Runestone, you will place your hand upon it, and if it finds you compatible, it will bestow an appropriate rune into you. That rune will determine your place in our spires. If the report that led you here was a fluke and nothing happens, you leave. If something does indicate that," Venric frowned, as if he could see what he was about to say was going to prolong this whole ordeal. He forced a smile. "Well, we will get there if we get there."

"Wait, that's it?" Tito asked. "No warning? No test?"

Venric sighed.

"The Runestone doesn't take questions, and my job is not to provide answers."

He turned back toward the far doors leading into the attunement chamber.

One of the attendants, a younger woman with pale braids and sharp eyes, leaned close and whispered something into Venric's ear.

Venric frowned.

"He what?"

She repeated it.

Venric looked over his shoulder at Tito, squinting.

"You're the one who...what...commanded the ocean?"

Tito hesitated.

"I...I helped pull it back...to save someone."

Ro leaned in.

"Well, a couple someones."

Venric rolled his eyes.

"Right. Well, I've seen eight year olds crack a hillside in half and a girl from Baras split a quarry stone with a sneeze. They were not who we were searching for. The stone will decide what it decides."

He turned fully now and gestured impatiently.

"Let's get on with it."

Venric didn't wait to see if the siblings were ready. He simply turned and began walking.

With a last glance toward the queen who was already turning down a separate corridor, flanked by her violet crested guards, the siblings followed.

The hallway was broad, built of ancient white stone streaked with veins of faded gold, leaving black carving underneath. It curved slowly to the right, the light soft and flickering as if filtered through unseen runes.

Tito sped up, his robe brushing against Ro's, and cleared his throat.

"Soren," he directed to the magus. It came out as a croak, indistinguishable between a question or a statement.

Why was that all that he managed to say?

Venric cast a backwards glance at Tito.

"Spit it out," he said. "Soren, what?"

"He was the only other one from Ethyrae," Tito managed, "where we are from. He was a boy they took ten years ago who underwent this same process."

Venric, a few paces ahead, let out a long, tired sigh.

"If you're about to ask what happened to him, save your breath. We don't know. That's the truth."

Tito frowned.

"No one? In ten years?"

The magus stopped walking for a beat, then turned his head just enough to look back at them.

"There's a reason the stories around the Runestone tend to end in whispers," he said. "The stone doesn't always respond gently. For most, it chooses a mark, an element, a path, and it shares its gift. But sometimes, the flood is too much. The Runestone tests potential on occasion, rather than simply measuring it. To answer you earlier, that is why we don't know anything before attunement."

Ro raised a brow.

"Test how?"

Venric turned fully now.

"Like a dam breaking. If a person touches it unprepared, or the Runestone seems to deem it so, it can drown them. Not in water, but in power."

He glanced at Tito with narrowing eyes.

"If no one's heard of Soren since he touched it, odds are the stone gave him more than he could hold. He likely didn't even leave the courtyard."

A hush followed.

The hall opened onto a colonnade, and beyond it, the sky blazed a bright, cloudless blue. The attunement courtyard.

It was larger than Tito expected, larger than any yard he had seen. It was massive, a wide circular space ringed by weathered pillars and old growth. Trees lined one edge, and a shallow reflective pool shimmered at the far side, but the serenity was a mask.

The stone and soil beneath their feet told a different story. There were scorch marks blackened across the far wall, sharp and wild, not like lightning, but like fire that had been forced against it. One of the columns was cracked clean through, bound together now with a lattice of magical threads that shined constantly. The grass in the center looked too green, unnaturally fresh. Some patches didn't quite match the rest.

A battle had happened here.

Tito felt it like an ache in the back of his throat. Magic had been let loose in this place. Or, remembering Venric's warnings, maybe something went wrong during an attunement. And yet...

At the center of the courtyard stood the Runestone.

He and Ro stopped walking.

Venric didn't, he simply gestured.

"There it is. The soul of Valcarta. The beginning and the end of the path."

Tito stared.

Whatever he had imagined was far surpassed.

The Runestone was a monolith, at least three times his height, towering from a circular platform carved with ancient sigils. Its surface was not smooth, but jagged and asymmetrical, like it had been pulled from the earth half shaped, half born.

Rather than sitting still, it pulsed lines of deep violet light, which ran beneath its surface in slow, shifting rivers, and cast strange patterns on the ground. Runes covered its face, some sharp and basic, others looping and intricate, some curling like flame and others fractal like frost. Alive. They rotated, shimmered, shifted shape. One blinked out entirely, only to reappear moments later on the opposite side.

Tito had heard a thousand stories. Some said the Runestone was raised by the first Magi, others said it fell from the sky. One tale claimed it was a sliver of an ancient god's spine, still humming with the memory of creation. He'd thought most of them were nonsense, but now he knew he'd been wrong. They were right about some of it. The hum of power in the bones, the runes on it pulsing in rhythm with seemingly every rune in Valcarta.

But none of the stories, not one, had captured the scale of it. Not just its size, but its presence. It commanded the space in a way that even the queen bowed her head as she stepped into its light in the ramparts above. The way the air bent around it, like the world had to make room for what it was.

Tito took a slow, shaking breath.

Venric stopped at the edge of the circle surrounding the Runestone. The ancient sigils carved into the stone beneath their feet lit up softly, responding to his proximity. He turned to face the siblings, robes brushing against the sigil lines, but seemed to focus more on the magi surrounding the outside of the courtyard instead.

"By decree of the Crown and the sanctity of the Runestone, you stand now at the threshold between the world you have known and the power that shapes what is to come.

"You stand beneath the gaze of the First Flame, before the bloodstone of our line, the heart of Valcarta's gift. Here, your will does not matter. Your desire holds no weight. You do not claim the Runestone, you submit to it.

"In silence, it shall judge you. In light, it may mark you. And should it choose to answer, your path will continue among our spires."

He motioned toward the balcony on the opposite side of the courtyard as the queen stood, flanked by her violet crested guards, who took formation a few paces behind her.

Venric bowed his head slightly.

"Behold Her Majesty, Queen Seraphina, the third queen of House Veradyn, the Radiant Flame of Atheron, Sovereign of the Spires."

Tito looked up.

This time, he really saw her. He had barely processed her earlier, his mind too clouded with nerves. Now, as the light shifted and her silhouette settled into view, something about her caught his breath. She wasn't what he expected.

She looked young, maybe only a few years older than him and Ro. She stepped forward from the archway as the later rays of sunlight kissed the courtyard, and for a moment, it was as if she walked with the light itself. Her posture was perfect, shoulders square, back straight, elegant in every movement of her body.

She wore a gown unlike anything Tito had ever seen. It clung to her frame like water poured into silk. It was a deep violet, near black at the hem, with silver stitching that shimmered as she moved. When it caught the light it glowed faintly as if charged with some quiet magic. Runes were woven in an elegant, curling script that seemed to shift subtly with every breath of wind.

Her crown was delicate yet unmistakable, a slender band of gold set with five small gemstones, one for each elemental school. They glowed with a muted light, as though the very spires in the distance pulsed in time with them. Her hair, black as night and threaded with fine strands of silver, was braided in a high, intricate coil beneath the crown's base, not a strand out of place.

And her face...

She *was* young, astonishingly so. Barely older than Tito, if at all. Her skin was smooth, and even from here he could see her eyes flick between the siblings with a quiet, calculating focus. Her cheekbones were high, her lips softly painted, and her expression, though composed, carried an almost unbearable intensity. Not cold exactly, and not cruel. Untouchable.

She was breathtaking. The stone beneath her feet seemed as if it had been carved to rise up and meet her presence. A living portrait of the impossible. Tito found himself staring, almost forgetting the Runestone entirely. This was the girl...no, the queen, who ruled Atheron? His queen?

She couldn't have been the one who wrote the decree. She looked like someone who should still be learning history, not making it. A girl like her hadn't torn families apart. She hadn't stood over screaming children and watched them taken away. She...

He blinked. A cold knot twisted in his gut.

No. Maybe she hadn't written the decree, but she hadn't stopped it either. She had let it stand. She could have watched Soren and whatever happened to him. She watched boys and girls dragged from homes, their power tested, their names forgotten if they didn't survive the surge. She had ascended that throne, inherited its laws. Sat silent while the ships kept sailing. She was not a monster, but she had done nothing to stop the monsters. And that, Tito realized, might be worse.

At long last, the queen spoke.

"Few are chosen," she began, "and fewer still endure. All who stand before the Runestone do so with the knowledge that their path, no matter its end, becomes a thread in the tapestry of Valcarta."

Ro nodded slightly, focused. Steady.

Tito didn't hear the rest. His eyes were still on her. Seraphina.

She wasn't the monster he imagined. She wasn't some old tyrant casting spells from a throne of skulls. She looked like someone who might have grown up in Ethyrae if the gods had shuffled the deck differently; yet, she sat on a throne built from those choices. She wore violet silk while boys were ripped from their mothers, while little girls walked into the light of the Runestone and never came back.

Tito's jaw tensed.

Venric's voice returned, cutting through the haze.

"Step forward."

Tito blinked.

Ro was already moving.

The Runestone pulsed once more, runes shifting like a heartbeat just beneath the surface.

There was no more waiting.

CHAPTER 11

No one spoke. No wind stirred. The only sound was the low, steady hum of the Runestone which pulsed with ancient rhythm, like the breathing of something older than kings.

Above them, on a high stone rampart, Queen Seraphina stood beneath a flowing violet canopy. Her crown caught the light as she observed with stillness more commanding than any roar. She said nothing now, her speech already given, but her presence alone silenced the wind.

Ro stepped away from Tito, light on their feet, hands loose at their sides. For all the weight in the air, Ro moved as if they were walking across sand back home in Ethyrae, chasing the last line of tide before sunset.

But Tito knew better, he saw the tension in their shoulders, the way their fingers curled in the hem of the ceremonial robe, the defiance of their firmed jaw.

Purpose moved Ro with squared shoulders and as they ascended the central dais their ceremonial robe fluttered softly behind them. Their boots met the engraved stone at the base of the Runestone, and the moment their feet crossed into its circle, the ground itself seemed to wake.

The Runestone flared, deep violet lines ignited as if the monolith had been dormant until this exact moment. Runes that had shifted lazily before now swirled and danced across its surface in fevered arcs and cast light up the trees and pillars that ringed the courtyard.

Ro drew in a breath, then they raised their hand and placed it against the stone. The response was immediate. The air snapped like a rope pulled too tight. A pulse of light surged outward from the point of contact, rippling across the courtyard in a wave of force that sent two of the nearest attendants stumbling backward; but Ro stood firm with outstretched arms, as if locked in place. The runes turned brilliant white against the obsidian surface, then fractured and split into spiraling shapes that no longer obeyed the expected forms of elemental alignment. Shapes twisted inward. The air around Ro wavered, then broke.

Mirrored copies of Ro began to spin outward; not identical, but fragmented echoes. Some of them older, some dressed in armor, some bleeding from unseen wounds, some cloaked in flame. Dozens of them shimmered and danced around the stone like ghosts pulled from a hundred possible futures.

Gasps echoed from the gathered Magi.

One of them, a stern woman in dark violet robes, took a step forward.

"That can't be…"

Venric's voice was hoarse now, stripped of his earlier arrogance.

"Illusion."

The word hit the courtyard like thunder.

Above, the queen straightened. The magi flanking her leaned in slightly, their conversation halted.

Tito's chest tightened.

The Runestone pulsed again as a new rune ignited across its surface, shimmering in iridescent silver, traced with violet. It writhed like a serpent, coiling and turning in impossible shapes, shifting too fast for the eye to follow. Light surged along Ro's arm, and with a sudden flare, the rune carved itself into their skin. It wrote itself in spirals from wrist to elbow, burning with divine precision, searing its presence into their very being.

Ro gasped but didn't cry out, their eyes seemed to return from some far out place. The air screamed instead with a sound like glass bending, or wind in a sealed chamber.

The Runestone pulsed one final time, then stilled.

The mirrored copies of Ro flickered and shattered like broken reflections. Silence fell.

Ro stumbled back, breathing hard.

Tito was at their side in an instant, catching them just as they dropped to one knee. Their arm trembled. The rune still glowed.

Venric approached slowly, his eyes wide for the first time.

"Only a handful in our records," he said softly. "One illusion touched every few generations, if that. Most don't survive the attunement…"

Then the old magi broke off, he was shaking and out of breath.

Ro looked up at him with a breathless grin.

"Guess I'm not like most."

Tito stared at the mark on Ro's arm. It was still moving slightly, like ink swimming in glass.

The Magi began whispering among themselves.

Above, Queen Seraphina remained silent, but her eyes were locked on Ro now, narrowed and unblinking. The illusion attunement had not gone unnoticed.

Ro leaned into Tito's hold to catch their breath. Their skin was slick with sweat, and the glowing rune on their arm had just begun to dim. They looked up at him, lips parted in half a grin, half disbelief.

Tito laughed, more in shock than amusement.

"You weren't even supposed to be here."

Ro exhaled.

"And yet…"

Tito shook his head, still wide-eyed.

"Good thing you came, then."

Ro leaned back on one hand to look upon the place where the Runestone had marked them, where the violet and silver still swirled under the skin like starlight in water.

"I never even thought I had anything," they said, as if waking up from a dream. "They only came for you. You were always the one with power, I was just the tagalong begging you to use it."

"Not anymore," Tito said in reverence. "That was...I mean...," out of the corner of his vision he saw a crowd of the magi and royal court gather round, "...everyone saw that."

Ro nodded.

"Yeah. It felt right."

"You were incredible."

Ro looked toward the Runestone, then up to the queen's rampart above.

"They're not gonna forget that, are they?"

Tito glanced at the magi still whispering behind them.

"I doubt it."

Ro went quiet for a beat, their gaze distant.

"I saw something," they said softly.

"During the attunement?"

Ro nodded slowly.

"It wasn't clear. Like a dream, or a memory that's not mine. A figure surrounded by light, and...," they paused, eyes narrowing, "...me, shattering. Not quite dying, just...," they seemed lost for words, "...breaking apart."

Tito's smile faded.

"Ro..."

"Alright, enough," Venric snapped from the edge of the circle. "Touching, truly. Being the rarity you now are, we have much paperwork to process, so I would like to get out sooner rather than later."

Ro groaned, pushing themself up.

"Charming."

Tito rose too, but his eyes stayed on Ro a moment longer. A vision? Of being broken?

Before he could ask more, Venric gestured impatiently.

"Let's go, waterboy. Let's get this over with."

Tito stepped forward, breath catching in his chest. Whatever had just happened with Ro, his moment was next. He stepped toward the Runestone. Where Ro's attunement had drawn whispers, Tito's drew silence.

Even the Magi, still murmuring from the rare illusion mark, fell quiet as they watched him ascend the platform.

The Runestone reacted immediately. Its color darkened, from violet to black, then surged outward in a flash of molten indigo light. The veins beneath its surface pulsed not just with power, but with pressure. Something about the stone now felt wrong, that much was clear, but he couldn't back away now.

Tito took one last breath and placed his hand on it.

A shockwave burst from the Runestone with force. Violent. The outer ring of the dais shattered like brittle glass, and the closest Magi were thrown backward. One crashed into a column with a crack of bone, another tumbled headfirst into the stone railing and didn't rise. Two more were knocked flat and groaned, their runes dimmed, and robes torn.

Barriers snapped up across the courtyard, spherical runic domes flared into place around the queen, the attendants, and the remaining Magi. The guards raised their arms, weapons half-drawn, unsure if this was an attack or something worse.

Ro staggered forward, only to be held back by a fresh shimmer of violet light, a containment ward flaring up between them and Tito, but the Runestone had ensnared him. Its runes surged with light, every color. They spiraled too fast to follow, overlapping, collapsing, forming impossible shapes.

Tito couldn't breathe. He felt the ocean in his lungs, waves crashing against his ribs. He felt heat flooding his veins, the roar of fire burning beneath his skin. He felt the immovable weight of stone dragging at his bones, the sting of wind knifing through his chest.

He opened his mouth to scream, but no sound came. Light began to crawl up his arm in forking, jagged lines, burning a path into his skin. Not one rune, but four. They overlapped, twisted, melted into one another.

The platform cracked under his knees. Then the Runestone itself cracked, a thin fracture splitting its face, glowing like molten glass.

Queen Seraphina, high above, surged to her feet.

"Contain him!" she shouted, her voice cutting through the chaos like a blade.

But no one moved.

No one could.

The stone was pouring magic into Tito, and he couldn't pull away. His body convulsed, back arched, eyes wide and blazing with shifting light. The power surged again and just before the platform shattered completely, it all collapsed inward.

His knees buckled, his eyes burned. And then...

He wasn't there anymore. The courtyard, the Runestone, the queen, were all gone.

Tito stood alone in a field of ash. The sky above him was dark and streaked with orange, as if fire had torn it open. The land around him was cracked and broken, vast fissures split the earth, rivers boiled away, forests were reduced to blackened spires.

In the distance, a city burned, and standing in the center of the ruin, backlit by swirling embers and churning storm clouds, was a figure. A man. He wore no crown, but his presence towered. Cloaked in flame and shadow, wind swirled at his feet, water coiled in streams around his shoulders, and stone cracked beneath his step. His skin glowed faintly with lines of light, and his hair...

Before Tito could get a better look, the figure turned his head slowly toward him.

Tito gasped.

"Eryon!"

The name escaped him like instinct.

The man did not speak. Instead, he stepped forward, and the very ground rumbled underfoot. A great tremor rolled through the valley, as if the bones of the world were shifting.

The figure came with firelight dancing across his skin. The skies above churned, heavy with ash and thunder, and the broken world at his feet pulsed like a dying heartbeat. Tito stared, unmoving. Then the man raised a slow, commanding hand.

"The Earth remembers..."

And the land obeyed.

Cracks spread across the ash strewn field like veins, and from them rose cloaked figures, faceless and shrouded in smoke. Their robes fluttered despite the still air, and from beneath their hoods came nothing save the hollow impression of presence. One. Then three. Then five. Then dozens.

"...and so shall you."

The cloaked ones charged.

Tito raised his hands instinctively, and magic surged through him as raw energy. He lashed out with a blast of force that crushed the first figure to ash, but three more replaced it. One swung a blade of solid shadow, and Tito ducked, rolled across crumbling stone and flung a wave of water behind him. Another lunged with spear like arms. Tito shouted, summoning a swirl of wind that tore it apart.

But they kept coming from all sides. The cloaked forms didn't bleed. Didn't fall. They unmade and reformed, over and over, dragging him down. Tito shouted, pushed, fought, but the land buckled under him, and one by one the shadows overtook him, dragging him down into the ash.

Eryon, or the being that looked like that hero of old, watched in silence. And as the darkness surged around Tito's eyes, he heard the voice one last time, echoing from everywhere at once, no longer gentle, no longer wise.

"You were not meant to bear this. But it was carved into blood. You are the echo of their sin, and the answer to it."

And then...

Light. The courtyard returned. And then everything shattered. The light vanished. The shockwave reversed like a breath sucked inward.

Tito fell to the ground.

CHAPTER 12

The first thing Tito felt was pressure. A deep, aching throb that pulsed up from his shoulder and chest, where something warm and heavy lingered beneath the skin.

The second was silk. His fingers curled into the sheet beneath him. It wasn't coarse like home. It was smooth, embroidered along the edges, and smelled faintly floral.

Then came the light. Soft, golden rays filtered through tall lattice windows rimmed with arching silver vines. The glass windows were set with colored panes, lining the ceiling above him that stretched high and curved like a dome, painted with a fading mural of stars circling a massive rune in the center.

Tito blinked slowly. This wasn't Ethyrae.

This wasn't anywhere he'd ever known.

A grunt escaped his throat as he tried to push himself upright, pain flared from his upper arm where something burned beneath the skin.

He looked down. The rune was still there. It covered almost the entirety of his forearm, longer and more intricate than Ro's mark. The skin beneath it was darkened, not with a scab or bruise, but with a deep, shifting hue, like spent embers in a dying hearth, threaded with veins of deep ocean blue and faint streaks of ash white.

It wasn't a single shape, not entirely. Instead, the rune was made up of four sigils like layers of writing etched on top of each other by different hands. One curled inward like a flame devouring itself, another spiraled in a slow loop like a whirlpool. A third fractured along sharp, rigid angles, and the last fluttered at the edges, breaking apart and reforming like wind caught in a glass jar.

It moved infrequently with lines that shifted subtly beneath the skin. The edges shimmered faintly when the light hit it, giving the illusion that it wasn't inked or burned into him at all, but grown, as if the magic had taken root inside him and was still settling.

"Don't move too fast."

Ro's voice came from beside the bed.

They were sitting on a nearby cushioned bench, elbows on knees, looking up with relief and something close to awe. Their robe was wrinkled, their hair a mess, but their eyes sparkled.

"You're awake."

Tito swallowed.

"Barely."

Ro grinned.

"Yeah, well. That was something. I was worried I was going to see what happened to Soren first hand."

Tito glanced at the room again, his eyes having adjusted to the light and his thoughts clear through the pain. The walls were smooth stone inlaid with gold trim, and a faint line of runes ran just beneath the ceiling, glowing softly like starlight. A tray of untouched fruit and cheese sat on a table carved from dark wood and shell. Every corner whispered luxury.

"Where are we?"

"In the Citadel. The queen's personal guest wing, apparently," Ro said. "You went a bit...well, you went overboard."

Tito frowned.

"What happened?"

"Oh, just a light magical apocalypse."

Tito stared.

Ro held up their hands.

"Okay, okay, maybe not an apocalypse, but it was wild. The Runestone cracked, the platform under you collapsed. Half the courtyard is gone! There was so much magic flooding into you it tore through the ground. I'm pretty sure three magi are still unconscious, and another one broke a leg getting blown off their feet."

Panic made Tito's heart flutter.

"I didn't mean to!" he said desperately.

"I know," Ro said gently. "No one thinks you did. It wasn't just you. The stone, it was giving you too much. You were glowing, and the air was warping around you. Venric even shut up for once. And the queen," they laughed. "You should've seen her face."

Tito laid back with a groan.

"Gods!"

Ro nudged his arm carefully.

"But seriously? It was kind of awesome."

Tito raised his eyebrows, his eyes still closed.

"I mean, not the whole near-death thing," Ro added, "but the way they all just stared after, surprised like a bunch of idiots! Whatever happened wasn't normal, Maldito. Then they gave us this room! I mean this is nicer than the governor's mansion back when Dad let us travel to Noret. They don't give this kind of space to just anyone."

Tito stared back at the rune on his arm.

It still pulsed softly, flickering in rhythm like a storm waiting to break again.

"What does it mean?" he asked.

Ro looked at him, serious for the first time.

"From what I've heard," they leaned back, folding their arms behind their head, "it means they don't know what to do with you."

There was a soft knock followed by a low hum of runes that shifted along the doorframe. Tito looked up just as the tall, curved door to their chamber parted with a whisper of enchanted wind. A woman stepped through, robed in deep emerald with silver thread woven like branches across the sleeves. Her eyes found Tito immediately.

"Oh," she breathed, one hand coming to rest against her chest. "You're awake."

Ro sat up straighter, brushing their hair back instinctively.

"He woke up just a few minutes ago."

The woman smiled softly, almost in awe.

"I am Magus Salindra, healer to the Citadel and caretaker of initiates during attunement recovery." She bowed her head in a full, deliberate motion, hands together. "It is an honor to speak with you, Maldito Vandero of Ethyrae."

Tito blinked.

"I... uh, thanks?"

"You've been unconscious for three days," she continued, stepping closer. "The strain your body endured during the attunement should have been fatal, your heartbeat almost immediately dropped to a whisper. There were moments...," she hesitated, then smiled again. "There were moments we believed the Runestone had consumed you entirely."

Tito grimaced, glancing down at the mark on his arm.

"I feel like it tried," he muttered.

Salindra gave a knowing nod.

"Perhaps, but you endured, that is what matters."

She took a step back and clasped her hands.

"Now that you are awake, I have been instructed to inform you, Her Majesty Queen Seraphina requests your presence. Personally."

Tito stiffened.

Ro let out a low whistle beside him.

"She's asked for me?" Tito said.

"She's asked for you," Salindra confirmed. "She has questions and perhaps answers, as well."

The healer hesitated only a moment longer, her eyes dipped to the shifting rune on his arm.

"I imagine the queen wishes to know why the Runestone reacted the way it did."

Her gaze lifted again, meeting his evenly. She opened her mouth to say more, before she stopped and bowed her head.

"I will return soon to escort you to her chambers, please get dressed in any clothing in the room."

And just like that, she turned and swept silently from the room, leaving only the soft sound of the enchanted door closing behind her.

Tito and Ro were left in a quiet state made suddenly heavier.

Three days.

Tito sat up straighter, the ache in his limbs returning like a long forgotten bruise. His gaze drifted toward the rune again.

"Three days," he repeated under his breath.

Ro let out a low whistle and flopped back dramatically onto the couch cushions.

"You really don't do anything halfway, huh?"

Tito didn't answer right away.

He stared across the room, toward the wardrobe Salindra had motioned to when she'd first entered. It stood tall in the corner, carved from deep wood with gold filigree worked into the doors, another artifact of luxury that didn't belong to boys from fishing villages.

Ro sat up, nudging him with a toe.

"You good?"

Tito exhaled slowly.

"She wants to meet me. Not us, me."

"You just cracked the Runestone," Ro said. "I'm not sure I would want to meet her after that."

Tito shook his head, standing carefully.

"It's not that. I just...I didn't ask for this!"

Ro's expression softened.

"I know."

Tito moved toward the wardrobe and pulled open the doors. Inside, several sets of clothes hung neatly in enchanted stillness, robes of deep navy, charcoal, and bronze, all etched with faint stitching that shimmered in the light. One set sat facing forward, a tunic of midnight blue with narrow silver embroidery at the collar and cuffs, layered with a sleeveless outer robe marked at the hem with the fivefold sigil of the Citadel. Matching boots sat below, freshly cleaned. He ran a hand over the fabric. Everything felt expensive. He could almost feel the royalty stitched into the seams.

Ro whistled again, peering over his shoulder.

"Well, you're going to look like a proper magical noble disaster. I get second pickings of those clothes, though."

Tito snorted under his breath.

"Want help?"

"I got it."

He dressed slowly, every motion deliberate.

The clothing wasn't stiff like he'd expected. It was flexible, clearly designed for movement, despite its ornate appearance. The robe fit perfectly, almost too perfectly.

He caught his reflection in the golden lines tracing the wardrobe and stopped. He barely recognized himself. He looked older, he looked like someone important.

Ro stepped beside him, brushing a loose thread from his shoulder.

"Hey," they said softly, "whatever she says, whatever happens, you're still just my Tito. Still the same guy who couldn't lie to save a fish."

Tito cracked a small smile.

"I just hope," he said, voice low, "that's who she sees."

Ro nudged him once more.

"Then make her."

A faint knock sounded again at the door. The siblings ended their conversation with a shared glance. Tito, after a moment's hesitation, opened the door.

CHAPTER 13

It was Salindra, punctual, waiting outside.

She stood in the hallway under the ever glowing lanterns that lined the corridor. Her emerald robes glinted faintly. Tito stepped out, Ro at his side, dressed in the deep charcoal tunic stitched with swirling violet thread.

The moment Tito's boots touched the polished stone floor, he realized he had never seen anything like this in his life. The hallway stretched out before them in a long curve of white marble, laced through with veins of gold and dusky violet, as though the stone itself had been drawn from the roots of the Runestone. Elegant arches lined the walls, each set between carved pillars etched with symbols of the five magical disciplines - fire, water, earth, wind, and illusion.

Between each archway hung wide, vertical murals, their surfaces not painted but inlaid with fine threads of colored glass glowing faintly under the flicker of floating torches suspended in brackets above. The torches gave off no smoke, only a quiet, shifting glow that rippled between silver and soft amber.

Tito's eyes caught on one mural in particular, he slowed without realizing it. It was larger than the others, spanning nearly twice the space, and set deeper into the stone, as if the wall had made room for it. On it showed a figure cloaked in crimson and ash, standing alone at the heart of a broken battlefield. Storm clouds swirled overhead, rendered in curling silver thread, and around the figure, the spires of Atheron burned in hues of orange and gold. The hero's arms were outstretched with water coiling down one arm, fire spiraling from the other, stone encasing his boots, and wind shredding the edges of his cloak.

In front of him loomed a great shadow, only half formed in the depiction, as though the artists dared not give it shape. It was made of jagged lines and fractured patterns, and it bled red runes into the sky like venom. The figure in crimson stood between the shadow and the burning city, sacrificing himself in a wave of blinding light that burst from his chest and rippled outward, scouring the next part of the mural in a wave of elemental fury.

It was not the light that struck Tito most, it was the man kneeling beside him.

Near the edge of the mural, barely visible under the glow of the elements, was a second figure that looked older, gray bearded, robed in tattered white and green. His face was twisted in grief as he clutched the fallen hero's shoulder, one hand reached toward the collapsing sigils, as though trying to hold the magic together, or simply stop the sacrifice from happening. He wept openly, his face worn not by battle, but by the weight of loss.

Tito's chest tightened. He'd known the stories of Eryon, the hero who ended the civil war, who saved Atheron and wielded all four elements; and the man who had trained him, Uldris, the Rune-Father. Nobody spoke about this mural of them. Tito wondered if anyone he knew had ever seen it.

Just as he was about to move on, something in the mural caught Tito's eye. The sigils, the four elemental runes etched into the hero's arm, were arranged in a unique spiral across his forearm, the same as Tito's; but it was more than that.

It was exact.

Tito's breath caught as he turned his arm slightly and pulled back the fabric of his robe to look at the mark burned into his skin. The lines of fire, water, earth, and wind, while they shifted, they formed a consistent shape. One that wasn't random. One that was in this mural.

Mouth dry, he staggered back a step with a pounding heart, as if the walls themselves had turned to look at him. The burning city in the background, the shadow bearing down, the man collapsing beneath the weight of what he carried...

Ro turned, catching the shift in his breathing.

"What is it?"

Tito didn't answer right away.

He only whispered, "That's my mark."

He didn't even realize how shallow his breaths had become until a firm hand touched his shoulder.

Salindra. She had stepped back from where she'd been walking ahead, her brows creased in sudden alarm as she examined him with the quiet precision of a healer.

"Tito? Are you...," her voice cut off as she followed his gaze. Her eyes widened, just slightly, "Ah."

There was no surprise in her voice.

"Yes," she said quietly. "This was meant to be discussed later, but that is why Her Majesty has summoned you to speak with her."

Tito blinked.

"So, it is him," he murmured. "Eryon."

Salindra straightened slowly, her gaze lingered on the mural, and then on Tito.

"This mural was crafted for us to remember. A vow for those who would come later to live by. That moment marked the end of the Flameward Rebellion when Atheron and even the Runestone itself was on the brink of collapse."

A change had come over her voice. There was reverence in it, a sense of the sacred.

"All seemed lost, but Eryon stood between destruction and the city. By his power alone was Atheron saved."

She took a careful step forward and looked down at Tito's arm.

"That mark," she whispered, "has only been carried by him. It was burned into his skin by the Runestone just as it was for you."

Her eyes lifted to meet his, and there was something like awe behind them.

"That mark symbolized what was expected of him...to be a living force of balance, of protection; and eventually, of sacrifice."

Why couldn't Tito find his breath?

"And now, the stone has given it to you. No one has seen it since his sacrifice. Not in twenty years. The Runestone didn't even seem happy to give it."

Ro took a half step closer.

"That's why they called you that name."

"What name?" Tito rasped.

"*Shardborne*," Ro said. "Maldito, your attunement cracked the Runestone."

Tito didn't respond immediately. His mouth had gone dry, and his pulse thundered in his ears.

"Why?" he muttered at last.

Salindra turned her head slightly.

"We are nearly to Queen Seraphina, but you should probably see this first."

She led him forward, just past the mural where they turned down another hall, wider and lined with open archways, and Tito's stomach dropped. The room was a sight. What was left of it, anyway.

The air hit him like a charging bull as the smell of smoke hung thick and heavy. It clung to the back of his throat like soot. His stomach turned as the heat of it ghosted against his skin. Beyond the fire and scorched stone was coagulated blood that left a copper taste on his tongue.

The attunement platform, once a beautiful ring of ceremonial power, was now a ruin. The grass was blackened and burned through, scorched to ash in wide, uneven streaks that spidered out from the dais. Patches had already been carved out, laid bare to the soil beneath, and rolls of fresh sod waited nearby like a funeral shroud.

Tito's blood ran cold as his gaze swept toward the far end of the courtyard. One of the white stone pillars that had once stood tall and immaculate was now stained with a long smear of dried blood, just above eye level. The red had darkened to a dull brown now, but the violence of it still clung there, untouched. Below, the base of the pillar had cracked, stone caved inward, the clear imprint of a body embedded in the marble like a ghost refusing to leave. Someone had hit it hard.

He heard whispering, low and hurried. A group of attendants in pale robes worked slowly across the field, quiet and cautious. Their hands moved with precision, guided by rune staves and soft incantations, lifting debris and binding split stone with golden thread. One of them looked up, a boy barely older than Tito.

Tito saw it. Recognition, like a flash of lighting across his face. The boy looked away quickly.

Tito turned, heart thudding, and let his eyes drift to the platform where it had all happened. What was once a ring of polished stone, etched with old magic and ceremonial grace, was now shattered, its surface split into wild, concentric arcs, like something had ripped outward from the center and broken the world beneath it.

Several magi stood in a ring around the site, their arms raised, repairing what could be repaired. Around them were floating tiles, sigils being reformed, and the dais slowly being reassembled with ritual steadiness, as though moving too fast might risk it fracturing again.

But then he saw it.

Just beyond the altar, near the heart of the Runestone was a hairline fracture. It ran like a sliver of lightning up the stone's jagged edge. It was small, but it was real, barely wider than a fingernail, glowing faintly at the seam with residual light.

The Runestone had cracked, and he had done it.

His mark was still on it, written in absence, in breakage, in blood and scorched earth and the silence of the magi who had watched it happen.

How many had been hurt?

How many hadn't woken up?

How many had tried to stop it or save others, and failed?

Tito's legs felt weak beneath him, but he was still walking.

Ro reached out and gripped Tito's wrist lightly, grounding him.

"I did this," Tito whispered.

Ro didn't try to deny it. They just held his arm a little tighter.

Salindra waited a respectful distance ahead, but when she turned to look back, there was no judgment in her expression, only understanding. She didn't rush them, but she did give an expectant look.

When Tito finally moved again, it was slower. He didn't look at the Runestone, he didn't look at the damage. He kept walking.

The queen was waiting, and there would be no hiding from what he had done.

CHAPTER 14

Tito barely heard the sound of his boots against the polished floor.

The corridors of the Citadel passed in a blur, gold veined marble, enchanted lanterns, columns etched with runes that pulsed like stars trapped in stone. His mind was elsewhere, his thoughts spiraling too fast, looping back again and again to the blood on the pillar, the bent stone, and the fracture running like a wound up the Runestone's edge.

He had done that. He had seen himself in the mural and worn the same mark. He had felt the Runestone tear through him like it was trying to dig something out.

He didn't remember how long they walked, only that Ro walked beside him, quiet for once, and Salindra led them forward with the same steady pace. Even the magic humming through the Citadel's bones didn't break through the noise in his head.

Until they stopped.

Before them loomed a pair of high doors, smooth as glass, carved from dark polished stone that shimmered with faint violet light. Intricate runes formed a crest across the surface, five interlocking spirals circling a sixth, smaller symbol in the center...the mark of the queen's own seal.

Salindra turned and faced them.

"This chamber is Her Majesty's personal sanctum," she said quietly. "You will address her as 'Your Majesty' when first speaking, and simply 'my queen' thereafter. Speak only when acknowledged. Do not turn your back until dismissed."

Ro gave a theatrical bow, murmuring, "So, none of the usual charm, then."

Tito nudged them, but Salindra's lips twitched ever so slightly before she inclined her head.

"You may be spoken to informally," she added, "But you should not assume it is permission to respond in kind. She is still new to the throne, and young, but she bears its weight."

Salindra lifted a hand. The runes on the door shimmered once, then parted down the center with a sound like silk torn in slow motion.

Tito swallowed hard as they stepped through.

The queen's chamber was not what he expected. It was not some cold throne room lined with guards and tapestries of conquest. It was open, elegant, lined with high windows draped in violet and silver, with smooth columns shaped to look like branches reaching toward the sky. Sunlight poured in from a circular skylight far above which cast a soft glow onto the polished floor, where Queen Seraphina stood alone, without her crown.

She turned as they entered.

Her gown was of pale violet with silver embroidery that glittered in delicate lines across the sleeves and bodice, stitched in symbols that Tito couldn't name. Her dark hair was coiled into an intricate braid, fixed in place by five crystal pins, one for each of the magical disciplines. Her eyes were sharp, an amber gold focus far too aware for someone so young. And yet, there was something soft about her. Not weak, but not hardened like the women of Ethyrae, who were weathered by salt and storms.

She stepped forward.

"Maldito and Espero Vandero of Ethyrae."

Her voice was even, no doubt having practiced that tone a thousand times. It had the cadence of royalty, of law, of rehearsed certainty.

"I've been told you are well enough to walk. I trust the chamber provided was sufficient?"

Tito nodded, slowly.

"Yes, my queen."

Ro managed a slight bow.

"We didn't break anything."

She glanced over at Ro, her eyes flashed for only a second.

"I asked for you because what happened during your attunements cannot be ignored."

She stepped closer.

"Ro, you've awakened power that hasn't been seen in a generation. And Tito, you've cracked a sacred stone no one believed could be broken, let alone the rune currently on your arm."

Tito looked down for a moment, the weight of her words falling like anchors into his gut.

"I do not believe the Runestone makes mistakes," she said, "but I do believe it sometimes shows us things we are not yet prepared to understand."

Her gaze lingered on Tito a moment longer.

He straightened slightly, uncertain whether to speak. When he noticed Seraphina pause further, he began.

"I saw the murals," he said. "I saw the mark on Eryon... and I saw it again on me."

His fingers brushed the edge of his sleeve where the glowing lines pulsed beneath the cloth.

"I want to know why."

That admission landed with weight, the first crack in the silence.

Seraphina's expression didn't falter.

"I want to know that too, along with how you fractured the Runestone. I have ruled this kingdom for four years. In that time, I have read every recorded account of attunement within these walls. I have seen children blessed with fire enough to burn half a village. I've seen those blessed with water that would have flooded the entire inner ring without our defense runes in place. I've seen prodigies."

Her eyes met his.

"But I have never seen the stone crack."

Tito shifted under her gaze, unsure whether it was a threat or warning.

"I am told," she continued, "That your attunement was unstable. That the stone poured too much into you, as if it didn't know how to stop. Or worse, chose not to. It would have killed anyone else."

She let the words hang there.

Ro looked ready to interrupt, but Seraphina raised a single hand, and they paused.

"You bear a mark once worn by our most celebrated hero," she said, quieter now. "And yet, that is not what unsettles the magi most."

Tito's voice was hoarse when he finally spoke.

"Then what does?"

She regarded him for a breath too long.

"That it did so on your first touch."

A beat passed. Her posture didn't shift, but something in her tone did.

"Your attunement was unstable. Violent, even. It overwhelmed even the stone's enchantments. The damage," she hesitated, just slightly, "was not entirely magical, or even just to the grounds."

Tito looked down, the image of the blood streaked pillar flashing again in his mind.

Seraphina continued, her voice composed.

"There are those who would ask what gives you the right to bear that mark, who wonder what was awakened in you, and whether it can be trained, or *contained*."

She took another step forward, close enough now that he could see the faint shimmer of protective runes woven into her gown's embroidery.

"I would like to understand what happened, Tito. From you."

Her tone remained formal, poised, but there was a subtle shift in the phrasing, an almost imperceptible narrowing of her authority.

Tito's knack for picking out truths in stories was not without the benefit of noticing changes in how they were told. He opened his mouth to continue, but Ro started first.

"And if he doesn't want to?"

Seraphina met Ro's eyes, calm and measured.

"Then I thank him for his honesty."

She turned, gently reclaiming the center of the room with ease.

"I have no intention of treating you like prisoners," she said. "You're not. The crown has extended hospitality in good faith, and I expect that courtesy to continue. You must understand, however, when something breaks the Runestone it is not a matter of ceremony."

There it was again. That carefully selected language.

Not *"I* will decide", but *"You* must understand".

Not "I *command*", but "I *expect*".

Tito stood still for a long moment, eyes fixed somewhere past Seraphina's shoulder, as if staring down a corridor only he could see.

Then he spoke.

"It felt like I was being torn open," he said quietly.

Ro turned silently toward Tito, watching him closely now.

Tito drew a breath, then another. The words came slowly, but once they began, they didn't stop.

"I don't know what attunement is supposed to feel like," he said, "but I don't think it was meant to feel like that."

He glanced down at his arm, the rune pulsing faintly beneath the fabric, then looked up, eyes distant, haunted.

"It was like being...split open...wide open! Like something had been buried in me, and the stone just tore the ground apart to find it."

His breath hitched, but the words kept coming.

"I felt everything. Water in my lungs, fire under my skin, wind slicing behind my eyes, stone holding down my bones... It flowed into me, through me, and out again, like I wasn't even there. Like I was just the space the magic decided to tear through."

He clenched his jaw.

"And then the courtyard was gone."

Tito's voice dropped lower.

"I was somewhere else. A field that had burned to ash. The sky was the color of fire behind smoke, dark and hazy and red, like something had torn a hole in the world. I couldn't breathe. The air even tasted like blood and ruin. In the distance, there was a city. A burning city."

He swallowed, his eyes looking at the ornate far wall, but the images in his mind recounting the attunement.

"There was someone waiting for me. A man. He was wrapped in fire and wind, stone cracked beneath his steps, and water spun around him like it belonged there. He didn't say who he was, but I... I thought he was Eryon. He looked like the paintings, like the stories."

"You saw Eryon?" Seraphina whispered.

Tito nodded.

Seraphina didn't move, but something in the set of her shoulders changed, tightened.

"Then, figures came out of the ground. Cloaked, silent. Dozens of them, almost perfect copies of one another. They didn't speak, didn't breathe, didn't hesitate. They came at me all at once. They were like pieces of him, all focused on getting rid of me.

"I tried to fight them. I used everything. I felt the Runestone reach into me, but it was like pouring water into sand. They just kept coming. I wasn't fast enough, I wasn't strong enough. I..."

He looked down again.

"I thought I was going to die."

He pushed back his sleeve.

The rune was still glowing, barely, cycling between the four sigils in the same rough shape. The chamber went quiet.

And then Tito said, almost as if to himself.

"Right before it ended, he said one more thing. '*You are the echo of their sin, and the answer to it.*'"

The words echoed off the stone, and when they fell away, the room felt heavier, as though it had tilted around him.

For a long moment, Queen Seraphina said nothing. Her hands were still folded, but her fingers had begun to tighten around one another.

Finally, she spoke.

"It makes sense. The vision, the battle. Visions are not irregular for powerful attunements. If you were lashing out against shadow forms with all four elements that could explain the secondary surges after the attunement. We've seen isolated elemental responses in early initiates like outbursts or collapses, but never a reaction that sustained across multiple forms. Fire and air together are already dangerous. Add water into the mix and..." She stopped abruptly, eyes flicking back to the two of them.

Ro raised an eyebrow.

Tito just stared.

Seraphina exhaled, clearly catching herself.

"That might explain the elemental damage," she said more carefully, "but it doesn't explain the fracture."

Her gaze drifted toward the high window behind her, where sunlight slanted down in a perfect blade of light across the stone floor.

"The Runestone is bound, enchanted, and protected by forces older than any single person still alive in the Citadel. It's withstood thousands of attunements, possibly even more than we have recorded; and catastrophic ones at that. Even Eryon's hadn't done this level of damage. And yet...," she trailed off.

Tito didn't realize he was holding his breath until Ro gently bumped his arm.

Seraphina seemed to catch their unease.

"I'm sorry," she said. "I'm not trying to make this sound like a mystery you're expected to solve overnight. We're still trying to understand exactly what happened. Investigators from the Citadel will continue their analysis."

She stepped back, regathering her composure with a breath so subtle it could have been scripted.

"For now, your task is to learn control. You cannot be allowed outside of the Citadel's wards with what you have shown during your attunement. Even you, Ro, for illusion can twist the mind easily if it is not properly given an outlet."

She looked at each of them in turn.

"Venric will meet with you both in the morning. He'll oversee your introduction into the Citadel's regimen. You'll be assigned mentors in due time, those best suited to your discipline. Or multiple, in your case Tito. Until then, you are expected to remain within the Citadel grounds and adhere to the Citadel's magical containment protocols."

Ro crossed their arms.

"Containment?"

"A precaution," Seraphina said quickly. "Not a punishment."

She folded her hands again.

"Venric will talk further. You'll find he's not the warmest of men," she added, "but he is capable. He has taught students who showed less promise than either of you...and they survived."

Her tone hinted at humor, but neither of the siblings smiled.

Tito nodded slowly.

"We'll be ready."

Seraphina gave one last, measured nod, then turned back toward the arched windows, where light spilled across the floor like melted gold.

"You may go."

The echo of the queen's parting words still bounced in Ro's ears, though their boots made no sound on the polished floor.

Tito walked beside them, quiet and thoughtful. A little too quiet, even for him.

Ro tried to break the silence with a joke, something lighthearted like, *"Well, at least we didn't get thrown off the balcony,"* but the words became stuck somewhere behind their teeth.

This whole place had a way of draining the humor right out of them. Atheron sparkled with wealth and mystery, and the Citadel practically bled importance, but ever since the attunement, it felt like every hallway whispered about them. First about Ro, now about Tito; or about what he might become.

Ro side eyed their brother as they passed a stained-glass arch of swirling runes and elemental sigils. Tito looked like he hadn't slept in a century even though he was just out for the longest three days of their lives.

"Hey," Ro finally said, bumping his elbow against Tito's. "You okay in there?"

Tito gave a vague nod.

"Just a lot to process."

"Yeah," Ro muttered. "No kidding."

They didn't press him further. They never did. Tito would talk when he was ready, and Ro knew the signs. He wasn't shutting them out. He was holding back the storm within.

Still, it didn't make Ro's own thoughts any quieter.

They reached the chamber again, the same lush one where Ro spent every waking and unconscious moment after the attunement at their brother's side.

Ro let Tito drift toward the cushioned bench by the window and watched as he sat down heavily, gazing out toward the towering spires in the distance.

Ro didn't follow, not yet. They lingered near the doorway, arms crossed, gaze fixed on the floor like the stone might whisper answers if they stared hard enough.

Three days.

Three long, uncomfortable, overwhelming days while Tito lay unconscious.

Three days while Ro tried to keep their head on straight and act like everything was normal in a place they had no idea how to navigate or where they were allowed. Like they hadn't seen their brother become a tempest of raw elemental force. Like they hadn't watched illusions of themselves disintegrate in flame and water and wind. They ate, assisted Salindra with care for their brother, and slept at his side as often as they could.

They hadn't told Tito entirely yet. Probably not ever, but *gods* that vision!

It started the moment their hand met the Runestone. A rush of cold, the snapping of light across their spine. A thousand thoughts at once. And then, suddenly, stillness.

Ro stood somewhere they were unfamiliar with, watching versions of themselves walk confidently across an open plain. Dozens of them, each one grinning, defiant, radiant. All of them perfect

Then the wind screamed, the ground cracked, and he arrived, smoke and fire curling in the air from a town well behind him.

It was Tito, but he didn't look exactly like the brother Ro knew. His eyes burned too bright, and his mouth was twisted in anguish or rage, they couldn't quite tell. Magic bled from every limb, fire licked from his fingertips, water surged around his feet. Air howled behind him, and stone rose to meet his steps.

And the versions of Ro in his path were nothing to him.

One by one, the copies tried to flee, to fight, to reason. And one by one, he destroyed them. No hesitation, no remorse. Just unyielding, overwhelming power.

And Ro, the real Ro, stood paralyzed. They were unable to scream, unable to move. They watched themselves die a dozen deaths through tricks and shadows and shattered selves.

And then, silence.

He turned toward them. The real them and began to raise his arms. Then, the vision faded.

Now, standing in the quiet chamber while Tito traced invisible runes in the glass, Ro clenched their fists. They didn't want to believe it was him.

The Runestone wasn't exactly known for being generous with clarity.

And Tito, their Tito, was still here.

Still gentle, still thoughtful, still every bit the big brother who held their hand when they cried as a child, who stood in front of them when Magi came, who told bedtime stories when the nights in Ethyrae got too cold.

The storm in his veins, though, was real.

If Ro had seen Tito as the destroyer, and Tito had seen himself destroying copies of someone, could they really be unrelated?

Ro sank down onto one of the nearby chairs, resting their chin in their palm. They thought about the queen's words, about the elemental outbursts, the clones he fought. Her theory made sense, Tito's powers reacting to danger. Maybe those clones were a test by the Runestone, or maybe they were a threat.

Even if the person Ro saw in that vision was a future version of Tito twisted by pain or war or gods knew what else...

They still believed in him.

No, believing wasn't the right word.

Ro knew Tito, knew his heart, knew how scared he was to accidentally hurt anyone, or talk too loud in quiet places. Even if the world turned on him, even if he turned on himself, Ro never would.

They'd stand in the path of that storm, again and again, until he saw himself clearly again. They'd remind him who he was, even if they had to convince the whole damn world into seeing it.

They exhaled.

Tito hadn't moved from the bench along the windowsill.

Ro stood and walked over to him, then flopped dramatically onto the bench beside him.

"So, what do you think we're supposed to call Venric in the morning?" they asked. "Master Venric? Lord Venric? *Supreme Magus*?"

Tito blinked, startled from his thoughts. A faint, weary smile tugged at his lips.

"Probably just 'sir.'"

Ro smirked.

"I like mine better."

They sat there together in silence for a while longer. And even though Ro's heart still beat a little too fast, and shadows still lingered from the Runestone's visions, they leaned their shoulder against Tito's and closed their eyes as their head fell against his.

Whatever was coming, whatever that vision meant, Ro would face it.

Because even if the world cracked and burned and illusions shattered into ash, there were two truths that nothing could change...Tito was their brother, and Ro would never stop fighting for him.

CHAPTER 15

Tito watched the first traces of dawn bloom against the glass paneled walls of the chamber, where the red and gold crept in like fire licking across stone. And still, rest hadn't come. Not really. When the sun crested over the eastern rooftops of Atheron, Tito gave up on sleep completely.

His body felt fine, rested even; but his mind hadn't stopped moving.

The queen's voice echoed in his head. The shuddering pulse of the Runestone still etched into his bones. Every time he closed his eyes, he saw not just the clone illusions he had fought, but something deeper, darker. That moment during attunement where it felt like the elements had flooded him and then turned back outward, like they didn't belong in his body at all.

He'd thought it would feel like power, but it hadn't. It felt like being torn apart.

He stood by the window, arms folded against his chest, staring out toward the towering spires that stabbed the sky. From this angle, they looked almost weightless, like someone had painted them into the clouds.

Ro stirred behind him.

Tito didn't turn.

"Morning, storm cloud," came the groggy, familiar voice.

Tito didn't reply right away. He just nodded, eyes still fixed ahead.

Sooner or later, someone was going to come. There would be orders and instructions. They hadn't been dragged across the continent and forced into attunement just to be left in silence. The queen had promised training, promised control. Tito didn't know what that entailed, but he didn't want any more blood on his hands.

Behind him, Ro moved through the room, light-footed as always.

Tito didn't turn until the knock came at the door.

The door opened without waiting for a reply as Venric stepped inside, looking exactly as he had a few days before, robes crisp, posture flawless, expression like stone with the faintest trace of disdain carved into the edges.

"Good," he said. "You're awake.

Ro flopped into the nearest chair and bit into a fig like they were attending brunch, not a meeting.

"Well, if it isn't Sir Venric. Back to deliver more cryptic warnings?"

Tito didn't speak. He had a feeling Venric wouldn't bother answering.

He was right, as usual. The magus moved to the center of the room and clasped his hands behind his back, eyes flicking between them.

"Effective this morning," Venric began, "your attunement results have been evaluated. Based on the aftermath and your unique," a slight smile crept upon his lips, "*disruptions*, you will each undergo separate training protocols."

Tito felt his jaw tighten slightly.

Separate?

Ro beat him to the question.

"Separate? As in, we don't get the sibling system?"

"You are not children," Venric replied.

Ro made a face but stayed quiet.

Venric turned to them first.

"You are to report to the Illusia Spire this afternoon. Master Thalen will oversee your development in the Veiled Art. He is…"

"A ray of sunshine?" Ro offered.

"...Not a man who suffers fools," Venric continued flatly. "Your tower does not behave as others do. Illusia shifts. Adapts. It may test you in ways you will not understand. The path forward will be unclear by design. You must remain within its bounds until dismissed. Do not attempt to exit early."

Ro gave a two fingered salute, though something in their eyes had sharpened.

Tito caught the glimmer of unease there, quickly hidden beneath humor.

Ro played it off, as they always did.

Venric's gaze moved to Tito, and the weight of it hit like a stone.

"You," he said, "will not be entering a spire."

Tito didn't flinch, but it took effort.

Ro frowned, looking between them.

"Wait, why not?"

Venric barely acknowledged them.

"Your body is not ready to handle the gifts you have been given."

Tito felt the words like a slap.

"You collapsed during attunement. Your reaction to the elemental surge not only injured three attending magi but irreparably damaged a courtyard that has stood for over a century, let alone the Runestone that stood for centuries before. There is no foundation to build upon until your body can withstand the force of your gifts."

Tito stayed quiet.

Ro didn't.

"That's ridiculous! He didn't ask to blow up the courtyard. You threw him at a magical stone the size of a house and expected what, exactly? A gentle breeze?"

"It is not a matter of fault," Venric said. "It is a matter of fact."

Tito finally spoke.

"So, what do I do?"

Venric regarded him for a long, unreadable moment.

"You will begin physical training under the oversight of the Queen's Guard. The vice-captain will conduct your preliminary evaluation this afternoon. Starting tomorrow, you will join morning drills. Form, strength, endurance until your body is no longer a liability."

Ro let out a low whistle.

"So, you're being sent to the military."

Tito ignored them, focusing on Venric.

"And the elements?"

"When your body can endure them," Venric said, "we will assign appropriate instructors. Until then, you are not to attempt elemental conjuration or rune writing of any kind. Understood?"

Tito nodded once.

"Understood."

Venric gave a tight nod.

"You'll meet the vice-captain this evening in the lower training hall. They will assess your limits."

And that was it.

With no more ceremony, Venric turned and left.

Tito sat down slowly on the edge of the bench near the window, elbows resting on his knees.

Ro drifted toward him, then flopped dramatically onto the floor with a groan.

"Well, I'm off to the Tower Nobody Understands later. You're off to do pushups until your bones break. I guess we're really in it now."

Tito smirked faintly, but it didn't last long.

"I really thought I'd be ready. That I could handle it."

"Well, I mean nobody expected you to have Eryon's mark. We still don't even know how, or why, but you did handle it," Ro said, tilting their head to look up at him. "You just happened to break a few things along the way."

Tito rested his face in his hands with a sigh.

"Yeah, like myself."

For once, Ro didn't deflect.

"You're still here," they said. "That's more than most people could've done, the queen said that herself."

Tito didn't answer right away. The image of the Runestone still haunted his thoughts. The memory of that brief, unbearable moment when every element screamed through him, and how none of it had listened to him. He wanted to learn. He wanted to be strong.

"Ro?"

"Yeah?"

"Just stay safe...in that tower."

Ro tilted their head.

"You, too. Don't let the vice-captain punch your spine into your stomach."

They shared a quiet, weary laugh.

Tito pulled the hem of his borrowed tunic straight again for what must have been the fifth time. It still didn't feel right, too unfamiliar against his skin. He missed the old cotton shirts back in Ethyrae. The ones that smelled like salt and home; but those were gone now, as far away as the ocean itself.

Ro stood near the table, fidgeting with the straps of their belt. They'd packed what little they'd been given, a small satchel, a few coins, a charm from the queen's aide that allegedly reduced dizziness in reality shifting environments, and a slip of parchment with their tower's schedule written in some delicate, swirling script.

They'd be leaving soon.

Separately.

Tito kept his gaze on the far window, jaw tight. The spires still loomed outside like silent judges. He could feel it coming, the split. The moment when Ro's footsteps would fade in one direction and his would trudge in another. Though he wouldn't say it out loud, the thought hollowed something out in his chest.

Ro broke the silence first.

"You think we'll get to swap stories at the end of the week? Compare bruises and nightmares?"

Tito nodded, managing a faint smile.

"Only if you don't get eaten by your tower."

Ro grinned, then faltered slightly.

"Hey."

Tito turned to find his sibling frowning, lips pressed in that particular way they got when something serious was trying to claw its way out of their throat. Their illusionist confidence flickered, just for a second, and what peeked out underneath was that same fire eyed kid who'd clung to his side when the storms hit home.

"Just, don't let them break you," Ro said.

Tito blinked.

"What?"

"You heard me. These people? They're all formality and power," they huffed in disgust. "They see you as a thing to use, but you're not. You're *you*. The boy who caught fish by talking to the tide. The one who held my hand during the flood. Remember that?"

Tito felt the words hit something tender and looked down.

Ro stepped in and wrapped their arms around him without asking. Not a side hug, not a quick tap on the shoulder. A full, tight, protective embrace. And gods, Tito needed it more than he realized.

He returned it silently, burying his face against Ro's shoulder, letting out a long, slow breath. They stood like that for a long time. Long enough to feel the weight of everything they hadn't said.

Ro pulled back and gave him a light thump on the chest.

"Go. Show them you're more than the aftermath of a rock."

Tito nodded, swallowing hard.

"You stay safe, okay?"

Ro winked.

"Safe is boring."

The guards arrived not long after to escort them in opposite directions.

Ro shot him one last crooked smile before disappearing down the marble hall toward the illusion spire...or now, Illusia.

Tito stood in silence for a heartbeat too long before following his own path, flanked by two Citadel guards.

The guards said nothing, and Tito didn't try any conversation.

The further they walked, the more the tone of the Citadel shifted. The spires faded from view behind interior arches, replaced by long corridors of stone and steel. Banners bearing the queen's sigil hung overhead, an ornate golden crown set against a silver horizon, but down here, the halls felt different. Heavier, sharper. Built for discipline, not diplomacy.

They passed through two iron gates and descended a staircase lined with spears mounted to the wall. The air cooled the deeper they went. Eventually, the hallway widened into a large subterranean arena.

Tito slowed as he entered, boots clicking against the polished stone. The space was vast, nearly circular, with tiers of benches rising around the edges, and a combat ring at the center lined with silver runes. Weapons, training gear, and wooden dummies lined one far wall. A faint scent of metal and old sweat clung to the air. Standing alone in the center of it all was her. The vice-captain. She wasn't wearing a helmet this time.

Her face was exposed now, sharp angles softened by youth, high cheekbones and a strong jaw framed by dark hair woven into a tight braid that swept over her shoulder like a black cord. Her skin was a warm bronze tone that caught the light like polished copper, and her eyes watched him with the kind of unwavering stillness that made movement feel like a mistake. Even at rest, she looked dangerous. Not coiled like a snake. No, that would suggest she had to prepare to strike. This woman looked like she struck without needing to move at all.

She was beautiful, that much Tito couldn't ignore, but it wasn't the kind of beauty that begged for admiration. Her armor was a clean iron gray, laced with deep purple inlay that pulsed subtly at the joints and chest. Familiar, though Tito had seen many armors and colors since arriving at Atheron. His eyes drifted to her left pauldron, where a sigil shaped like a rising flame above a crown in the shape of a V was carved into a crimson plate and set with gold.

Tito's breath hitched slightly.

It was her.

The armored figure who had led them into the Citadel from the gates. The one who hadn't spoken a word but whose presence had cut through their escort to the Citadel like a blade.

Tito stepped forward, feeling the weight of her gaze settle fully on him. Her expression didn't shift, and she didn't offer any greeting or welcome, but her voice was clear, grounded, and completely self-assured.

"Maldito of Ethyrae," she said evenly, "you're here for your evaluation."

He gave a short nod.

"Yes."

"I am the vice-captain of the Queen's Guard," she said. "You may call me Vice Captain, or ma'am, if formality suits you."

Tito said nothing but made a note about the pauldron insignia referencing rank.

She crossed her arms, appraising him.

"You were the one who broke the courtyard and the Runestone."

He flinched.

"I didn't mean..."

"I didn't ask for an explanation," she said, cutting him off, "only for a confirmation of *what was*."

He bit the inside of his cheek.

"Yes. That was me."

She nodded once, then turned and gestured toward the ring.

"Inside, Shardborne. Strip to the waist."

Tito hesitated.

She raised an eyebrow.

"We evaluate everything, including muscular endurance, joint alignment, and range of movement. If modesty is more important than training, you may leave now."

Embarrassed, Tito tugged off the tunic, folding it quickly before stepping barefoot into the rune ringed center.

The stone was cold and the air sharp even though it was a sunny day. He felt exposed, more than just skin deep.

The vice-captain walked a slow circle around him, arms behind her back, her gaze clinical. She didn't leer or scoff, didn't linger over scars or softness, but she saw everything.

"Unbalanced shoulders," she said. "Left leg slightly favored when standing. Hands show signs of strain, probably from work involving ropes or grip intensive tools. You're used to physical labor, but not training. You carry your weight like someone prepared for drowning, not combat."

Tito winced.

She stepped in front of him.

"Punch me."

"What?"

"Punch me," she repeated.

He hesitated, then threw a slow, cautious jab toward her chest. She dodged it like she was brushing away a leaf.

"Again...with intent."

He narrowed his eyes, stepped forward, and punched.

This time, she caught his wrist mid-motion, spun it, and twisted him to the ground before he could blink. His breath left him in a gasp as his back hit the stone. Pain flared across his shoulder.

She let go and stepped back.

"You're not completely untrained," she said. "Your instincts aren't terrible, but instincts without discipline are just a slow death."

Tito sat up, breathing hard.

"You're not a weapon yet," she added, "but you could be."

He looked up at her, heart pounding.

"And if I don't want to be?"

She didn't smile. But something in her voice softened by a fraction.

"Then train harder so you can choose what you become. Otherwise, you will not become what we need."

He accepted her proffered hand. Her grip was strong, steady, and unapologetic as she pulled him up.

"We start at dawn," she said. "If you survive the first week, you'll move to your elemental integration. Until then, you run, you fight, you build, you break."

Tito nodded slowly.

"Understood, ma'am."

She studied him for a second longer, then gestured toward the stairs.

"You're dismissed. Eat well. Hydrate. Pray, if it helps."

She gave a single nod and turned from him, already walking back toward the weapons rack with the confidence of someone who had nothing to prove.

Tito lingered at the edge of the ring, chest still rising with exertion. He turned toward the exit, legs sore and mind racing, every part of him bracing for whatever tomorrow would bring.

Before he reached the threshold, her voice called out again.

"Maldito."

He froze.

"You looked scared when you walked into the Citadel. Scared, but determined." A pause. Not judgment. Not praise, just a fact. "Inexperienced, but raw. I want to see if that version of you survives."

CHAPTER 16

The dining hall was colder than Tito expected. Not in temperature, though the stone walls and vaulted ceiling seemed to take enough space to hog the warm air. He felt it more in the sense of the sparse and functional atmosphere. Here there were no golden banners or carved columns like those on the Citadel's main floors. Just long tables, iron sconces, and a heavy silence broken only by the occasional clatter of cutlery. It was a place devoid of character.

Tito sat near the end of one of the tables, alone, chewing slowly through a piece of dense, oat crusted bread and watching the clusters of what he could only guess were new recruits preparing for the day. The food was good enough. He'd taken some roasted root vegetables, a boiled egg, and what looked like a strip of cured meat. It was hearty, obviously meant to fuel soldiers, not please nobles. He appreciated it for exactly that reason.

The silence helped too. He had time to think or, more accurately, review. The barracks weren't what he expected. After his evaluation with the vice-captain, he'd been escorted down another flight of stairs, past a small training yard built into the side of the inner wall, and into a chamber built for thirty men easily.

However, at present it held only two. It was clean and symmetrical, not lavish like the guest room in the upper Citadel where Tito and Ro had stayed, but well-made. Stone walls, a line of unclaimed beds with footlockers at the base, and two beds actually occupied, one tucked in the corner with folded linens, and his.

No one had spoken a word to him. The two guards who led him down simply pointed at the bed and left. He hadn't minded. Truth be told, he preferred the quiet, it was a nice change from the last couple days.

There was a chest at the foot of the bed, polished wood banded with a silver medal, already unlocked. Inside were the basics, two folded sets of training gear, a sealed water skin, a flint kit, and a slip of parchment with a training schedule. Beneath it all, an armband with the Queen's Guard insignia, dyed in crimson but with no gold trim, an outsider's mark probably, or an initiate's.

The clothes themselves had the same feel, there was no flourish like the incredible work of the robes in the wardrobe of his previous chamber. Thick black trousers reinforced at the knees. A sleeveless gray tunic stitched with crimson thread and rune etching at the collar. Matching wraps for his hands and forearms, and a pair of hardened boots with flexible soles meant for running or combat.

Everything was sized precisely, not generous, nor tight, but measured, as if someone had taken note of his frame the moment he stepped off the ship, which, honestly they probably had. That or the vice-captain was really good at taking measurements from her evaluation, and really fast to get them made. As incredible as she seemed, Tito was inclined to believe the former rather than the latter.

After he'd washed up and eaten dinner in near silence, surrounded by fully armored guards who didn't acknowledge his presence except for the ones who spared him wary glances, he'd gone straight to bed.

Sleep came fast. Exhaustion had made sure of it.

His back ached from where the vice-captain had thrown him. His arm still felt the twist of that wrist lock, but more than that, his mind had finally shut up.

For the first time since the attunement, there was no storm of questions. Just silence, breath, and the weight of everything catching up.

And now, morning.

Tito took another bite of bread and looked around the dining hall again. A few guards sat scattered at the far end of the room, eating and talking in hushed tones. No one sat close, not out of hostility, only that distance was normal. Tito supposed he couldn't blame them. They probably didn't want to be flung into any columns.

He reached for the mug beside his plate - tea surprisingly - and took a slow sip. Bitter, but not bad, definitely meant to wake him up. And gods, he needed it.

He'd dressed in the gear from the chest. The shirt was heavier than he liked, but it moved well. The boots were quiet. His arms already ached slightly from how tightly the wraps pulled across the forearms, but they grounded him, reminded him what today was. No elements, just body. Break, build, repeat. He wouldn't let his power flare without control and hurt others again.

He stared into the mug, catching his reflection on the surface. His eyes looked tired, and he didn't even notice the cut on his lip from the spar yesterday. He was pretty unshaven now, but cleaner than he'd been in days. He didn't look like the same boy who'd boarded the magi's ship with Ro.

Maybe that boy had already burned away, taken instead of whatever the Runestone was trying to search for.

A distant bell began to toll in the hallway beyond the mess. He stood slowly, the sound vibrating in his ribs. Time to find the vice-captain.

Sweat clung to Tito's skin before the drills even began.

The training yard was already hot, and the sun which had barely broken the horizon scalded the stone beneath his boots. They were still warm from the day before, even before the coming of the sun, like they hadn't cooled overnight. Heat radiated off the walls of the Citadel's lower grounds and rose in waves. No wind, no relief. Just stillness and the sharp bark of orders cutting through it.

He stood in formation with twenty-six others, most of them recruits, though there were a few proper guards in training; but all of them were leaner, faster, and better prepared than he. His new tunic stuck to his back, his legs ached from the day before, his shoulder still remembered the vice-captain's throw, and the day hadn't even started.

A stocky man with a broken nose and voice like a dropped anvil paced before them, eyeing the line like he was inspecting fish for rot.

"You'll move until I say stop," the man barked. "You'll run until your legs forget what stillness is. You'll speak only when your lungs work well enough to form a sentence. Understood?"

The recruits shouted back, "Yes, Drillmaster!"

Tito added his voice half a beat too late.

Then it began. Running. Sprint drills around the yard, laps around the sparring pits and elemental trenches.

Tito kept pace at first, legs burning as they thundered over the packed dirt and stone, but it didn't take long before the heat clamped onto him like armor.

By the second lap, sweat streamed down his temples. By the third, his legs trembled. By the fourth, he was behind.

Worse still, he wasn't the only one who noticed. He could hear the sharper footfalls of the others pulling away. A few looked back, not unkind, but not patient either. Measuring him, gauging whether he'd drop. The drillmaster never broke pace.

When the laps ended, they were thrown straight into more drills. Pushups, sit-ups, striking form, and grappling. Every task exact, every repetition counted loud by a guard standing overhead. There were no breaks, just water from a single shared trough and the weight of exhaustion rolling in hotter than the sun itself.

And then there were the elemental exercises.

Not for him, of course. He wasn't allowed.

But they trained close by, in separate lines along the side of the yard, attuned recruits working through focused drills.

Tito tried not to look, but he couldn't help it.

One boy ignited a controlled flame across his forearms, striking at wooden dummies with bursts of heat that blackened the air.

Another formed a thin shield of water, arcing it in front of her just before a partner's strike landed. Someone further down summoned stone from the ground, dragging up jagged slabs and slamming them into place with practiced motion.

They made it look easy.

I had all of that, Tito thought bitterly, knuckles white around the wooden staff in his hand. *All four, just for a moment.*

But now, nothing. Not even a spark. He couldn't even feel the pull of the water that used to yearn to be moved by his hands. He wasn't entirely sure it was still there after the attunement if not for the constant reminder of the rune shifting on his arm.

"Ethyrae," the drillmaster barked suddenly. "Focus!"

Tito snapped his attention forward just as a padded staff smacked him across the ribs.

A grunt escaped before he could help it.

"If you want to daydream, do it while crawling back to your healer," the drillmaster said, stepping back. "Again!"

He stumbled into another bout of striking drills that were rhythmic, punishing, and endless.

By midday, the yard stank of sweat, dirt, and burning pride. Even the air felt thick enough to choke on. When they were given water, Tito dropped by the trough, gulping until his vision steadied.

"You're leaking heat like a broken forge," said a voice beside him.

He looked up, expecting mockery, and saw a girl, mid-twenties maybe, braid tied up, shoulders broad from years of drills, who expressed no mockery at all. She wore a crimson under sash marked with the sigil of the water element, her skin glistening with exertion, not struggle.

"Drink slower," she said, tipping her water skin toward his mouth. "Else you'll cramp mid-fall."

Tito nodded, too tired to waste words. She didn't wait for thanks.

They ended the day with sparring.

Tito's partner was a younger fire attuned guard, judging by the crest on his shoulder. He was fast and calculated, who sweat less than Tito and maintained his strength. The moment their staves met, Tito knew he was outmatched. His grip was too slow, his shoulders too tight. He blocked high and caught a jab to the ribs that stole his breath.

He hit the ground again.

The drillmaster's voice cracked across the yard, cutting through the clamor of clashing staves.

"You're soft, Shardborne."

Tito staggered to his feet with a heaving chest. He blinked the sweat from his eyes. Nobody called him that outside of the time Ro mentioned it. Well, come to think about it, so had the vice-captain, but she had privileged information. He assumed nobody outside of the magi and queen would know about what he did to the Runestone.

The man stepped forward slowly, boots grinding into the dirt.

"I heard you stood at the Runestone, cracked it even as your mark was given. Heard that it even matches Eryon's. That true?"

Tito didn't hesitate.

"Yes, Drillmaster."

He barely got the words out before the air around them shifted. A ripple passed through the other recruits as they stared, stilled hands and sparring matches, and whispers blooming like sparks in dry grass.

"Did he say Runestone?"

"He's the one from the courtyard?"

"Gods, I thought the mark was just decorative."

"Is that why his eyes are like that?"

Tito could feel the heat rising in his cheeks.

The sudden weight of being noticed, for the first time that day, no one was measuring his footwork or posture. They were staring at the rune etched into his forearm. He resisted the urge to cover it, but the drillmaster didn't let it go on.

"Enough," he snapped, his voice cracked like a whip. "He's still breathing, still bleeding. Same as you. You want to gawk, join the damn magi."

The whispers died immediately. Then the drillmaster turned his attention back to Tito, and his words struck like steel.

"You lived through that, Shardborne. Fight like it."

The words dug deep, echoing through Tito's chest as he stepped back into the ring. No fire rose in his palms. No stone crawled from the ground to lift him, but something else stirred. Not power, and not something graceful. Refusal. Refusal to be small, to be whispered about like a myth while he crawled through the dirt like a failure.

The next bout started. Tito lunged, no hesitation this time.

His grip was firm, his stance lower. He picked up some notes while watching the others fight. He didn't block so much as drive forward, forcing his opponent to backpedal for the first time. He swung harder, faster, finding rhythm in rage. Momentum.

He didn't win.

But he didn't fall.

And when the whistle blew and the bout ended, he was still on his feet.

By the time they were dismissed for the day, the sun hung low behind the spires. The light had shifted into a lazy gold and cast long shadows across the stone walkways. The training yard, once alive with shouts and clashing weapons, now stood quiet except for the occasional clang of gear being stored or boots shuffling toward the barracks.

Tito moved slowly. Every muscle ached. His shoulders screamed from drills, his legs felt like wood, his arms trembled.

The mess hall loomed ahead. Warm light glowed from the archway like an invitation he hadn't earned. He found a seat near the far edge of one long table and set his tray down, roasted squash, spiced grains, and a hunk of dense bread. He didn't even make it through the first bite before a voice broke the expected quiet.

"Hey, you really the one they called Shardborne?"

Tito looked up mid-chew. A tall recruit with storm colored eyes and a bandaged elbow stood over him, grinning.

"You're the one who broke the courtyard, right?"

Tito hesitated, then nodded.

That was enough.

In minutes, the seat across from him was filled. Then the one next to it, then the bench beside Tito groaned under the weight of bodies as more recruits slid in, plates in hand, voices eager. It was like someone had flung a whole bucket of fish guts into hungry waters. Conversation roared to life all around him.

"I heard you collapsed the entire training ring."

"No, it wasn't the ring, it was the Runestone itself that cracked, right?"

"Is it true your eyes glowed when it happened?"

"I heard one of the Magi tried to attack you and you knocked him out while attuning before passing out!"

"Did you see the queen? Like see her up close?"

"What's the rune feel like when it channels?"

Tito tried to answer politely at first, then more casually, then he simply tried to keep up. He had no idea who half of them were. A few wore the red threaded tunics of fire attuned initiates, while others had water sashes or stone pendants. A handful were nonmagical guards in training, wide-eyed and loud, each tossing stories back and forth, trying to confirm which parts of the tale were true. He gave them the facts he could.

"Yes, the courtyard cracked, but I don't know how or why."

"Yes, the queen was there, but she didn't say much."

"Yes, it hurt, like holding too much lightning in your chest while also drowning in water. Oh, and you're also trapped underground."

They hung on every word.

For a while, he forgot how tired he was, forgot how badly his legs ached or how sore his arms felt. He drank water. Somehow he finished his food.

Someone slid an extra slice of bread to his plate without asking.

Another asked to see the rune and he hesitated but finally twisted his forearm just long enough for them to glimpse the dark, shifting lines beneath his skin.

It pulsed faintly, even now. Like it breathed.

They whispered like it was holy.

He wasn't sure how long he was there. Time got strange in the mess of voices and questions. Someone recited a passage about

Eryon from memory, comparing Tito's eyes to some ancient warrior's. Another insisted the magi saw Tito's arms glow like molten steel during the attunement, even though he knew that couldn't possibly be true.

He didn't correct them, he just listened until, slowly, the table emptied.

Some left proudly, as if they'd touched history. Others gave him a firm clap on the back or a nod of respect before disappearing toward the barracks. But not all of them left with admiration. A few slipped away with something colder in their eyes.

One in particular lingered longer than the rest. He stood across the table from Tito long after the others had left. Taller by a head, maybe nineteen or twenty, with sharp cheekbones, perfectly cut hair, and the stone threaded sash of a trained earth attuned. His skin was clean, hands unscarred, his uniform pristine like someone who'd never lifted anything heavier than a training blade, unless a steward handed it to him.

He hadn't asked any questions, hadn't laughed. Hadn't even eaten. Now he just stared.

"Are you really from Ethyrae?" the boy asked at last.

Tito nodded slowly, "Yeah."

The boy let out a soft, humorless breath, "Figures."

Tito furrowed his brow.

"What's that supposed to mean?"

The boy leaned forward slightly, both hands braced on the table.

"That a fisherman's son from the coast gets handed Eryon's rune and a training regimen while the rest of us claw our way up from years of training. Family legacy, guard records, and trials. And you, what? You break a courtyard and suddenly you're a legend?"

Tito's stomach knotted, but he stayed still.

"I didn't ask for this."

"No," the boy said, "but you got it."

He glanced around, then stepped closer, and said in a low voice, "You know what you looked like out there? During your attunement? Like a poisoned sword wielded by an infant. You scorched the field, nearly crushed a magus, and killed two. You don't even know how to hold what you've been given, and yet here you are, center table, full audience, drinking it in like you earned it."

Tito's jaw tightened, "If you're trying to..."

"I'm trying to warn you," the boy snapped. "That rune is a fuse. You think these people cheering you on won't be the first to run if you lose control again?"

He took a step back, looking Tito up and down.

"You don't belong with that mark. Not from where you came from."

The last words dripped like venom, like even referencing his home was taboo.

Tito stood up slowly, the bench groaning beneath him. His body ached, his bones throbbed, but his spine held firm.

"All your records, legacy, bloodline," he said quietly, "and the stone still chose a fisherman's son. Wonder what that says about your bloodline."

Tito didn't wait to see if his words stuck. He stood up and turned back to the barracks.

CHAPTER 17

The days blurred. Tito lost track of how many mornings began with aching bones and ended with bruised pride, how many meals came with whispers, or how many nights he collapsed onto the hard barracks' bed only to be woken before the sun dared to rise.

He hadn't known how long a week could stretch, how it could feel both endless and like it vanished in a heartbeat. He'd lived by bells and barked orders, by drills and bruises, and by the rhythm of dirt underfoot and sweat in his eyes.

Slowly, it began to shape him.

By the third day, the drillmaster started calling him Shardborne again. By the fourth, the name spread. Not just among recruits, but whispered between younger guards, muttered by instructors, etched in chalk onto the sparring wall when someone wanted to call him out.

Tito didn't rise to it. Truth be told, he didn't have time. Every morning brought a new gauntlet of laps around the yard, weighted climbs, weapon drills, grappling rotations, and exercises designed not to train but to break everything weak inside so the rest could be rebuilt stronger.

Always nearby, watching, was Kael Morran.

That was the name the watermarked girl gave him. She'd found Tito after their second grappling rotation, during the short water break when everyone leaned on whatever wall or bench they could find. Her braid was already coming undone from sweat and impact, and she passed him her water skin without asking.

"Name's Callyn," she'd said between gulps. "You looked like you were ready to bite through your tongue back there."

He coughed, then laughed.

She smirked.

"And that stiff-necked brat who gave you the talk last night? Kael Morran. Family's old Inner Ring. They train elemental engineers or something. Think they're better than half the magi."

Tito didn't say anything, but he remembered the boy's words. The tone, *you don't belong here*, dripping from every syllable.

Callyn read it on his face.

"Don't waste your fire on him," she said, slinging her braid over one shoulder. "He's been training for years and still didn't get half the attention you did in one day. That kind of burn doesn't go away easily."

He thanked her.

She grinned, and just like that they fell into an easy rhythm.

They didn't talk constantly, there wasn't time for that, but she started nodding to him before drills. Sometimes she'd correct his form with a sharp tap or a motion. Sometimes she'd share water without a word. She didn't coddle him or cheer him on. She just showed up.

For Tito, that was enough.

Kael, on the other hand, did the opposite. He never laid a hand on Tito during training and never spoke to him again directly; but every time they were assigned to the same rotation, he watched Tito more closely during spars. He smirked when Tito stumbled, scoffed when instructors corrected him. And once during a sandbag carry drill, he *accidentally* bumped Tito hard enough to send his sack spilling over.

Tito didn't lash out, but he remembered.

The rivalry simmered beneath the skin of every drill. The other recruits began to notice, began to whisper again, not about the rune, but about the fisher boy and the Morran son circling each other like storms waiting to break.

And through it all, Tito trained. Gods, he trained. The soreness didn't fade, it just became normal. The aches stopped feeling like punishment and started feeling like progress. His hands hardened, his grip steadied. His movements, once sluggish and unbalanced, began to tighten.

Five days in, he was matching pace with recruits who'd been here for years, much to Kael's dismay.

Tito wasn't besting them, the progress still came slow, but he just stood his ground. For someone who'd come to this place with nothing but a cracked courtyard behind him, that was enough.

It wasn't until the end of the seventh day that everything truly paused.

The final drill had ended. The sun had begun to dip behind the towers again, casting long shadows across the yard.

Tito was leaning against the training wall, forearms resting on his knees, sweat dripping from his chin onto the packed dirt. Callyn dropped beside him, handing him her water skin.

"You survived."

He took it with a tired smirk, "Barely."

She stretched out her legs.

"Next week won't be easier. They're testing us again."

Tito wiped his forehead.

"Us?"

She nodded.

"Everyone in our intake group. There's only five of us, but the drillmaster says the vice-captain is reviewing evaluations herself. I assume that's because of you. Valeria is rarely out with the recruits."

Tito sat up a little straighter.

"Valeria?"

"You don't know her name?"

He shook his head.

She grinned.

"Valeria. Daughter of the Guard's High Commander. I've personally seen her disarm a man twice her size in three seconds flat."

Tito blinked. The woman who threw him like a sack of potatoes had a name.

Valeria.

There was something alluring and dangerous to that name. Why he felt that way, however, Tito had no way of explaining.

"She likes watching," Callyn added. "Won't say anything until she has to, but she sees everything. Every flaw, every advantage."

Tito felt a bead of sweat trail down his temple.

She would be watching again, and this time he wanted to prove himself. Not just that he was improving, but that he belonged.

Later that night, when the yard lights had dimmed and the barracks had quieted into the soft shuffle of bodies settling into beds after dinner, Tito lay staring at the ceiling above his cot. His arms ached, his knees were bruised. He'd torn a muscle in his left calf three days ago and hadn't even noticed until the adrenaline wore off.

None of that kept him awake. What did was the silence. Rather, there was no Ro to fill that silence. No sarcastic banter or laughter about how "ridiculously dramatic" the magi were. Just Tito, alone. And even though he'd forged something here, small bonds, earned respect and grit, he still missed his sibling.

I hope you're okay, he thought as he stared up into the shadows. *I hope your tower's not eating you alive.*

He let out a slow breath.

And I hope, wherever you are, that you miss me too.

CHAPTER 18

The sky was still more gray than gold when Tito stepped into the yard.

A pale sun hovered just over the outer spires, casting a soft haze across the stonework. Everything was quiet, almost reverent. No barking drillmaster, no rhythmic drills. Just five recruits waiting in a single row at the edge of the arena. Sweat already lined Tito's neck beneath the tunic, even though the early morning heat had yet to sink in.

He knew the true source was today's purpose...Evaluation Day.

Tito took his place second from the left. To his right stood Callyn, arms crossed. On the far end, a pair of older recruits he barely knew, both whispering about who might make rank by year's end.

And between them, like a darkened scale, was Kael Morran who gave a long, deliberate glance down the line, then rested his eyes on Tito.

"You look cleaner than usual," he said flatly. "Finally figure out how to scrub the gutter off?"

Callyn sighed beside him, "Gods, you're exhausting."

Tito didn't rise to it. His eyes stayed forward.

"I'll be sure to bleed carefully when we spar."

Callyn smirked.

"Only fair. Kael's already bled on most of the training grounds this week."

Kael scoffed softly, "It's not the blood I'm worried about. It's whether the ground shatters again when the Shardborne tries to punch above his weight."

The others quieted at that.

Callyn scoffed, "He's already been punching at your weight. So, what does that say about you?"

Kael's jaw flexed, but before he could retort, a horn gave a single sharp note from the far gate.

The air changed instantly as all eyes turned to watch Valeria enter without any more ceremony.

Today, she donned no armor, but dressed herself in a dark, sleeveless leather training cuirass with matching bracers. Pale crimson runes were etched into the bracers, and a long crimson sash tied at her hip. Her hair was braided back into a tight coil, and her gaze moved over them like a drawn blade. She stopped in front of the group and folded her arms behind her back.

"I don't care what you've heard about today," she said ceremonially. "This is not your graduation. There are no ranks, no one gets a sword. The only thing you leave with is pain, and whether you wore it well."

No one dared move.

"You've been chosen for this evaluation because the drillmaster believes you may be worth more than cannon fodder," she continued. "But belief means nothing. Show me your worth."

She let the silence settle like heat across the yard.

"Step forward when I call your name. One at a time. You will be tested on form, instinct, resilience, and focus. You will not be graded on showmanship. You will be watched, and you will be remembered. For better or worse."

Her eyes scanned the line again.

No banners, no ceremony. Just the crackling energy of an audience, not just Kael, but guards watching from balconies, Drillmaster Varin near the gate with his arms folded, and Valeria, the vice-captain of the Queen's Guard, commanding the center of the ring like the yard itself bent around her presence.

"Rannon."

The first recruit, a tall, lean boy with a sharp jaw, stepped forward from beside Tito and cracked his knuckles. Valeria motioned to the center.

"You'll be sparring me?" he asked, flashing a grin. "No offense, Vice-Captain. I was raised to avoid hitting women."

Callyn exhaled sharply.

Tito bit the inside of his cheek, remembering how easily she flipped him to the ground.

Valeria said nothing, she just lifted one hand and beckoned him forward.

Rannon moved quickly, too quickly. The way he lunged was confident, the kind of speed that earned cheers in the sparring yard across this week. Valeria didn't even blink. She sidestepped, caught his arm mid-swing, pivoted behind him, and in a single, fluid motion, snapped his elbow the wrong way with a sound that made everyone in the line flinch.

Rannon collapsed with a scream. Valeria stood over him like the moment had barely registered.

"You'll speak less when the pain teaches you more."

A nearby guard rushed in to lift the man up. He was still groaning while cradling his arm.

Valeria never turned her head.

"Next, Thorne."

A quiet, stockier recruit with broad shoulders and a scar above his eye stepped forward from the end of the line. No words, just a bow of the head and a ready stance.

Valeria circled him once, like a predator testing distance. Then she struck. Their clash was heavier, slower, with steel behind each strike. Thorne blocked well, dodged better, but she pushed him...tested him.

Her staff was a blur. Tito never even noticed her pull it out, and though Thorne held ground longer than expected, it ended similarly. A sweep to the leg, the staff end to his throat, and it was over in less than a minute.

The vice-captain stepped back and nodded once to a guard who approached and gestured for Thorne to follow. He did, head held high despite the bruises forming under his eye.

"Yren."

The third recruit stepped in with a confident, almost theatrical turn of his wrists. He flashed his rune, orange pulsing briefly through it. His movements were bold, strong, and surprisingly imprecise. He struck like he was used to winning. Valeria let him come, let him throw a full series of wide, powerful arcs that she parried down before she struck back, fast and clean. She didn't dismantle him instantly, she let the spar stretch, letting him hang himself on momentum and poor footwork. When it ended, she stepped back, not even winded. Three fights in a row now.

"You have ability," she said at last. "but you treat your body like it's a weapon already forged. It's still raw steel. Come back when you've learned to temper it."

Yren nodded with wounded pride. He left with slower steps than the others.

"Callyn."

Tito turned.

She stepped forward with no bravado, no fire in her eyes, just readiness. Her braid hung low over her shoulder, skin glistening from the heat already rising off the stone. Her face remained unreadable, but her stance was clean.

Valeria gave her a single nod.

"Your evaluation will be different, you may use your element as you see fit."

Callyn didn't respond, just bowed slightly and raised her hands.

The fight began fast.

Tito watched, barely blinking, excited to see Callyn's magic in action.

At first, Callyn met every strike with pure technique. She spun to deflect, ducked beneath wide sweeps, and countered with sharp, explosive movements of her legs and shoulders. It was graceful, with no wasted energy and no panic. She even managed to land a glancing hit to Valeria's hip that would've earned praise from any other instructor, especially from the other initiates considering how the other evaluations went.

But Valeria had no such praise. She turned like the wind and returned fire twice as fast.

Callyn stumbled. Her footing recovered, but now she was sweating, breathing faster.

Tito clenched his fists.

Then, just as Valeria swept a staff strike toward her ribs, water erupted from Callyn's hand.

Tito was amazed. He watched the water flow from her sash along her runed arm and back out.

A twisting arc surged up in a burst of mist and pressure, intercepting Valeria's blow with a crack of magic against wood. The vapor clouded the air briefly, and for a half-second, she vanished behind it, reappearing low, spinning to land another quick shot to Valeria's calf.

It worked.

But Valeria recovered instantly and spun through the mist, grabbed Callyn by the wrist, and brought her to the ground in a single, fluid movement. She didn't strike again, but hovered there, knee poised just above the point of pain.

"You waited too long to call on what is yours," Valeria said.

Callyn didn't answer.

Valeria stood, released her, and nodded.

"Good instinct, better composure. You may wait here."

As Callyn walked back to the line, Tito caught the faint shake in her arms.

She didn't meet his gaze, but he knew she felt his eyes. She'd fought beautifully. And still, Valeria had bested her like it was nothing.

Tito's name hadn't been called yet. He could feel the sun now, high and hot overhead, the light making his breath feel heavier than it had all week. Sweat trickled down his back, but he stayed still.

"Vandero! *Shardborne.*"

All sound, all sense of time, vanished. He stepped forward. The weight in his legs from training, the soreness in his ribs, all fell away under the press of anticipation. His palms tingled with nerves.

Valeria stood across from him, still calm, watching him with full attention. He moved into his stance and tried not to look at the way the light caught the curve of her jawline, or the fine lines around her eyes when she narrowed them in focus. She was undeniably beautiful. He found that he couldn't look at her directly.

He swallowed, tightening his grip on his staff, the comfort of the wood between his hands grounding him.

You're ready. Show her.

Valeria moved like the air knew her. She didn't sprint, didn't shout, didn't roar her way into combat. She stepped, spun, pivoted, all precision with no waste. Her staff came down in a clean diagonal. He blocked it, barely. The shock ran through his forearms like lightning.

She didn't stop. One strike became two, then five.

He parried low, then rolled beneath the next swing. His boots skidded slightly, the barren ground beneath him slick with sweat. He rose back to stance, staff raised, breath tight.

She came again and again, until he lost count, not only of her attacks, but of how many of his own missed. She was there, then she wasn't. A sweep at his legs, a jab at his ribs, a short, quick blow toward his shoulder that nearly broke through his guard.

He pivoted, ducked, and spun away, feeling the air shift around her like she was reshaping the very space they fought in. It almost felt like dancing.

The thought hit him unbidden. Tito had never danced before, only watched it growing up with Jaro and his old wife, or Eira before her husband moved.

He immediately cursed himself for it. What kind of thought was that? But even as he tried to shove it away, he couldn't unsee it, the rhythm of it all. He was keeping pace with something choreographed, and he was barely keeping up.

His arms burned, his feet ached. Every block came just in time, every counterattack was met with something sharper; but he hadn't fallen yet. That mattered.

Then...a feint. A jab. A sharp strike to his side that nearly cracked through his defense.

He grunted, twisting too late, and her staff came in hard across his chest.

Crack!

The impact didn't knock him down, but it staggered him. His heel skidded back.

And then she stopped. Just as she had with the others. Watching, waiting for him to yield. And gods, he almost did. But as the staff hovered there, just inches from his collarbone, he moved.

His staff twisted up clumsily and caught hers just off the shaft. It shouldn't have worked. She was stronger and faster, but for a single breath, the wind shifted. A whisper, a flicker of something inside him, not called by will but by need, nudged him. It curled beneath his heel and behind his shoulder, accelerating him. A surge forward, just enough, just barely, to give his body the edge it needed.

He lashed out. His staff came up in a tight arc, powered by every ounce of desperation he had, and Valeria staggered and stepped back. Just one step, and for a heartbeat, the world froze. The wind vanished as fast as it had come. No one spoke. No one moved.

Valeria stared at him.

Tito stared back, chest heaving, arms trembling, eyes wide. *Did I...?*

Then her staff spun low, cracked his stance, and swept his legs clean out from under him. He hit the ground hard, dust bloomed around his shoulders as his back met the stone. She stood over him, staff pressed lightly to his throat. A beat passed. Then she spoke.

"Up. On your feet, Maldito of Ethyrae."

CHAPTER 19

The dust still clung to Tito's shoulders as he stood up, breath shallow, arms heavy.

Valeria's staff withdrew from his neck with a flick. She said nothing, just motioned with her fingers, subtle but firm, pointing him back toward the line outside the ring where they started.

Tito turned, legs still shaky, and made his way across the yard to stand beside Callyn. She gave him a look as he passed, a half nod to *you're not unconscious, so that's something*. He gave a tired nod back and took his place beside her in the line.

Valeria remained in the center of the yard, speaking now with Drillmaster Varin and two guards who had stood at the perimeter through the evaluation. Their voices were low, too distant to hear, but Tito could see the shift in posture, the deference in how the guards stood, the way the drillmaster nodded once and stepped back.

When Valeria finally turned to face them again, her eyes swept across Tito and Callyn alone.

"The two of you," she said, her tone precise, "have demonstrated readiness. You have shown that your training has had an effect."

Tito straightened.

Callyn's brows lifted slightly.

"You are not finished, not even close," Valeria continued, "but your performance today has proven sufficient for what comes next."

She let that hang in the air for a breath.

"You are being reassigned."

Tito blinked.

"To what, ma'am?" Callyn asked.

"A weeklong assignment outside the Citadel. A controlled training exercise structured to test your elemental progression and your ability to adapt without Citadel wards. A scouting mission in name, but you will be observed, and you will be challenged."

Outside the Citadel.

They hadn't been allowed outside since the day they'd arrived. The thought was thrilling and unnerving.

"You will be issued new quarters, upper chambers, in the east hall. There are only two rooms in the east chamber. One is reserved for the magi initiates who will accompany you, the other will be yours," she added, glancing toward Tito. "You'll sleep light, move fast, and you'll be expected to supply yourselves."

Tito blinked.

"Ours?"

He hadn't meant to say it aloud.

Valeria arched an eyebrow but didn't elaborate.

"Yes."

And that was that. No further explanation.

Tito nodded slowly, trying to keep his expression neutral. *Right, military lodging, bunks. Nothing weird.* He'd shared sleeping space with Ro his whole life. This would be the same. Probably.

Callyn, of course, didn't blink.

"Are the magi initiates assigned yet?" she asked, already moving past it.

"You'll meet them during final prep. For now, focus on your time. One day for research and another for gathering supplies. Once you leave the Citadel, you won't get another chance to resupply."

Then Valeria turned her eyes briefly to Tito.

"Lean on her judgment. Don't waste your time playing soldier."

Tito nodded quickly, "Understood."

"Good," she stepped back. "Dismissed."

Valeria turned to the guards nearby and gestured, "Escort them to their new quarters."

They began to walk, slowly at first, crossing the yard, but just before they reached the inner gate, Valeria's voice rang out again, "Tito. Stay a moment."

He paused.

Callyn glanced at Tito questionably but said nothing, stepping ahead with the guards.

Tito turned back.

Valeria stood alone again in the center of the yard, the sun still high above her. She didn't speak until he stood directly in front of her. Her eyes, sharp as always, locked onto his.

"You channeled wind during our sparring match."

Tito swallowed.

"I didn't mean to. It just…"

"I know," she said, calm but firm. "I should report it. Venric would want to know. The moment your control slips, he'll call it a risk, an instability. That's how the magi work."

She took a slow breath.

"But I saw something else."

Tito's pulse quickened.

"You didn't summon it. You responded on instinct without ego, it wasn't forced." She studied him for a long moment. "So, for now, I'll refrain from telling him."

His throat tightened.

"Why?"

"Because you're not ready to answer the questions that would follow," she said, "and you deserve the chance to learn what you are before others try to decide it for you."

Her voice softened, but only slightly.

"Don't make me regret that choice."

Tito nodded, voice low, "I won't."

Valeria stepped back, "Go, get ready. And try not to burn anything down."

Tito turned quickly as soon as Valeria dismissed him, trying to spot the guards or Callyn, but the courtyard was already clearing.

Drillmaster Varin was gone. The two guards who'd flanked Valeria were nowhere in sight, even Valeria had managed to leave. The only sound left was the faint whistle of wind catching between stone columns, and the slow clatter of weapon racks being restocked near the edge of the training yard.

Tito jogged toward the nearest path out that Callyn was heading towards. He glanced left, then right, past tiled corridors and open balconies, but there was no sign of Callyn's braid or the armor of the escorts.

"Great," he muttered.

Out of habit, his steps pulled him toward the Citadel's mess hall. The food wouldn't be glamorous, but after a fight like that, after a week like this, he could practically taste the grain bread and roasted squash already.

As he stepped up toward the archway, though, voices rose from within. Laughter, spoons clinking, the familiar scrape of boots on stone. And then, worse...whispers. His name. *Shardborne*. He hadn't even entered the hall yet and they were already talking. He lingered just beyond the edge of the doorway, hidden in the shadow of the arch, and caught snippets.

"...took a swing at Valeria, I swear!"

"...even assigned a training mission! Bet Kael's furious. Heard he stormed out early..."

Tito exhaled through his nose. He wasn't in the mood for the looks or the questions, the hero-worship when he wasn't allowed to call elements still for fear of destroying half the ground. And he definitely didn't want to see Kael post assignment from Valeria.

His stomach twisted as he remembered Valeria offering to not turn him in. The sudden burst of air that had swept through him mid-fight, not summoned, not shaped, just there. It hadn't even been conscious, and yet it felt good. For one moment, everything had lined up. His stance, his breath and the staff in his hands. The world felt light, like wind moving through a tightened sail. And then it was gone. Tito wanted it back.

He turned from the mess hall before anyone could spot him, footsteps echoing off the narrow hallway walls as he made his way toward the eastern corridors.

Finding the upper chambers wasn't easy, he hadn't been anywhere near this part of the Citadel.

The stonework was different here, less worn. The torches mounted in wall brackets were newer, clean even. A subtle pattern lined the floor tiles, and the crests on the walls were the emblems of the magi, the tower orders, and something else he didn't recognize.

He moved quietly as he let his thoughts spin. Upper chamber...shared room. That was still bouncing around in his head. He told himself it didn't matter. Soldiers did it all the time. This wasn't strange. Callyn certainly hadn't made it strange.

But everything was changing so fast, and he didn't know where to put half the things he was feeling. Including the one thing that had stayed quiet in the back of his mind through all the drills and bruises and dust...Ro.

His pace slowed as he turned into another corridor, light catching on a polished brass lantern overhead. He hadn't seen his sibling in a week, not once.

He didn't even know what hallways led to the illusion spire now, Illusia as Venric called it. The only thing Tito knew is that Ro was training with someone called Thalen, that they were probably doing something completely ridiculous and laughing about it, driving Thalen insane. Or crying. And Tito wouldn't know which until it was too late.

I should've found you at the end of the first night, he thought. *I should've pushed harder, or asked someone, or something.*

But he hadn't and now, with this new assignment, he'd be even further away. He ran a hand through his hair and sighed, then looked up at the corridor sign engraved into the stone above him.

East Hall – Field Assignment Quarters.

Finally.

His shoulders sagged slightly, the adrenaline from his evaluation with Valeria had long since worn off, leaving nothing but aching limbs and churning thoughts. He barely had time to turn before a fist slammed into his ribs.

Tito stumbled back, air gone from his lungs, eyes watering as he fell into the wall. Before he could react, a boot caught him in the side, sending him skidding across the polished stone.

Laughter followed.

"I was almost convinced you got lost, *Shardborne*."

Tito coughed, chest burning, and looked up.

Kael Morran stood just outside the bend in the corridor with two others wearing initiate insignia flanking him. They were both taller, older, and built like they'd been raised on stone and soldiering. One wore the pendant of earth, the other the beaded necklace for wind. Tito's stomach dropped.

"You think they'll really let you represent the Citadel?" Kael asked. "Let you walk out that gate like you earned it?"

Tito stood slowly, jaw tight, legs already screaming in protest.

"You're not going to stop me," he muttered.

Kael smiled, no humor in it.

"Oh, I'm not here to stop you...just to delay things."

The others moved.

Tito raised his arms just in time to catch the first blow to his shoulder, then a knee cracked against his hip. He twisted, hands instinctively half raised, and struck one of them in the side hard enough to stagger him.

Kael cursed and came in swinging.

Tito ducked low and dodged it. He caught Kael with a shove, sending him off balance, but the second recruit grabbed Tito from behind, pinning his arms. A fist slammed into his side again, then across his jaw.

White flashed in his vision.

He fought, he struggled, but it was not enough. Something was screaming from deep within his mind. *Let it out! You have the power, show them what they are jealous of.*

Two on one, then back to three on one. They didn't want to kill him, just ensure that he couldn't walk the next day. Every strike was meant to break something without breaking everything.

And it might've worked.

The stone beneath their feet split with a sharp, thunderous snap, and suddenly a wall of jagged rock surged up between them, forcing the attackers to leap back.

A voice rang out like steel drawn across stone.

"That's enough."

Everyone froze, except for Tito who collapsed to one knee, bleeding from the lip, ribs pulsing in agony.

A figure stood at the far end of the corridor now, robes of gray and deep violet, sleeves threaded with sigils. He lowered his hood to reveal sharp, weathered features and a large, ornate pendant from his neck.

A magus.

Someone in front of Tito moved to run. The magus lifted a hand and more stone erupted, snatching their ankles, yanking them down with a thud. Tito blinked through something wet running into his eye and swore he could make out Kael being the one to fall.

"You dare attack a rune marked initiate under assignment?" The magus didn't raise his voice, the weight of it was enough. "Cowardice in the halls of the Citadel. Treason against command."

Kael spat blood.

"He doesn't deserve the rune."

The magus tilted his head, gaze sharp.

"You don't deserve the walls you stand in."

He turned.

"Guards."

Two armored soldiers appeared at the end of the hall like summoned ghosts, stepping quickly into the corridor. The magus gestured to the restrained initiates.

"Take them to holding. Evaluation pending disciplinary tribunal. They are not to leave the south chambers until further notice."

The guards moved swiftly, dragging Kael and his cohorts out.

The magus exhaled, then turned to Tito.

"You're lucky they didn't aim lower," he said, voice dry. "Still walking?"

"Barely," Tito muttered, trying not to wince as he stood.

"I would ask who you are, but word spreads quick," the magus started as he glanced at Tito's rune marked arm.

"You'll want the next corridor," the magus said, already turning away. "Second door on the left. Move fast before someone else decides to test your balance."

Tito didn't reply.

The magus raised a hand lazily, and the stone walls that had erupted now folded back into the floor like they'd never been there. The floor was polished as ever, save a small little crack between the patterns on the floor. Then he was gone.

Tito stood alone in the corridor, blood trickled from his lip and now from his head. His ribs ached with every breath, and the faint whisper of wind moving past his ear. Not summoned, not present. Just like it was waiting, watching.

He turned slowly and limped toward the next hallway, heart pounding, hands trembling, not just from pain, but from the knowledge that, for the second time today, he'd survived.

The pain was very much still there, and the hallway tilted with each step.

Tito just needed to rest, to lay his head down. His legs felt like they belonged to someone else. They were stiff, unresponsive, trembling with effort. His ribs throbbed with every breath, the bruises from Kael's boots already darkened beneath his tunic. The pain anchored him, but barely.

He rounded the corner, his eyes hyperactive to not be caught off guard again. There it was...second door on the left, the Field Quarters. Tito made a mental note to not confuse that with Field *Assignment* Quarters.

The corridor was dim, the sunlight of the fading evening bled in just enough to show the polished stone beneath Tito's feet and the brass plating along the archways. His body felt numb. He reached the second door on the left and pressed a trembling hand to the bronze handle.

A pulse met him. The runes in the metal hummed faintly at his touch, like a held breath recognizing him. Something flashed through his body, almost like a cold chill, as the door unlocked without a sound.

He pushed it open.

Callyn stood with her back to the door, bare feet on the marble, fully nude. She was mid-motion, arms raised to pull on a thin linen gown, nothing yet covering her, no armor to shield her or sarcasm in her mouth to warn him off.

She was there.

Sunlight from the arched window poured across her skin in long, warm ribbons, gilding every inch of her with gold.

His breath hitched.

Her dark wet hair waved over her shoulders which were broad, sculpted by years of training, but still carried the natural softness of her femininity. Her back curved in a long, graceful slope, tapering at the waist before flaring into hips that tilted slightly as she shifted her weight. The lines of her body were striking, not polished like a statue, but lived in, real, radiant. Strength and softness, elegance and danger, woven together into something utterly captivating.

His gaze moved down before he could stop it.

The swell of her backside, tight and shaped by years of lunges and drills, flexed slightly with the motion of her arms. There were faint marks across her thighs, training scars, bruises in the shape of impact. A life in motion.

The gown whispered down her arms as she tugged it on. Slow, delicate linen caught the light as she turned. It passed over the swell of her breasts, which were small, high, and round, gravity barely touching them.

Tito saw them fully, silhouetted for one unbearable second in the sun.

The darker skin of her nipples stood out starkly against her tone, dusky and stiff from the open air.

His mind seized on the curve of them, the way they moved slightly as the fabric passed over, the softness surrounded by the hard plane of her torso, the way they...

He'd never seen anything like it. He'd never seen anyone like her. His mouth was dry. His heart pounded like he'd just run laps. His eyes traced her back up until they met hers.

It was a thunderclap.

Her expression flashed pure flame, wide-eyed and furious, cheeks instantly flushed with rage and embarrassment. She snatched the gown down the rest of the way, pulling it over her thighs, fingers gripping the hem.

Tito didn't have time to apologize. The breath left his lungs. His vision fractured. He staggered forward once, lips parted to apologize and then dropped in the doorway like a taught fishing line snapping.

The last thing he saw before the black took him was her. Gown half-hanging, eyes alight with something between fury and disbelief.

Then, nothing.

CHAPTER 20

Cotton slid between Tito's fingertips.

The first thing he noticed was the comfort of the sheets on top of him. The second was someone standing over him. He opened his eyes, and Salindra stared back.

Her dark robe framed her like a painted silhouette, one hand on her hip, the other gently lifting the edge of a damp cloth that had been laid across his brow. She was frowning, but there was no alarm in her eyes, just that familiar *what did you do now* kind of concern that somehow made him feel both guilty and comforted.

It reminded Tito of the way Eryx would look at him when he overheated and collapsed while helping repair the docks.

"You're awake," she said simply.

Tito sat up too quickly and instantly regretted it as his bruised ribs protested.

"Where's...? I...Callyn!"

He scrambled upright, legs tangled in the sheet, face flushing with immediate memory. The gown. The light. Her skin...gods!

"I didn't mean to... I wasn't...!" he stammered, half standing, already looking toward the far side of the chamber. "I have to apologize. She's probably furious, and I didn't..."

"She left an hour or two ago," Salindra said, unmoved.

Tito froze mid motion, heart still racing.

"What?"

"She waited longer than she needed to," Salindra said, adjusting the tray of herbal salves beside the bed. "She sat beside you until I arrived, even stayed through half of my usual midday tea. Then she left for the archives."

Tito blinked.

"She waited?"

Salindra arched an eyebrow.

"Slightly worried, I'd say. You hit the stone hard."

He ran a hand down his face, heat still burning in his cheeks.

"I didn't mean to... I wasn't trying to..."

"Sit still before you open something that was already barely closed."

Tito flopped back onto the bed with a grunt.

His eyes darted around the chamber. The room was large and spacious compared to the barracks. It had two beds, one neatly made, wardrobes on either end and a window which let in soft daylight that shifted to pale beams.

"Did you have dinner last night?" Salindra asked, already knowing the answer.

"I was going to," he offered weakly.

She snorted.

"That's a no."

"I wasn't hungry."

"You're bruised, you're underfed, and you're about to be sent beyond the walls for a full week of field exercise," she said, rolling her sleeves. "You will eat, and you will pack more food than you think you need. Until then, I'm having dinner delivered here, sizable portions, for both of you."

Tito blinked.

"Thank you."

"Don't thank me. Just eat."

She turned back to gather her bag of tinctures and cloth, then paused before the door.

"I'm not going to ask about the state you arrived in," she said quietly, "but I will remind you this... you have power in your veins and, thanks to Morran, a target on your back. Walk carefully."

Tito sat for a long second then nodded, "I will."

She reached for the door handle.

"Oh, one last thing..." he added quickly. "The archives. How do I get there?"

Salindra turned, a knowing flicker in her eye.

"Spiral stairs, north wing. Fifth landing. Look for the mirrored arch. If you hit a hallway lined with floating orbs, you've gone too far."

"That specific, huh?" he asked with all the humor he could muster.

"Not enough," she said, and then, with a swirl of fabric and a faint scent of incense clinging to the air behind her, she was gone.

Tito sat up on the edge of the bed and slowly pulled a clean tunic over his shoulders, careful not to twist too fast. His body still hurt, but less than before. The worst of the ache had dulled to a low throb in his ribs and across his side. His lip felt puffy, and his jaw was stiff when he clenched it, but something about the way Salindra worked with her precise hands and warm salves had soothed him back from the edge.

He didn't know how long he'd been asleep, but the light pouring in through the window was pouring almost directly inside.

Half the day's gone, he thought. *And I haven't done anything.*

A tray sat waiting for him on the low table near the foot of the bed full of fruit, oat bread, a boiled egg, slices of cured meat, and a cup of still-warm tea that smelled faintly of citrus and earth.

Salindra, of course.

He ate slowly at first, half-expecting his body to rebel, but it didn't. The nausea faded, the lightheadedness cleared; and the more his body steadied, the more his mind began to wander.

The memory flashed again without permission, the curve of her back, the slope of her breasts, the golden light making her skin glow like flame painted marble.

His face flushed all over again, and he wiped his hands on the cloth napkin too hard. He hadn't meant to look. He hadn't meant to see *that* much, but gods, he *had* seen it, and it was carved into the back of his mind like a brand. So now what?

Apologize? Pretend it didn't happen? What if she was angry enough to report it? It couldn't be that rare of an occurrence between men and women sharing rooms, right?

She waited and stayed with him longer than she needed to. That meant something.

Still, a knot lingered in his chest.

Was it better to speak to her first or dive into the mission? Time was already slipping. Valeria had said one day for research, one day for supplies. There wasn't room to hesitate.

He stood, careful as he tightened the belt of his tunic. If he saw her, he would figure out what to say. If he didn't, then he would complete his research and hope to clear it up in the evening.

He rolled his shoulders, hissed slightly at the sting in his side, then made his way to the door, pressing one hand against the runed latch.

It clicked open.

The Citadel was not made to be navigated by instinct. Tito realized this somewhere between the third fork in a corridor he swore he'd already passed, and the winding gallery full of statues that all looked vaguely like Queen Seraphina from different angles.

"Spiral stairs, north wing," he muttered aloud, recounting the instructions Salindra had given him. "Fifth landing. Mirrored arch."

He looked up. No spiral stairs, no arch. Just another hallway and a mosaic of the five towers arranged in a swirling constellation of polished tile. He sighed. Callyn probably walked this path blindfolded.

She had known exactly where to go when Valeria gave the order and had practically led the guards herself. She hadn't paused, hadn't checked a map, or even asked for clarity. She just moved, like she'd done it a hundred times before.

How long has she trained here? How did she know Kael's background?

It hadn't struck him before, but now it itched at the back of his mind. Callyn was a seasoned fighter, but beyond that she moved like someone who had been allowed to belong here long before he ever walked through the gate. Tito quickly realized he didn't know her at all.

You can ask her after the archives.

He took a deep breath and stepped through the next archway. The hallway narrowed here, stone shifting from polished gray to a pale, veined marble etched with narrow silver runes...and cold. A faint prickle ran up the back of his neck. He took two more steps before he noticed the carved title above the threshold he had just passed under. *Magus Hall – Tiered Access Only.*

Tito froze.

He turned, ready to backpedal, but stopped. If it were truly off limits, surely there would have been barriers like the ones separating the rings. It was, however, not the way to the archives. He turned before several voices stopped him.

"...No, I'm telling you, it pulsed again, after the evaluation," came the voice. Crisp and familiar. Clipped with frustration.

Venric.

Tito ducked low, hugging the wall just beneath a recessed archway, heart suddenly thudding far too loudly in his chest. Another voice answered. Male and older, a deep resonance echoing off the marble just far enough for Tito to pick it up.

"And you're sure it wasn't triggered by any other initiates?"

"It responded to him," Venric hissed. "I watched it. He was supposed to be exhausted...drained, but he summoned wind reflexively. No training, no uncontrolled outburst, just pure will."

"You've said this before," the second voice replied. "You don't trust him."

"I don't trust what's inside him." Venric's footsteps paced now. Closer. "Just like I didn't trust who it was inside before, and if anyone listened then I could've saved us twenty years of searching."

There was a pause.

Tito didn't dare breathe.

The older voice sighed, "You want to test him early."

"If it doesn't work then we just do it again," Venric snapped. "We know what to avoid now."

"You're walking a line," the other warned. "We gave them permission to go on a field exercise. The instructors know what to do. If the council catches you wanting to retry after having waited 20 years..."

Venric's tone dipped colder.

"The Council hears everything eventually."

The conversation moved on further down the corridor, the voices fading beneath the quiet crackle of torches and distant magical energy vibrating through the walls.

Tito stayed frozen, pulse hammering in his ears.

Trust what's inside me? Who was it inside before?

Did Venric mean Eryon? Surely not. The hero that ended the Flameward Rebellion saved Atheron from so much more blood.

He slowly backed out of the hall the way he came, careful not to make a sound. The mirrored arch and the archives could wait five more minutes.

First, he needed to breathe and decide just what the hell he was walking into.

CHAPTER 21

Tito moved like a ghost through the upper corridors. The voices still rang in his ears. He couldn't unhear it.

Do it again? Retry?

And worst of all, *who it was inside before.*

His breath came in shallow bursts as he climbed, but he took the time to check the sigils carved into each marble threshold, confirming he hadn't veered off course again.

Fifth landing, mirrored arch.

When he reached the final turn of the spiral staircase, the hallway narrowed, flanked by two great bronze sconces shaped like open books. Between them stood a tall stone arch, its frame etched with faintly shimmering runes, and at its peak a perfect silver mirror.

Tito slowed. His reflection stared back, bruised, tired, the tunic from that morning with a small bit of blood from something that opened along his chest. He glanced down to his rune, half hidden by his sleeve, and it seemed darker somehow.

He stepped forward.

The mirror shimmered as he approached, and then parted, opening up to a whole new world that was The Archives of Atheron. This was no mere place.

The moment Tito passed beneath the mirrored arch, the air stilled and cooled. He walked into a long, descending corridor, simple at first, with stone floors and walls lit with torches that never danced.

As he reached the base, the world truly opened. A grand, circular chamber unfolded around him, vast enough to hold a forest. Shelves spiraled upward like tower balconies, five levels high, each filled wall to wall with tomes, scrolls, etched stones, and crystalline discs. A glowing chandelier of floating orbs hovered at the center, illuminating the room in soft golden hues. Ladders glided along the walls on their own, and every so often a book would recall itself to the shelves. It was beautiful...overwhelming even.

Tito felt as if he had stepped into the living mind of the kingdom itself. He turned slowly in place, neck craned back to try and take it all in.

Sigils glowed faintly beneath his feet, marking walkways between various wings. Each bore a symbol above the archways, a flame, a tide, a gust, a mountain, a shimmering veil. Beyond them, deeper still, was a vault in the center chamber guarded by two silent stone statues, their hands resting on the hilts of swords that reached the floor.

He had never seen so much grandeur in his life. Not even in the queen's audience chamber. Not even in the Citadel for his attunement. Now that he stood in the heart of it, Tito felt something shift. If the answers were anywhere, they were here. Not just for the exercise given to him and Callyn and the others, but even what Venric and the other magus were talking about.

He took a breath and squared his shoulders.

The archive's main desk stood like an altar in the heart of the great chamber, an immense, crescent-shaped structure of dark oak wrapped in veins of copper and runes that pulsed gently with stored energy. Papers fluttered on their own nearby, cataloging themselves. A single scribe sat at the desk, hunched over an ink stained logbook. He didn't look up as Tito approached.

"Name?" the scribe asked flatly.

"Maldito," he answered, voice soft with lingering uncertainty, "uh.. Espero."

The quill paused.

A moment later the man lifted his head. His eyes were tired, sunken from too many years reading in dim light, but alert. "And what is it you're seeking, Maldito uh Espero?"

Tito opened his mouth, then hesitated.

What was he looking for? Maps for the training mission? Details on the terrain outside Atheron? Intel on the cursed lands? He had no clarity on what the actual field exercise was for.

Tito decided to trust his hunch.

"I want everything you have on Eryon," he said finally, "and the end of the war."

The scribe raised a brow but said nothing. He simply turned to his left, plucked a glowing token from a carved niche in the wall, carved something, and handed it to Tito.

"Slot that into the access terminal on the second ring. Western section, flame crest."

Tito nodded his thanks, accepted the token and turned back toward the spiraling path.

He found the reading alcove easily enough, tucked behind a section marked Historical Accounts – Post-Flameward Reconciliation.

The moment he inserted the token into the console, a soft hum filled the space. Shelves behind the desk shifted with a low grind, and a sliding shelf rolled into place, brimming with tomes and etched glass tablets.

Tito pulled the first book free.

The Hero's Flame: Eryon and the War's Final Breath. He read. Then a second. *A Kingdom Saved by One.* Then a third. *The Bright End.* The more he read, the more discomfort he felt in his gut. They all said the same things.

They spoke of Eryon being glorious, powerful, and selfless. They spoke of the rebellion's leaders, of the great siege of Atheron's outer walls, and the massive counter strike led by the queen's forces under Eryon's command. No matter which account of different tellings he flipped through, the ending never changed.

"And so, at the height of the bloodshed, Eryon summoned the full strength of his unique rune and its connection to the Runestone. In a final, brilliant blaze of elemental unity, he

channeled unbelievable power and sacrificed himself to end the rebellion and preserve the realm. The tide fell, the flames ceased, and Valcarta wept for its golden son."

That same phrasing, over and over. Every book, every source.

Sacrificed himself.

Every account concluded as if Eryon had simply dissolved in the light of pure unbridled power from the Runestone.

Tito had grown up on the stories. He had read variations and heard dramatizations in the streets of Ethyrae. No matter the story, they had details. Something more human. These were... sanitized.

Even Uldris, who was sometimes painted as the cold-eyed magus who mentored Eryon, was shown in a strangely softened light. Some records described him leaving the Citadel shortly after the war ended, "grieving the cost." Others said he retired in solitude, "disillusioned with victory." None of them asked why. None of them questioned it, not a single one.

Tito's fingers tightened around the edge of one of the glass tablets, the words frozen mid change as he looked away. Was this all they wanted remembered? Or was that actually it?

Had even the archives, this massive, monumental collection of knowledge, decided to preserve only the version that made people feel better?

The knot in his stomach grew heavier. He looked again at the last paragraph of *The Hero's Flame*, whispering it aloud under his breath.

"Eryon sacrificed himself to preserve the realm."

Then he thought of Venric's voice.

"Just like I didn't trust who it was inside before..."

Tito's hands trembled slightly as he placed the book back onto the shelf.

Whatever happened twenty years ago, this wasn't the truth. This was a story. Tito lingered at the shelf for a second longer, eyes still on the title of the book as he slid it back into place.

The Hero's Flame.

He wanted to yank it out again, toss it across the marble and shout that it wasn't enough. That it didn't answer anything. That it possibly even lied.

Instead, he exhaled through his nose and gently let the spine slide home.

"You know you just put that on the wrong shelf, right?"

Tito froze.

His heart skipped as he turned to see Callyn standing just a few paces away, one hip cocked, arms crossed over her chest and an unmistakable smirk curled at the corner of her lips. Her hair was tied back today in a tight braid, a few strands falling loose across her brow. Her tone wasn't biting, but it wasn't warm either.

She was teasing him. Of course she was.

He cleared his throat.

"I, uh, just finished reading it."

Callyn's brow lifted slightly.

"Mm hm. Looked more like you were trying to bury it."

He rubbed the back of his neck, caught between guilt and embarrassment.

"I didn't really know where to start, so I figured I'd look up Eryon. End of the war. Just to get a feel for the world outside."

Callyn stepped closer. Her hand brushed along the edge of the nearest reading console.

"You thought you were gonna find marching orders in a history book?"

He opened his mouth to defend himself, only to close it again with a sigh.

She smiled.

"Relax, Shardborne. I figured you'd be lost here." Her smirk never quite faded. "These archives are meant to confuse people. Half the fun is pretending you know what you're doing while the shelves rearrange behind you."

Tito gave her a sidelong glance.

"I'm not used to places where books act alive."

"Then you'll hate the second tier. Some of them bite."

He snorted. And for a breath, the tension between them cracked just enough to breathe, but it returned a second later when he started to speak.

"Callyn, about last night..."

She raised a firm hand.

"Later," she said, "when we're back in the room."

He hesitated, then nodded.

"That works. Dinner should be delivered by then anyway."

Now it was Callyn's turn to pause.

"Delivered?"

Tito coughed lightly.

"Salindra. Said she'd make sure we ate, didn't really give me a choice."

Callyn considered that for a moment, then gave a small shrug.

"Honestly? Might be the nicest thing anyone's done for me all month. If it's not gray and congealed, I'll call it a luxury."

He grinned.

"You're easy to impress."

"You say that, and yet you're the one who passed out in the doorway after catching one look at me."

His face turned scarlet.

"You said we'd talk about it later."

She was already moving toward a console, fingers trailing along the carved runes as the shelves behind her began to shift with quiet grace.

"Right," she said. "Later."

The shelves rearranged in response to her touch. Dozens of texts emerged, most with blackened spines and strange glyphs that pulsed faintly when held. She guided Tito toward a table already stacked with open books, scrolls partially unraveled and pinned beneath polished brass weights.

"This is what I've found," she said, gesturing for him to sit. "Standard maps of the outer ring and the valley beyond the northern ridge. Some field reports from previous scouting parties, mostly magi sponsored excursions or training exercises like ours. There's some mention of elemental disturbances past the perimeter runes."

Tito sat, eyes scanning the materials.

"Disturbances?"

"Something's wrong out there. Trees warped in place, wind that doesn't behave naturally. No sightings of anything alive, but there's tension in the records. They never say it out loud, but it's there."

Tito traced his fingers across a passage written in tight, angular script.

"Like they're scared?"

"Like they're censored."

They spent the next stretch in quiet focus.

Callyn had bookmarked pages with references to ancient attunement failures, lands still under elemental instability, and reports filed from scouts who'd never returned. Her notes were clear and neat, organized in a way Tito could barely follow but respected all the same.

She was as sharp as she was thorough. He watched her as she spoke, not just absorbing her words but the way she moved, confident without needing to be loud, precise without showing off. She was brilliant in a way he hadn't fully understood before, when physicality was the only showcased trait.

He leaned forward on his elbows, hands folded as he took it all in.

"You were really meant for this, weren't you?"

Callyn didn't look up.

"What, digging through dead men's words?"

"No, all of it. The Citadel, the training. The magic. You fit here."

She was silent for a moment. Then she looked up, just briefly, her eyes met his.

"Sometimes fitting in just means you got used to the edges cutting less."

CHAPTER 22

"I think we've mapped most of what's worth knowing," Callyn said, stretching her arms over her head and cracking her neck before returning to her notes. "These reports go back nearly forty years, though most of the recent activity picks up about twenty years ago right after the war ended."

Tito leaned forward, elbows on the desk as he flipped through a pile of field logs they had sorted from the archives' second tier. The parchment was worn and brittle in places, but the writing was clean and methodical...military hand.

Callyn continued, sweeping her finger across a map pinned to the corner of the table.

"The patrols report minor anomalies, crops refusing to root, trees growing in twisted spirals, patches of earth that randomly harden or sink overnight. It gets worse the farther north you go."

Tito frowned.

"Worse how?"

She pulled a different scroll into view, half-unraveled already.

"Some entries mention water evaporating instantly from pools near cave mouths. Wind gusts strong enough to knock scouts off their horses when the skies were clear and still. One patrol captain even wrote that his compass spun in circles for two days straight before the needle melted."

"That doesn't sound like nature."

"No," she said, "it sounds like magic. Angry magic."

They both fell quiet.

Tito's eyes skimmed a particularly sharp piece of text written by a scout captain near the border. *Three of my men refused to step further. Claimed the wind carried whispers. Couldn't sleep the night we camped beside the blackened trees. One of them swore the bark bled when he cut it. I don't blame him. The leaves didn't burn right. Smoke was wrong.*

Callyn tapped it lightly.

"That's from a decade ago. They still won't send that captain out again."

Tito shook his head slowly.

"And we're just walking into this?"

"It's a 'training mission,' remember?" she said, rolling her eyes as she began stacking reports. "We're not supposed to go far. Just close enough to 'feel the wind,' get some practical exposure, and then scurry back with a few notes to make the magi feel clever. Plus, it gives us more open areas to test our element. Or elements, in your case."

She leaned across the table, collecting the last few texts into a tidy pile.

"I say we finish up here and go eat," she added. "I need something that didn't come out of a pot scraped for the last dregs of salt."

Tito smiled and was about to respond when Callyn paused. Her fingers brushed the corner of a thin, charcoal bound report tucked behind a larger stack of weather journals. She tilted her head slightly, eyes narrowing.

"This wasn't here before."

Tito straightened.

"What?"

Callyn slid the new report forward. The parchment was pristine, the ink still wet in places. The spine hadn't even creased. Her eyes scanned the heading.

Scout Report – Regimental Return South of the Veiled Ridge, Logged: Solin, Velmara, 6th bell.

Filed by: Lyra Venel Issara, Ranger-Captain, 3rd Northern Regiment.

Tito's stomach dropped at the date.

"This was filed today! Was it just dropped off? Or did it get mixed in with your request?"

Callyn's eyes had already skipped lower.

Initial contact with northern fissure in canyon mouth yielded anomalous showings. Stone door embedded with unknown runic structure, similar to elemental runes, dormant but intact. Too large to be burial. No previous charted records of artificial structure in this sector. Door held a sigil similar to those above attunement chamber. Marked coordinates and withdrew.

She looked up sharply.

"There's no mention of this in any older field reports," she said. "I would've seen it. This vault wasn't on any map."

"Vault," Tito repeated, the word foreign on his tongue. "What does that even mean?"

Callyn shook her head.

"I don't know, but whatever it is, it was just filed. Not even fully archived. This was meant to be logged today and probably sorted for review before anyone saw it."

Tito's pulse began to rise.

"What if we weren't meant to see it?"

Before she could answer, a voice like frost cracked through the air behind them.

"You weren't."

Venric's voice cracked through the air like ice snapping underfoot.

They turned.

Venric stood at the edge of the research wing, eyes locked on the report in Callyn's hand.

"That report was not yet cleared for access," he said in a low, cold voice.

Tito swallowed.

"It was sitting on the shelf."

"And yet you read it."

Tito turned fast, Callyn slower.

The report still rested in her hands, but her fingers tightened around it instinctively as Magus Venric approached, shoulders stiff, fury coiled just beneath his controlled movements. He stopped just shy of the desk.

"That report was filed incorrectly," he said. "It wasn't approved for initiate review."

Callyn flipped the page over, as if hoping she'd missed something. No clearance rune, no seal. Nothing.

"It didn't have a stamp," she admitted, "but it was shelved openly."

Venric's eyes flared.

"Because someone failed to route it through the correct channels. It was logged prematurely, before it was reviewed for classification or security. That is more than just a clerical error. I expected you to know better, Initiate Callyn. You know what you've just risked!"

Tito frowned.

"A risk to who?"

"To you," Venric snapped. "To anyone reading something that hasn't been properly vetted. You think reports go through us just for style? They are reviewed to assess the sensitivity, context, and implications of what's found. You don't get to walk into the Archives and start parsing field anomalies like it's recreational reading."

He snatched the parchment from Callyn's grip, folding it once with precise force.

"This," he said, holding it up, "has not yet been processed. You weren't meant to see it because it hasn't been deemed safe or appropriate for initiates without full understanding of the terrain or the risks involved."

Callyn's jaw flexed but remained silent.

Venric looked between them.

"You are both under the queen's directive, yes, but that doesn't entitle you to bypass the structure that keeps this city intact. There are reasons information is withheld until reviewed."

He tucked the report beneath his arm.

"If you come across another document without proper clearance markings, you will not read it. You will not speculate. You will leave it for those who have earned the burden of knowing first."

His gaze lingered on Tito, longer than necessary. Then he turned, robes whispering against the stone, and vanished into the shadows of the upper tier.

Silence returned to the table.

Callyn slowly exhaled.

Tito stared at the empty space where Venric had stood.

They left the reading tier without speaking. Steps echoed lightly through the hushed spiral of the archives. The air was still cool, still dusted with that faint scent of old paper and burning runes. Only now, every corner felt like it held its breath. They were halfway down the second tier stair when they heard him again. His voice wasn't loud, but it was unmistakable, dripping with fury held barely in check.

"I don't care if it wasn't filed in the correct spot, if you followed the *system,* it should have been flagged for review and locked down."

Tito and Callyn slowed instinctively, glancing to the lower floor where Venric stood near the archive's main desk. The scribe from earlier looked pale and tightlipped, fingers clutching the edge of the record ledger like it might save him from being burned alive.

"It was logged and tagged as urgent. Urgent doesn't mean accessible. It means restricted until processed," Venric seethed. "You are not new here. If you can't differentiate between a scout log and a classified tier report, then you should not be tasked with physical intake."

The scribe began to stammer something, but Tito and Callyn didn't stay to hear it. They walked past, slow and quiet, their boots against the steps swallowed by the tension below.

Venric didn't look up, his voice followed them in fragments, sharp as broken glass.

"I want it off the shelves, no initiate level routing. Do you understand me?"

They heard the heavy sound of something being slammed shut followed by silence. Tito and Callyn remained quiet until they were past the mirrored arch and into the north wing's corridor, where the lamps adorned with runes glowed soft gold and the Citadel's breath felt normal again. Even then, it was Callyn who broke the silence first.

"So," she said under her breath, "not processed, not for initiates."

Tito's mouth was dry.

"You'd think it was the queen's diary the way he acted."

Callyn shook her head, walking close enough for their shoulders to nearly brush.

"You heard what he said. 'Not safe to read without context.'"

"Yeah," Tito murmured. "Like he's protecting us. It makes sense if we are planning the goals for our own scouting training missions."

"Or protecting something from us," she added quietly.

They turned a corner, passing a set of high arched windows glowing with the last light of day. The Citadel sprawled below, spires cutting into the sky like needles dipped in starlight.

"I've been reading these reports for months," Callyn said. "I've seen some classified stuff, even things filed incorrectly or submitted without stamps. I've never seen anything pulled that fast."

Tito nodded.

"And that name? Lyra Issara?"

"She's a Ranger-Captain," Callyn replied, lowering her voice even more. "Pulled from the outer regiments a few months ago. She was supposed to be heading the scouts along the border."

"So why was she at a canyon just a couple days away from Atheron?" he asked.

Callyn didn't answer.

The corridor quieted even further as they approached the east hall, just past a narrow arch flanked by two statues with rune lit eyes. Tito opened the door, the familiar search and click of the runic lock being an odd comfort.

Inside, soft light glowed from the enchanted torches set into the corners. The beds were made, the air smelled faintly of herbs and spice, and...

He stopped.

There, on the nightstand between the beds, sat two large bowls. Steam still drifted from them lazily, curling in the warm air. The bowls were simple but beautiful, dark ceramic etched with glowing runes that pulsed every few seconds, a quiet heartbeat of heat magic.

Callyn stepped in beside him, setting her books down with a long exhale. She caught sight of the food and gave a dry, exhausted smile.

"Well," she muttered, "guess she meant it when she said she'd make sure we ate."

Tito couldn't help but smile. He sat cross-legged on his bed and found the warm bowl in his hands ground him more than he expected. The soft pulse of the heat runes beneath the ceramic sent gentle waves into his palms and wrists, soothing the ache that still lingered from training and... other things.

Callyn sat on the opposite bed, back against the wall, knees tucked up, bowl already half-finished. The food was simple, but richer than anything he'd tasted in the last week. Sliced sweetroot and seasoned lentils rested beneath a blanket of soft rice, soaked in a spiced tomato broth that clung to every grain. Soft strips of grilled meat, venison if Tito had to guess, rested along the rim of the bowl, their edges crisp with a flame-sear. Small wedges of fried plantain floated at the surface, and every few bites revealed crushed nuts or dried pepper hiding just beneath the rice.

It was hearty. Earthy. Just enough kick to make him sweat.

Callyn made a sound somewhere between a sigh and a groan.

"This is unfair," she muttered. "Barracks should revolt."

Tito grinned behind his spoon.

"We should write Salindra a thank you poem."

"I'm not a poet. I'd stab a guy for a second helping though."

They ate in companionable silence for another few minutes, save for the occasional crunch or satisfied grunt. The air felt comfortable until Tito set his bowl aside and looked up.

He shifted his posture, nervous energy coiling just behind his ribs. His hand rested across the runes shifting on his arm as he tried to distance himself.

She raised an eyebrow.

"Alright. Out with it."

He hesitated.

Then finally, "About last night…"

Callyn stared at him.

Tito held up his hands immediately.

"I wasn't trying to… I didn't know… I mean, I did walk in, but I didn't expect…"

"You fainted," she said dryly, setting her empty bowl beside her. "Not exactly scandalous."

"I saw you."

"You did," she said with the most unreadable inflection.

Tito swallowed.

"And I… I didn't mean to. I was barely standing, and I wasn't thinking, and…"

"You stared, even," she cut in.

He froze and looked down at his hands, then up at her again.

"I did. I'm not proud of it. It wasn't respectful. You didn't deserve that."

Callyn studied him for a long moment. Then she leaned forward slightly, elbows on her knees.

"I'm not made of glass, Tito."

He blinked.

"I'm a soldier. I've trained with countless others, men and women, all day for close to a year now. Privacy's a luxury I rarely get. That doesn't mean I enjoyed it," she added, "but I've had worse things happen than being seen."

He didn't know what to say.

She softened, just slightly.

"You were exhausted, and barely conscious. You passed out like a kid who snuck his first drink."

He let out a breath that might have been a laugh, hand dragging down his face.

"Still, I haven't been able to stop thinking about it."

"Oh?"

Tito shook his head quickly.

"Not like that. I mean, I *have*, but not just that. I saw you and—"

He hesitated.

She waited.

"I saw someone strong," he finally said. "Not just in combat. Not just training. You looked powerful. In control. Not like a statue or something out of reach. Just real."

He swallowed for his throat had gone dry.

"And beautiful."

Callyn blinked. For the first time in a week, her expression faltered, just slightly. The smirk didn't return. Her eyes dropped for a half-second before meeting his again. She reached for her water and sipped it slowly.

"Well," she said, "that's better than I expected."

Tito stared.

"Better?"

"I figured you'd stammer through it, blame exhaustion, and beg forgiveness for the next three days."

"I still might."

She smirked.

"Don't. You said what mattered. Just don't make it a thing."

He nodded.

"It's not a thing."

Callyn let out a long breath and leaned back slightly on her hands.

"Alright. Then here's a better question."

Tito looked up.

"What happened to you? Last night, before you got to the door, you looked like you fought a glassworm and lost."

The warmth in his chest cooled slightly, replaced by a dull knot.

He looked down at his hands, flexed his fingers.

"I'm not sure what a glassworm is, but I did find Kael and two of his buddies. They were waiting for me a hall or two away."

Callyn's posture shifted instantly.

"They said I didn't deserve the rune. That they couldn't let someone like me go on a mission so soon," he said, voice low. "I tried to hold my own, but there were three of them. I got in a couple hits, but it didn't matter."

Her brow furrowed.

"And then?"

"A magus stepped in. I don't know who, gray and violet robes, older. He cracked the floor with stone and pulled them off me. Took them away. Told me where to find the new quarters. If he stopped to ask me questions, I wouldn't have even made it this far."

Callyn stared at him.

"You didn't think to mention this sooner?"

"I was overwhelmed," he said honestly. "And then I walked in on you and passed out, and, well, you know the rest."

She sighed through her nose, but not in frustration.

"You should've told someone."

"I'm telling *you.*"

That earned him a glance that lingered longer than before.

She reached for her water again and murmured, "Next time, tell someone you're hurt sooner, especially if they step in to save you. You're lucky Salindra's wing is so close."

He nodded slowly, "I will."

A silence settled between them again, but it wasn't awkward anymore and was broken only by their comforted breathing and... footsteps?

Tito's head snapped up.

They were light but fast, accompanied by the soft scuff of boots against polished stone. The kind of footsteps that weren't meant to be heard but were moving too quickly to stay quiet. The footsteps Tito had after stealing bread from Eira's outer shelf.

Callyn was already rising, shoulders squared, her earlier calm gone in a blink.

Then came the voices, low and urgent. Two of them, one hushed and tense, the other faster.

Tito's breath hitched. One of the voices sounded familiar and something about it tugged at his memory.

No, it couldn't be.

The sound came closer, just on the other side of the door now. A bag hit the wall, coupled with a muttered curse.

Callyn moved beside the door like a shadow, hand resting on the hilt of her training dagger. She glanced at Tito, and he could see the same question in her eyes he felt churning in his chest. The whispering stopped directly outside their room.

Tito didn't wait. He surged forward the same moment Callyn moved.

CHAPTER 23

Tito crashed into the cloaked figure and drove them into the wall with a thud that echoed down the corridor.

Callyn bolted beside him, one arm braced across the second figure's chest, the glint of her dagger held low.

Both strangers yelped, their attempts at quiet now gone.

Tito shoved back the hood of the figure beneath him, ready to attack, but then stopped cold.

"Ro?!"

A pair of wide, familiar eyes blinked back at him from beneath a mop of tousled curls.

"Tito?" Ro wheezed, breathless from impact. "Are you always going to attack me after not seeing me?"

Tito stumbled off them immediately.

"I-I thought!" He held back a moment, not quite yet processing what he was seeing. "Why are you sneaking around in the middle of the night?"

Callyn's grip on the second figure relaxed.

The girl she had pinned had a slim build and wavy brown hair now loose from her hood, her sharp cheekbones flushed with surprise and irritation.

"She's yours, too?" Callyn asked Ro.

Ro groaned and rubbed their ribs, adjusted the wrinkled, half-slid bag of food now clutched against their stomach.

"This is Thena. She's my incredibly subtle roommate who decided we needed snacks after nearly exploding our eyebrows off in glyph practice."

"I said quietly," Thena snapped, "and you said, 'just one stop by the bakery stall, I swear.' You bought six."

"I was emotionally compromised," Ro muttered.

Tito turned to get a look at the girl Callyn still had partially restrained.

She stood stiff, cloak twisted around her shoulders, cheeks flushed with frustration and a hint of embarrassment.

"Thena Morran," Ro added offhandedly. "She thinks pastries can replace eyebrows."

Tito froze.

Callyn's fingers tightened back around Thena's arm like a reflex.

"Morran?" Tito repeated, voice going taut. "As in Kael Morran?"

Thena rolled her eyes so hard it looked painful.

"Unfortunately, yes."

Callyn didn't loosen her grip.

Thena's voice turned sharp.

"And before either of you assume anything, yes, I hate him; and no, I didn't pick my bloodline."

Ro raised a brow and grinned.

"Believe me, you've never heard someone say 'Kael's an arrogant sack of compost' with such venom. It was actually how we became roommates, making fun of everyone around."

Thena smirked, then glanced back at Callyn.

"Do you mind letting me go now?"

Callyn held her gaze for a beat longer, then stepped back, still watching her carefully.

Tito looked between them, still trying to recalibrate.

"You're the magi initiates staying beside us?"

"Surprise," Ro said with a grin, brushing off their cloak.

"You could've checked in with us first, since we are going on the same mission," Callyn muttered with folded her arms.

Ro shrugged.

"Could've, but that felt too formal somehow."

Tito exhaled, finally letting his staff drop. His pulse was still winding down from panic.

"I thought it was Kael coming back for round two."

Ro grimaced.

"That dirtbag? No thanks. I'm way prettier."

Thena adjusted the sack in her arms, the scent of warm sugar and roasted nuts wafted into the room.

"And less punchable, most days."

Tito rubbed his face. His disbelief melted slowly into awkward relief.

"I can't believe you're here!"

Ro opened the door to their room.

"Well, come in! I have enough to share!"

The chamber was similar to Tito and Callyn's. There were two beds, a central table, minimal furnishings, but somehow it felt lived-in. The air smelled of ink, citrus balm, and floral. Books were stacked unevenly near Ro's side, scrolls half opened, and a cracked lantern glowed faintly in the corner.

Thena stepped inside first and tugged off her cloak in one practiced motion, tossing it onto her bed with a sigh. The long-sleeved tunic beneath hugged her frame, dusted faintly with powdered sugar from the hidden pastry stash.

Tito followed behind her. He caught himself glancing at her as she moved.

The resemblance was subtle, but undeniable...the same angled jaw as Kael, with high cheekbones, and that cool sharpness in the eyes like she was always calculating something; but where Kael's posture screamed entitlement, Thena's carried precision. It reminded him of Callyn, the way she was always coiled. Where Kael's smile was smug, Thena's was razor-edged. Whatever blood they shared, she wore it differently.

Ro kicked off their boots and collapsed backward onto the bed with a dramatic sigh before tossing the cloak across the footboard.

"Okay. Emergency protocol...pastries and proper stories."

They reached into the crumpled bag on the table and tossed Tito a warm, syrup-glazed triangle wrapped in soft cloth. He caught it on instinct.

"Now," Ro said, propping themselves up on bended elbows, "why in the world did you think we were Kael, and what did you mean coming back for round two?"

Tito looked at the pastry, then at Ro, then slowly sat down at the edge of the bed.

"Because he already came for round one."

Ro's smile vanished and the room shifted again.

Callyn stepped in last, closed the door behind her, and leaned against the far wall with arms crossed. She watched Tito as closely as she had watched Thena earlier.

Thena, cross-legged on the bed, unwrapped her own pastry with an expression that turned careful and guarded.

Ro straightened, "Wait, what happened?"

Tito kept staring at his pastry like it might change shape if he waited long enough.

Ro waited silently.

Tito didn't look up as he spoke.

"I was heading to the hall, shortly after we were assigned the upper chambers. They were waiting, Kael and two of his friends. They attacked me just outside the corridor. They said I didn't deserve the rune. That a fisherman's son had no place carrying it. Said they couldn't let me walk into the field like this meant anything."

His voice lowered.

"I fought back. I got some hits in, but it was three on one. They beat me, kicked me while I was down."

Ro looked like they wanted to throw something.

Thena's brow creased, the pastry in her hand forgotten.

Tito continued.

"A magus stepped in. I don't know his name. He pulled them off me, cracked the stone with earth magic, and ordered some guards to take them away."

Ro let out a slow breath.

Tito finally looked up.

"So, when I heard voices outside the room tonight, I thought maybe Kael wanted to try again. After that," he rubbed the back of his neck, "I finally got to our room."

There was a pause.

Ro tilted their head, "And?"

Tito cleared his throat, cheeks coloring.

"And I sort of... I might've... fainted."

"Fainted?" Ro asked.

"I was exhausted," Tito protested, "beaten...bleeding. The magus didn't send a healer for me, just gave me directions to the field rooms. I opened the door and then..." he paused. He felt heat rise to his cheeks.

"He saw me naked," Callyn said flatly from the wall.

Tito went still.

Ro's eyes widened, then howled with laughter.

"Oh, my gods! You what?! You passed out after walking in on her?!"

"It wasn't like that!"

"You fainted like a kid!"

"I was injured!"

"And blessed, apparently!"

Callyn rolled her eyes but didn't bother correcting them.

Thena watched with thin amusement, slowly taking another bite of her pastry.

"To be fair, it is a way to better bond with your training partner."

"Is that what we're calling it now?" Ro cackled.

Tito groaned and flopped back onto the mattress.

"Remind me never to tell you anything again," he sighed again, but caught the smirk Callyn gave him across the room.

"Too late," Ro said. Their grin wasn't going anywhere. "This one's going in the vault."

At the word vault, Callyn's expression shifted. She stirred from the wall and moved to pour herself a glass of water from the basin beside Ro's desk.

Ro sat up.

"Alright, alright," they said, and nudged Tito's leg. "You got me. I deserved the tackle, but it's still your turn."

"My turn?"

Ro gave him a look.

"Yeah, how was your week?"

Tito let out a breath.

"Hard. Brutal, actually. I've been doing nothing but physical conditioning and weapons drills. They're delaying elemental work until we are out on this field exercise."

"That explains the bruises," Ro said.

"They had me running drills with a whole regiment. Valeria's no joke."

Callyn scoffed quietly at that, still facing the wall.

Ro grinned.

"I'd love to meet her."

"You might, yet," Tito said. "I think she said she was briefing us tomorrow."

Ro tossed a glance at Thena.

"We didn't know what we were being assigned to. They kind of just had us move up here today and said they would call for us tomorrow. I was hoping it was a break."

"Break?" Tito asked.

"Sort of," Ro said. "We've been pushing nonstop. Especially me with illusion exercises, channeling, resistance drills and projection forms. You should've seen it. Earlier this week I managed to split six mirror clones at once and walk them across a collapsing field."

Tito's eyes widened.

"None of that sentence made any sense, but that sounds incredible."

"I'd say. I think I even scared one of the magi."

Thena spoke up without looking away from her food.

"He absolutely did, and he should've."

"And you?" Tito asked Thena

She brushed a few stray crumbs from her shirt.

"Wind. Been in rotation since I was fifteen. I like force more than finesse, but I can keep formation grounded in a hurricane if I have to."

Callyn gave a small, surprised noise.

Thena, clearly satisfied with herself, smirked.

"Kael's not the only one with power in the family. Just the only one who wastes it."

"So, you've both just been training?" Tito asked both of them.

"Nonstop," Ro confirmed. "No research. No briefings. They told us we were chosen for our aptitude, but they haven't said much about where we're going or why."

"Guess they expected us to do the research for you," Callyn cut in. Her arms were crossed again.

Thena's posture stiffened, "Excuse me?"

Callyn didn't miss a beat.

"You're initiates of the magi," she said. "Most magi think they're above groundwork. You two being chosen was probably more about showing how much better you are than our military groups."

Ro stayed quiet, but Thena sat up fully.

"That's a hell of an assumption."

"It's not," Callyn replied. "We've been pulling reports from field logs all day. They've sent over two dozen units toward the outer perimeter over the last forty years, half of them magi initiates like you two, half of them more like us. Most of them didn't know what they were walking into."

Tito spoke softly, "And most of them didn't come back. The non-magi, that is."

Callyn and Ro both shared a look.

"So, what are we walking into?" Ro asked.

Callyn stepped to the center of the room.

"Elemental anomalies. Territory where magic behaves like it's alive and angry. Wind that shifts direction mid breath. Earth that caves in even while it's solid. Patches of trees twisted like they grew in pain. Reports of smoke that just hovers."

Ro frowned, "They told us we were going to the ridge at most."

"They didn't lie," Callyn said. "They just didn't finish the sentence."

Silence followed.

Tito looked down at the pastry still half-wrapped in his hands. A knock came at the door. All four of them froze slightly before Ro hopped up and opened the door.

A young man stood outside in trimmed robes of slate gray and indigo. Tito pieced together that those colors signified the Citadel's couriers.

The courier nodded once, polite but efficient.

"Field assignment initiates?"

Ro raised a lazy hand.

"That's us, the whole four."

"You're to report to the briefing chamber just after the midday bell tomorrow," the courier announced. "Field assignment quarters, supplies and updated mission orders will be provided there. Come prepared from your own research."

He turned and walked back down the hall before any of them could ask questions. The door clicked shut.

Callyn ran a hand down her face.

"Well," she muttered, "guess we're officially in it now. At least we don't have to worry about buying our own gear."

"Well, I would offer to recite what you just told us to them, but your notes might be more detailed than mine, so I will let you lead that conversation," said Ro to Callyn.

Thena dropped back onto her bed with a quiet exhale and muttered something about needing a full night's sleep if they expected her to survive more briefing nonsense.

Callyn gave a small nod to Ro and moved toward the door, but Tito didn't move right away.

He turned to Ro who was still standing near the doorway and stepped forward without a word and wrapped them in a tight embrace.

Ro immediately melted into it.

Neither spoke.

Tito held them for longer than he expected to. Long enough to remember what it felt like to have someone in his arms who knew him, who believed in him, before the rune, before the clouds building at their backs.

Ro squeezed him once.

"I'm not planning to explain to the Magi that I lost my brother because he tripped into a pit of angry air."

Tito huffed a laugh into their collar.

"Only if you promise not to set any illusions of me fainting while we are out there. I know you thought of it."

"No promises."

They pulled apart, but Ro kept a hand briefly on Tito's arm, a tether they weren't quite ready to cut.

Tito gave one last nod, then turned.

Callyn was already by the door, watching with quiet patience.

The two of them slipped out into the corridor and walked in silence back across the stone to their quarters. Their door clicked shut behind them.

Callyn stepped a few paces in and unstrapped the thin belt from around her waist.

"So," she said when she tossed the belt onto the nearby chest. "That was your brother?"

"Oh, gods. I didn't even introduce them."

Callyn arched her brow as she turned to face him.

Tito rubbed the back of his neck.

"Ro's my sibling," he corrected gently, "not brother."

Callyn paused, then nodded.

"Got it." Her voice softened. "Sorry."

Tito shrugged, "You didn't know. Now you do."

Callyn lowered herself onto the edge of her bed and began unlacing her boots.

"Still, that was nice. Seeing you two together like that."

"Yeah?"

She didn't look up as she said it.

"Must be something, having someone who knows the world with you before all this."

He didn't respond. The silence said enough.

Callyn kicked off her boots and reached for the hem of her tunic.

"If you turn around for just five seconds, I promise not to make you faint again."

Tito quickly spun around with ears already turning red.

"You're impossible."

"You're the one who kept pace with me after just a week," she called lightly. "You earned this."

He shook his head, smiling in spite of himself. A minute passed, maybe two.

"Alright. You're clear."

Tito turned back around, cautiously.

She was already under the covers. The room was quiet again. Comfortable.

Tito crossed to his bed, slid beneath the blankets, and finally closed his eyes.

CHAPTER 24

Morning came early. The Citadel stirred. Light crept in through arched windows and filtered through inscribed runes that hummed along the stone walls.

Tito and Callyn were already awake when the first bell sounded in the distance. Neither spoke as they dressed. The urgency of the day didn't need to be spoken aloud.

They were among the first in the mess hall which carried quiet conversation, a few guards spooning breakfast onto trays, the smell of fried dough and spice. The pair sat at the edge of the long table, bent close over their shared notes and crumpled parchment.

"Don't mention the unstable wind pockets unless they bring it up," Callyn murmured as she chewed absently on a dried fig. "It'll sound like we're overstating the risk."

Tito nodded, writing quickly.

"Got it. And the tree rot zone?"

"We can call it a 'biomagic flux sector.' Sounds more clinical."

He chuckled, "We're learning how to lie like real scouts."

"We're learning how to survive the mission. How to live in order to report back."

Their plates sat half-eaten as they went back and forth rehearsing phrases, trimming down the more alarming parts of the reports, and crafting something that would be considered useful. By the time the second bell chimed, the mess was filling up and they were already wrapping leftovers in soft cloth.

"Come on," Callyn said. She grabbed an extra handful of sliced fruit. "Let's go feed the prodigies."

The moment Tito stepped into his sibling's room, the smell of burnt sage and ink hit him again.

Ro's side of the room was already scattered with half-sketched glyph work and a pile of folded clothes that had never quite made it into the trunk.

Ro and Thena were still only half-awake.

Ro sat cross-legged on the bed, bleary-eyed but alert, combing fingers through their hair.

Thena leaned against the far wall, still tying her bootlaces and muttering something under her breath about "people who plan too early be cursed."

"We come bearing peace offerings," Tito said, setting down a cloth bundle on the edge of Ro's bed. "You missed the calm."

Ro perked up immediately.

"Tell me you brought the flatbread."

"Your brother made sure. That and melon slices," Callyn added as she dropped her parcel onto Thena's desk.

Thena grunted in approval, "Okay, early planning forgiven."

As the others unwrapped their food, Tito pulled out the parchment they'd been working on and set it between them.

"We drafted a version of the scouting overview. Since we don't have full maps, we tried to focus on the immediate sectors, tree warp, elemental drift zones, and that north eastern basin with the soft soil."

Ro leaned in, squinting at the notes while shoving a bite of bread into their mouth.

"Mm. This is good. Smart phrasing."

Thena scanned a line, chewing.

"I like the way you categorized the wind distortion here. Makes it sound like an environmental issue rather than active magic."

Callyn gave her a nod, "That was the idea."

Ro grinned, "I guess pairing nerds with bruisers *does* work."

Tito rolled his eyes but didn't argue. As they settled in to go over the final phrasing, Callyn rose and reached for her cloak.

"I'm going to grab something from the armory," she said, pulling her hair back into a quick bun. "I'll meet you at the room just before the bell."

"We'll be ready," said Tito.

The door clicked softly behind her. There was an awkward silence. The three sat there eating and not even Ro spoke. Thena had finished most of her flatbread by the time she spoke again.

"I want to say something," she said suddenly.

Tito looked up, startled.

She didn't wait for a response.

"I knew Kael was a pompous ass, but I didn't know he'd gone that far. We haven't spoken properly in months. I heard rumors about his behavior during training, but I didn't think..." she laughed, only to relieve the pressure. "I didn't think he was capable of that."

Tito shrugged lightly, "You're not responsible for him."

"No," she said, finally looking at him, "but I'm still sorry for what he did to you."

The apology lingered in the air between them.

"And I get it now," she added, "why he's so pissed. He's not in the upper chambers, he's not going on a field mission. Kael's sitting in a holding block while someone he thinks shouldn't have passed him did."

Tito stayed quiet for a long beat.

"Thank you," he said, and he meant it.

Thena didn't smile, but there was something less defensive in her shoulders as she leaned back in her chair again.

Ro watched the exchange, then flicked a crumb from Tito's sleeve.

"Not bad for your first political reconciliation," they said with a lopsided grin. "If you keep this up, you'll be too well-liked to fit in with the magi or the military."

"I'll take that risk," Tito said with a laugh.

Tito stood, stretched, and moved to sit on the edge of Ro's bed.

Thena, already flipping through the last few scouting notes again, tuned them out.

"So," Ro whispered, "you doing okay?"

"Aside from nearly being broken in half a couple times? Surprisingly, yes."

Ro bumped his shoulder with theirs.

"You're holding up better than I expected."

"I've had help," Tito replied. "Callyn's tough, but fair, and I think she's starting to respect me."

"You mean now that you've fought half your regiment and survived?"

"Ha! Something like that."

Ro studied Tito's face.

"You've changed, Maldito."

"So have you, *Espero*," Tito shot back, not sure what exactly Ro was seeing.

"I feel it," Ro admitted. "The magic, the runes, the training. It's like I'm bigger than I was before. Not just stronger, but brighter. Like my thoughts hum with the magic."

"I'm happy to hear that," said Tito, who tried not to reveal his own dejection. "I haven't felt that yet."

"Valeria's been working you hard, though. Right? I see some muscle that wasn't there a week ago."

"She's held nothing back," Tito said, rubbing his wrist. "She's not cruel, just relentless. She's not the main one, though. We have someone called the drillmaster."

"Makes sense. They're probably still scared to let you near anything magical. But still, you haven't practiced at all?"

Tito shook his head.

"Not since the attunement. I had an evaluation to be able to be chosen for the fieldwork and I could feel the wind helping me; but they don't let me do anything directly. They say I carry too much of it. Not just one element...all of them. They're afraid that if I start channeling now, I'll bring down part of the Citadel by accident."

"That might not be an exaggeration," Ro conceded.

"Valeria said this mission might be a chance. Away from the city, out in the field. Somewhere I can try without crushing anyone alive."

"Controlled chaos," Ro murmured.

"Yeah. Something like that."

They both sat in silence for a moment, the quiet enjoyment of being alone together.

"Do you think this really is just a test?" Tito asked. "This mission?"

Ro shrugged, "Field exercise, scouting test, weird political theater? Could be all three."

"Are you scared?"

Ro was quiet for a moment, then nodded.

"Yes. I wasn't really before because they don't tell us much."

"Then why?"

Ro met his eyes, serious now.

"If there's a chance of choosing between saving anyone or you, you are who I will choose every time. I'm just scared of what that means about me."

The conversation was cut short and Tito held that thought as the first toll of the midday bell echoed across the Citadel. He joined Ro and Thena out the door. Their body language was rigid as they crossed the final corridor and approached the doors of the field assignment chamber.

Callyn was already waiting, arms crossed as she straightened to meet them.

"Are you ready?" she asked.

Tito nodded, "As we'll ever be."

Without a word, she turned and pushed open the tall arched doors. The briefing chamber was not large, but a presence loomed. It was carved from pale stone and trimmed in blackened iron, with high windows that let in cold light and shadowed corners where large maps of lands Tito had never heard hung. The table in the center glowed faintly at the seams, pulsing in rhythm with the protective wards anchored into the building's foundations.

Four figures stood at the opposite end of the table.

Valeria stood closest to the entry, posture straight with a presence as unyielding as her armor. She didn't wear her helmet, but the black and crimson pauldron on her shoulder shimmered slightly with the ward sigil.

To her right stood Venric, his expression severe as ever. His gloved hands folded with exacting precision over a stack of untouched papers.

Next to him stood a short woman in dark green robes, hands gloved in rings of silver and copper, a massive brown and yellow beaded necklace lay against her chest. Her hair was braided in a high, tight braid. No name was offered, but Tito guessed her to be the Head Magus of the wind spire based on her dress.

The fourth figure stood furthest from the center, half in shadow. A tall man, broad-shouldered, draped in light-green robes. He wore no sigils or title pins. A long burn scar traced the side of his face and vanished beneath his collar. He didn't speak, but Valeria's subtle tilt of her head and straightening of her spine as she glanced toward him said enough. This man outranked her.

Tito exchanged a glance with Ro as they stepped forward in formation.

The older woman spoke first.

"You are the initiates assigned to the Solin Domaris Initiate Scouting Mission," she stated. "This is a rare opportunity and your advancement in ranks past initiate will be heavily regarded in reference to this training. I am told you were advised to review past field logs in preparation. We'd like to hear your assessments. Begin with your findings."

Tito started forward, but Callyn stepped out first.

"We reviewed reports mostly from the last twenty years, ones that were scout led, magus escorted, and a few conscript notes that didn't appear in the upper file lists." Her voice was crisp. "We focused on three key areas for our assessment. The first being the tree warped regions northwest of the Veiled Ridge; then a basin prone to elemental sink and soft earth degradation; and finally, the delta near the three ravines past the perimeter wards."

She stepped slightly to the side, giving Tito a glance. He picked up where she left off.

"There's a repeating pattern of instability in those zones. Changes in air pressure, wind movement without visible fronts, elemental drift in soil that doesn't align with seasonal patterns."

Venric's eyes never left Tito.

Callyn continued, "We've divided the terrain into three mapped zones and suggest testing each region by perception and elemental response, then track any signs of flux without engaging them directly."

The older woman spoke, "And your projection on cause?"

Thena stepped forward this time.

"We don't know enough to give a cause," she said, "but the behavior aligns with field distortion, specifically residual magic left behind by either massive anchoring spells or elemental ruptures."

"It's not behaving like wild magic," Ro added. "It's structured...or was. These shifts are too regular, too patterned. The tree growth, the way wind is drawn into certain canyons, the light fractures in low fog, this isn't natural."

Ro moved slightly in front of Tito and Callyn now, speaking with ease and confidence. In other words, Ro was in their element.

"My guess," Ro said, glancing at Thena, "is something was buried, either forgotten or sealed."

"We're not suggesting we dig it up," Thena clarified. "Only if this is a residual zone, we should be scouting for boundaries and leave the rest to those experienced."

The expression of the woman in green flickered for a moment, then was stilled.

"A measured approach."

The tall man in olive robes finally shifted slightly, his voice deep and gravel edged.

"And this summary, these zones and classifications, were concluded from a combination of your independent work?"

"Yes, sir," Callyn said.

He glanced at Valeria, who inclined her head slightly, as if confirming it.

"And you believe this information would help define the scope of your scouting mission?"

Tito stepped forward, just a fraction.

"It gives us starting points. A way to focus our attention instead of walking blind."

Venric's eyes slid to him with that same surgical stillness.

"And if what you find doesn't match your expectations?"

"Then we record what we find," Tito replied. "It's a field exercise, nothing more."

"Good," the woman magus said.

Venric finally spoke.

"Then the matter is simple. If this group is ready to observe, you'll be tested on your investigative prowess and your ability to observe and *to not draw attention to yourself.* You are not to solve anything."

There was a short silence, then the four leaned inward slightly, voices lowering into private discussion, their words swallowed by the steady thrum of the rune etched walls.

The initiates stepped back, falling into a loose circle near the room's edge.

Ro exhaled slowly.

"Well, I think we almost sounded like we knew what we were doing."

Thena tilted her head, "We did?"

Callyn's eyes lingered on the olive-robed man.

"That's the captain," she said under her breath, "of the Queen's Guard. Captain Garius."

Tito followed her gaze.

"He didn't say a word until the end."

The low conversation among the four officials quieted as the door to the chamber opened behind the initiates. A woman stepped inside, her gray cloak still dusted from travel. Or was it brown? Her boots clicked sharply against stone as she strode. She carried a satchel of scrolls tucked under one arm. She was striking, though perhaps not beautiful. Not in the conventional sense. Mid-twenties, maybe older. Her hair was pulled back into a tight braid, and her posture spoke of someone who had stood her ground before men twice her size and won.

Her eyes scanned the room as she entered and landed on the four initiates. She paused.

Tito saw it...the flicker of confusion as her gaze moved from him to Ro to Callyn, and then Thena.

Valeria inclined her head slightly toward the woman, showing a sliver of deference Tito hadn't seen from her before.

The tall man, Captain Garius, spoke first, "Ranger Issara, we've reviewed your submitted report. The council would like it confirmed verbally."

Where had Tito heard that name before?

The ranger acknowledged her superior, "Understood, sir."

"Don't worry about the initiates," Venric said with venom. "Due to a rather incompetent scribe, they stumbled upon your submission early. No point in preserving protocol now."

Ranger Issara narrowed her gaze, but she said nothing. Instead, she stepped forward toward the rune lit table and placed her satchel beside it.

"My regiment was returning from the western edge of the northern perimeter," she began. "We rerouted to avoid a collapsed ridge pass near the Veiled Ridge, something not previously reported."

Ro shifted slightly beside Tito, recognizing the location as a point that Callyn and Tito had mentioned for a focus in their scouting mission. That's when the name clicked.

Scout Report – Regimental Return South of the Veiled Ridge, Logged: Solin, Velmara, 6th bell. Filed by: Lyra Venel Issara, Ranger-Captain, 3rd Northern Regiment.

This was who was in charge of the scouting report.

"As we passed through the canyon mouth, we detected magnetic drag through one of the scouts' compasses," Lyra Issara said. "Wind gusts began funneling unnaturally low, but with no pressure system to support the movement."

She paused, adjusting one of the scrolls and unfurling a small, sketched diagram.

"There was a structure embedded in the cliff wall. It was stone, smooth-faced, with geometric carvings resembling ancient rune scaffolding. Door-like in shape but sealed. We noted no entrance, no enchantments, but the area around it was inert. It's several decades old at least. Moss has taken over several portions of the structure. I logged it and pulled the unit back before nightfall, no direct contact was made. Coordinates are noted in the submission."

A pause followed as the four senior figures absorbed the weight of her words.

The older magus woman, the one who had led the initial questioning, spoke again.

"Your findings align with several anomalies in the areas the initiates highlighted. We believe this is the ideal opportunity to test both your command ability and their preparedness."

She turned toward the initiates.

"You will be deployed to investigate the broader region surrounding the coordinates Lyra discovered. A simple survey. Excavations may come later."

Venric added, "If it is nothing, you return. If it is something, you observe, document, and wait. No involvement. We do not risk untested talent on forgotten ruins. Especially destructive talent."

Captain Garius crossed his arms, finally breaking his long silence.

"With respect," he said in a deep voice, "Valeria would be better suited to this assignment. These are her initiates. She's trained them, shaped their readiness, and they already follow her voice."

Lyra turned toward him.

"Captain, there are magi initiates that..."

"Your presence is still required," the magus woman cut in. "But he is right."

Her eyes drifted toward Valeria, who hadn't spoken, only stood firm as stone, eyes straight ahead.

"You've prepared them. You'll lead them. This will also be a council test for you and your ability to lead magi initiates."

Valeria bowed her head slightly.

"As the council commands."

Venric did not look pleased.

Garius gave a single, approving nod.

Lyra stepped back slightly, folding her arms.

"By the decree of the council," the green robed woman began. "I, Head-Magus Coralaine Thorne sanction the Solin Domaris 4 Initiate Scouting Mission led by Vice-Captain Valeria Serran and co-captained by Lyra Issara as testament to leading potential. You will be responsible for the protection and evaluation of barrack initiates Callyn Marvera and Maldito Vandero, and magi initiates Thena Morran and Espero Vandero. Your goal is to evaluate the initiates, test their physical and elemental capability, and measure their ability to confirm the scouting report submitted on Solin-Velmara 4 by Lyra Issara. You are to stay within the perimeter wards in response to the Liora initiate deaths. May Eliar protect you."

With that, Coralaine stamped a page on the table as orange light pulsed from the center.

"You are to meet at the northern Citadel gate immediately, where travel bags will be provided."

CHAPTER 25

It was late in the day when they set out. A breeze swept through the dirty streets of the outer ring. It was the final afternoon of Solin, when the heat still clung stubbornly to the stone, but this wind had already begun to shift. Tomorrow brought the season's change.

They walked in a quiet line through the outskirts of Atheron with the weight of departure pressing against their backs.

Valeria led them. She wore padded leather lined with light plate under a black travel cloak, her sword strapped across her back instead of her hip.

Beside her, Lyra walked in silence. Her gear matched the rest of them, standard issue, but she carried herself like someone used to more freedom. She kept perfect pace with Valeria, not a step ahead or behind, and didn't speak.

It wasn't out of respect, Tito noted.

The four initiates followed just behind, packs resting squarely on their shoulders, gear freshly distributed and already beginning to settle into new, unfamiliar shapes against their frames.

Callyn and Tito walked side by side, eyes forward, quiet and focused.

Ro and Thena trailed behind, occasionally muttering to each other as they adjusted straps and tugged on glove seams.

The streets here were quiet. All the attention seemed overcrowded at the front of Atheron with the docks that opened the world. At the edge of the corridor ahead stood a structure older than the rest of the city, a curved wall of obsidian and marble inlaid with iron veins and engraved with the sigil of the queen.

Tito kept a hopeful eye for Barrel.

It had been over two weeks, though. No matter his word, he had no reason to wait for no answer.

The northern gate, known as the Gate of Breath, was still sealed. A smooth disc of obsidian sat in the center, framed by a silver inlay etched with elemental runes all interlocked in an ancient ring. From behind the gate came the faint shimmer of the arcane barrier separating the inner ring.

Valeria stepped forward without a word, withdrawing a small silver token from her pouch. The guards stationed at the entrance nodded but did not stop her. She inserted the token into the slot beside the seal. The obsidian disc pulsed with soft light, first blue, then gold, then white. Then, the gate actually breathed. A slow exhale of mist slid from its seams, and the magical barrier began to dissolve, folding away in silklike ribbons of energy that shimmered and faded.

Beyond the threshold, the world stretched wide and warm. Fields lay just beyond the outer walls, dotted with low hills, a winding path of stone, and the first trees of the untamed ridge, now touched with the first hints of turning gold.

This was it. Valeria turned back.

"Finish gearing up. While the wards deter monsters and the like, it is still better to be prepared."

They began to move. Their travel armor wasn't made of plate or of the ceremonial kind, which was common for the guards at Atheron. The party's protection was designed for survival. Thick padded jackets reinforced with runes at the chest and joints, gloves with runes sewn into the knuckles, travel cloaks with heat and weather resistance folded inside the lining. Their boots were heavy but well-balanced, built for rock and trail alike.

Each of them was handed a pack by one of the waiting quartermasters. They were told it contained rations, flint kits, collapsible runestone lamps, compact tents, bedrolls, water cloths, binding wraps, and basic salves for injury or exhaustion.

Ro frowned at the weight of theirs.

"They really think I'm going to carry all of this?"

"You've got strong legs," Thena said, not looking up.

"I use them for incredible magic manipulation, not hiking."

Callyn adjusted the chest straps on her armor without a word, her hands steady and practiced.

Tito ran a quick check on the flask holsters sewn into the pack's side, then bent to secure the lacing along his boots.

Valeria turned toward Lyra, "You'll take the left flank, you know the perimeter."

Lyra gave a short nod, "I'll keep us in."

Valeria didn't return the glance, "Good."

She turned to the initiates.

"Once we're through the main perimeter, we follow the outer path for three hours to the second anchor for camp. No magic during, and no detours. Speak up if anything changes. Your awareness is being assessed."

They all nodded quietly as she turned back to lead them out.

The outer path was larger than any path Tito had seen. It was wide enough for a caravan, worn smooth by years of use, but flanked by grass that grew tall and trees that sheltered everything behind.

Three hours of walking wasn't far, but every step away from Atheron made the world feel a little less familiar. The city disappeared behind them slowly. The spires thinned in the haze as the walls became swallowed by the rise and fall of yellowed hills. Above them, the last warmth of Solin still kissed their cloaks, though a colder current rode the air beneath it with the breath of Vieren beginning to whisper along the ridge.

No one spoke for the first twenty minutes. Even Ro was quiet, eyes scanning the shifting grass, their fingers tapping lightly on the strap of their pack as if testing its weight against an unseen tempo.

It was Thena who broke the silence.

"That smell," she muttered. "What is that?"

Tito sniffed, "Metal?"

"Magical runoff," Lyra called from a short distance ahead. "The anchors pulse on a rotation. When the boundary seals flicker, trace energy seeps into the soil."

"Is that safe?" Ro asked, sidling up beside her.

"It dissipates within an hour," Lyra said without turning. "It won't kill you but might give you strange dreams."

"That explains so much," Ro muttered.

Tito smiled faintly, but his gaze shifted to the horizon toward a cluster of dark roofs just beginning to form from the curvature of the trail.

A village. Small and tucked between two low hills, its homes were squat and built from pale river stone. Smoke curled gently from a few chimneys, and a wind wheel spun slowly above the main barn. A scattering of farmers stood along the edge of the road, watching the travelers pass with cautious eyes. Children paused their play near a stack of hay bales, one holding a wooden sword and another with a ribbon in her hair that fluttered unnaturally, caught by wind that didn't exist within the city.

"Do they always stare like that?" Ro asked.

"Always," Valeria answered. "Most villages know we're not here for trade. When soldiers walk the path, something's wrong."

Tito caught the look one of the older farmers gave him, one full of a furrowed brow, then a resigned nod.

As they passed the last fence, the land dipped slightly, and that's when Tito saw it. The anchor. It rose like a mountain from the earth, a spire of hewn stone and metal, woven with ringed walkways and latticed with crystal ridges. Massive runes pulsed along its surface, timed to a silent rhythm that vibrated faintly in his chest. From this far out, it looked like something ancient, but Tito knew better. This was built by the magi. Recent history, not myth. A tool, not a monument.

Ro slowed, gazing in awe at the anchor.

"What is that?" they asked.

"The northern ward anchor," Valeria answered. "One of ten, actually. Each keeps a segment of the capital's protective shell stable. They also keep the outer paths clear of lesser creatures."

"So, monsters really can't get in?" Tito asked.

"They can't pass the seal's edge," Lyra added. "Not unless something breaks."

The tone she said it with made everyone quiet again. They moved closer, and the size of the anchor became real. It dwarfed the land, tall enough to pierce the sky, and hummed with restrained power. Birds didn't circle it, the wind even moved differently around its base as if shaped by the spire's presence.

Valeria raised a hand and signaled them to stop at a flat stone rest point near the anchor's edge, one of many left for guards, messengers, and scouts.

"We'll pause here," she said. "Check your gear, hydrate. We head north in ten."

Tito let his pack drop with a soft thud, rubbing his shoulder as he turned to look back the way they came.

Atheron was gone.

The pulsing of the anchor wasn't loud, but it was there. It was a quiet rhythm beneath their feet, like standing over the slow beat of a slumbering titan.

Tito sat on the edge of the resting stone, elbows rested on his knees, eyes drawn upward.

The northern ward anchor stretched impossibly high, its spire etched in runes that flickered faintly, like stars winking through gauze. Wind slid around the structure in long, slow waves, carrying a kind of hush with it, as if even the air was under orders not to speak too loudly here.

He adjusted the strap of his pack again, his fingers brushed one of the side buckles, more for something to do than from necessity.

Ro crouched nearby, sorting through their satchel with a furrowed brow and a strip of dried fruit hanging loosely from their mouth. A few sheets of half folded glyph paper sat between their knees, partially scrawled with illusion rune variations. Every so often, they glanced up at the anchor and muttered to themself under their breath.

"Is it weird," they said finally, "that I keep expecting it to move?"

Callyn looked over from where she stood, arms crossed near the base, "It doesn't move."

"Yeah, but it feels like it could. Like it's waiting."

"Resonant charge dispersal," Thena corrected as she adjusted the strap across her chest. "They build anchors to cycle outward. Like a heart pushing magic instead of blood."

Ro looked at her with mock offense.

"Can't I have one poetic moment without you explaining it to death?"

"No," she replied without hesitation.

Lyra stood a little apart from the group, watching the horizon. Her back was straight, her hand resting on the hilt of a short blade. The wind tousled a few strands of her hair, but she made no move to tuck them back. Her eyes scanned the tree line beyond the path ahead, even though the true edge of the wilderness was still a couple hours march north.

Tito stood, brushed his palms against his thighs, and moved closer to the anchor. The base was constructed of dark stone veined with pale metal that didn't look like gold or silver. Something that shimmered only when he didn't look directly at it. He placed a hand on the stone. It was warm. Not heat radiating onto it from the sun but more like the magic inside it had a temperature. It vibrated against his palm with a strange gentleness.

"You alright?" Callyn asked from behind him.

"Yeah," he said softly. "Just trying to feel it."

Ro stood up and stretched.

"Well, you've got about thirty seconds left of feeling things before Valeria gets tired of letting us sit still."

As if summoned, Valeria's voice rang out clearly from the far side of the rest station.

"Form up."

Tito stepped away from the anchor, and the connection faded like a hand sliding from a pulse. They gathered again, the six of them drawing close as the spire of the anchor loomed at their backs. Valeria waited until all eyes were on her.

"The moment we step past the radius," she said, "we're beyond the stabilizer ring. That means in about an hour, elemental behavior becomes inconsistent. That is the area the reports begin to cover."

She looked at each of them in turn.

"No magic until then unless I give the word. No rune tests, no illusions. We don't know what the land will do with it."

Lyra's eyes narrowed slightly but said nothing.

Callyn stood still, focused.

Thena nodded once.

Ro twirled a copper ring on their finger but didn't speak.

Tito felt the anchor's rhythm still echoing faintly through his wrist.

Valeria turned toward the narrowing path that veered beyond the spire's northern edge.

"Let's go."

CHAPTER 26

They marched in loose formation with Valeria at the lead and Lyra at the rear. Between them, the four initiates walked in pairs.

Tito and Callyn moved near the front. Behind them, Ro and Thena were deep in an apparently preexisting debate about magical theory, and how illusion spells might behave in terrain warped by elemental residue.

"It's not that the magic itself gets corrupted," Ro said, gesturing with a stick they'd picked up, "it's that the land holds echoes. Like casting an illusion over a mirror, it reflects itself weird."

Thena scoffed, "That's not how grounding works. The instability comes from poor anchoring. Elemental interference disrupts projected threads and destabilizes the weave."

"Or," Ro said with a smirk, "maybe the world just doesn't like being lied to."

Tito smiled faintly as their voices rose and fell behind him. It was more comforting than annoying, reminding him of home, of simpler arguments. They were really just excuses to keep talking.

The first hour passed without note. Then the world began to feel *off*, but it started small.

A patch of moss grew in a perfect circle around the base of a stone, but the same type of moss grew in a spiraling shape only two feet away.

The wind that had once flowed consistently from the southwest shifted without warning, blowing east for ten minutes before dying entirely. The sun was still out, the path still clear, but the silence between those oddities was thick.

By late afternoon, they reached the second anchor. It wasn't as tall as the first, but it was a broader, our-pillared structure ringed with a disk of metal that spun slowly, unnaturally, with no visible mechanism. The air around it felt tighter, like walking through a curtain of pressure, just enough to remind them that this space was claimed.

Valeria raised her hand, "We make camp here."

No one objected. They found a clearing near the base of the structure, a shallow slope tucked beneath a leaning tree whose trunk forked in a sharp Y, covered in bark with a natural sheen like polished lacquer. The ground was dry, and the warded presence of the anchor promised relative safety for the night.

Bedrolls were unfurled and a fire pit was dug.

Ro summoned a small, nonmagical flame the old-fashioned way with flint and steel, muttering the whole time about how insulted they felt by not being allowed to show off.

Callyn handled most of the meal prep, rationed bread softened with warmed water, dried vegetables rehydrated in a tin pot, and smoked meat cut thin and folded into tight bundles.

As dusk bled into deep blue, the stars began to emerge. They were sharper than they'd ever looked inside Atheron's ring. A sliver of moon hung overhead, and the air turned cooler with each hour past Solin's breath. They sat close around the fire, packs nestled near the base of the anchor.

Valeria passed out the watch schedule without ceremony.

"Two-hour shifts. I'll take first."

Callyn raised her hand for the second shift.

"I'll take third," Tito offered.

Ro and Thena were paired for the last.

With the details settled, the fire dimmed slightly, and the group leaned into the quiet.

It was Ro, of course, who broke it.

"So," they said around a mouthful of preserved berry, "what's the weirdest thing everyone's seen so far?"

"Besides you trying to make a joke at a fire?" Thena muttered.

Ro gave her a playful shove.

"I mean it," they said. "This area's off. The backwards wind? That tree with the leaves that all face down?"

"That stone back on the trail," Callyn added. "It had an impression under it like it moved recently. But there were no drag marks."

"There was frost," Lyra said from her post nearby, speaking for the first time in a while. "Just a sliver around one root. In late Solin."

Valeria didn't speak. She watched the dark beyond the fire, the outline of her jaw set like stone.

Tito poked at the fire and spoke low, as if he needed to say it aloud to believe it.

"I think the land's remembering things wrong."

They all looked at him.

"I don't know, it's just a feeling," he said, shrugging. "Like the world wants to behave normally, but something's thrown it off."

Ro exhaled.

"Well," they said, "good thing we brought a historian."

Things quieted after that. The fire crackled low. Its flames danced like half-hearted spirits in the growing dark. The six of them sat in a wide ring, gear close at hand.

Tito leaned back against his pack, his arms around his knees, watching the flickering light reflect off Ro's boots, then Callyn's gauntlets, then Thena's quiet stare. She was the one who broke the silence this time.

"You know," she said, not looking at anyone in particular, "twenty years ago, missions like this weren't scouting missions."

Ro glanced over, "No?"

Thena shook her head.

"They were just maintenance runs. Scouts would walk the outer paths, check for erosion, and make sure the anchor cores weren't overheating. Elemental residue was rare. Monsters were almost never sighted this close."

"And now?" Tito asked.

"Now we walk through cracked ground and watch trees grow sideways. Now we test memory against maps," Thena answered. She gave a sarcastic laugh. "Now we go out first, and if we're still breathing when we come back, the magi send a team of seven to 'make the tweaks.'"

"I noticed that in the reports," Callyn chimed in. "I forget there was a before. This is all we have ever known."

Ro was turning a twig over in their hand before choosing to toss it in the fire.

"Before what?"

"The Flameward Rebellion," Thena answered.

"I thought that was mostly internal. Magi and nobles, right?"

"Ha! That's what they put in the books."

She leaned forward, her hands near the fire, warming fingers made stiff from the march.

"There are rumors that say some of the anchors were targeted, maybe even sabotaged; but battles make for glorious history and are thus more widely discussed. Obviously, this sabotage was not enough to bring the anchors down, but enough to shake their balance. Elemental channels bent out of place. Seals warped."

Tito swallowed, "You think that's why the world is wrong out here?"

Thena shrugged, "Best guess the instructors ever gave me. When the anchors were first built, the land resisted. Earth cracked. Storms flared. Creatures we thought extinct started showing up again. And then, it stopped...for a while but can be contained forever. Especially the wild parts of the world."

Ro exhaled, "So, they keep sending teams like us. Poke the edges, map the weirdness, then call in the senior magi to 'fix' it."

"And hope," Thena finished, "that whatever broke the first time doesn't break worse."

The fire popped.

Valeria hadn't said a word. She stood near the edge of the light, arms folded, her silhouette sharp against the outline of the spire behind her. The glow from the anchor rim that caught the edge of her cloak gave her a spectral shimmer.

Tito watched her for a moment.

"You're quiet," he said.

Valeria's head tilted slightly.

Ro raised an eyebrow, "Everything okay, Vice-Captain?"

She was still for a beat. Then she said, "The woods are too quiet."

No one moved. The wind had died an hour ago. The insects had stopped, even the trees, once swaying gently, now stood utterly still.

Tito glanced past her into the dark, his throat dry.

"You think something's...?"

"No," Valeria said too fast, but her hand rested on the hilt of her sword the moment she'd spoken.

Ro exchanged a glance with Thena, then slowly reached into their cloak and palmed a small rune disk, just in case.

Valeria turned back to the fire.

"Keep talking," she said. "No sense in letting me ruin the night."

Tito felt like pressing further but thought better of it.

They settled down one by one as the moon hung above the spire of the anchor like a pale coin on the edge of spinning. The fire burned low as the sky deepened into full night.

Callyn was already asleep, her arms crossed beneath her head and one boot half loosened.

Ro had sprawled sideways atop their bedroll and was muttering softly in their sleep, something about trees and upside-down birds.

Thena lay still, her eyes closed, but her fingers were curled tight around the leather strap of her pack.

Tito tried to sleep, he really did. He lay on his back and watched the stars move. He counted them, traced imaginary lines between them. Tried to remember the names his father used to murmur on quiet nights in Ethyrae, names older than the Magi, names in a language neither of them spoke anymore. But his body was restless, humming with nerves and the memory of the anchor's pulse.

He sat up just to breathe and rubbed at his face, then noticed movement at the edge of the firelight. Two shadows. Valeria and Lyra.

They stood near the tree line, not far from the anchor's base, partially shrouded by a slope of dark stone. The fire behind Tito didn't reach them fully, just lit the edge of Valeria's cloak, and the faint motion of Lyra's hand gestured as she spoke.

Tito couldn't hear what was said. The wind had picked up again, soft and slow. Valeria simply listened to Lyra, then gave a short nod. She turned back toward camp first, boots silent over the grass, and disappeared into the darkness. Lyra remained for another moment longer, looking out into the woods, past where the anchor's safety radius would end. Then she followed.

By the time Tito shifted and stood, Valeria was already by the fire again, crouched low to stir the embers and feed it a few dry splinters from her satchel. The flames rose slightly, painting gold against her jaw, her hair drawn back and untouched by sleep. She looked up once at him and said nothing.

Tito didn't ask, he just moved toward the edge of the camp, where the night waited for him, and the woods whispered.

Tito sat on a smooth stone near the edge of camp. The fire behind him had dulled to embers, its extra warmth thinning by the minute. He tried to keep his eyes on the tree line, but the dark played tricks. Twice, he thought he saw movement, a figure just between the trees, too tall for an animal, too low to be windblown branches.

The first time, he straightened.

The second time, he reached for the staff lying across his bedroll. But both times, when he looked again, there was nothing. Just moonlight or grass or bark split in patterns that only almost looked like faces.

Tito shook his head and exhaled through his nose.

"Paranoia," he whispered to himself. "First time in the field. Probably just my nerves."

The forest didn't answer, it just stood there watching without eyes.

He sat back down, still gripping the staff, and forced himself to breathe slow and deep. He counted to five, then ten, then twelve. His thoughts drifted back to Ethyrae, to Ro's laughter echoing along the tide pools, to Jaro scolding them for forgetting the fish traps. Back when the only monsters were too deep to see, and the wind always smelled like salt and seaweed.

A twig snapped behind him.

He spun, staff raised and stopped just short of Callyn's shoulder.

She blinked at him, then curled an eyebrow.

"Terrible watchman," she said flatly. "I've been standing here for a solid ten seconds."

Tito lowered the staff slowly, swallowing his surprise and his embarrassment.

"You could've said something."

"I did," she replied. "You were too busy staring into the forest."

Tito glanced toward the trees again, still half expecting something to be there this time. He let out a breath and dropped his hand from the staff.

"Sorry."

She shrugged, sat down beside him, and pulled her cloak tighter around her shoulders.

"Don't apologize. Happens to all of us the first time, especially out here. I haven't been this far before, but I have been out once or twice."

"Have you ever seen something?"

"Once," she said. "Didn't stay long. Looked like a shadow trying to remember how legs worked. Next morning, our campfire was gone. No ash or stone or anything, just grass. I didn't come back out."

Tito looked at her sidelong.

"You're joking."

Callyn's eyes didn't leave the tree line.

"Nope. I hope I imagined it."

They sat together in silence for a while, their shoulders just close enough to share the warmth left from the fire.

CHAPTER 27

Dawn broke quietly over the second anchor. No bells, no birdsong. No waves lapping. Just a slow sweep of cool light across the uneven ground, painting long shadows from the leaning trees and catching the faint shimmer of the anchor's disk as it rotated above their heads.

By the time the sun crested the hills, the camp was already packed. The ritual of departure done with the silent coordination of people who knew that routine meant survival.

Tito chewed through a hard roll filled with a smear of root paste and dried fig. It wasn't good, but it was fuel. Around him, the others ate in similar fashion.

Valeria stood at the edge of the anchor's radius, scanning the faint perimeter sigils half buried in the soil.

Lyra stood not far off, arms crossed, waiting. She hadn't spoken much since the night before, but when Valeria gave her a short nod, she addressed the group.

"We're staying within the warded perimeter today," she said. "The line runs northeast for another five miles. The path won't be marked, so stay sharp and keep formation. I'll guide us."

"Still no spell work?" Ro asked, already bouncing on their heels.

"You can start your magic practice once we stop for midday." Valeria replied. She turned to look at the rest of the group, "That goes for everyone."

Ro groaned.

Still, the promise of magic in real, open practice kept a buzz of anticipation humming through the group.

The morning march was lighter than the day before. Here, the perimeter ring curved gently through the wilderness and the terrain alternated between gentle glades and dry, crooked groves. Patches of exposed roots twisted around rocks in patterns that almost looked intentional. A few rabbits darted across their path, silent and lean.

Thena murmured to Ro about the way the air felt lighter here, less heavy than beyond the anchor.

Tito stayed near the front, walking beside Callyn again. The two moved in a kind of rhythm now, falling into step without needing to speak.

"What do you think they'll let us do?" he asked as they crested a hill overlooking a small dell.

Callyn considered it.

"They still don't trust us not to light the woods on fire, so probably not much."

"Fair," Tito admitted.

Behind them, Ro said, "I will absolutely light the woods on fire. With style, of course. Maybe even in purple flames."

"You're not helping," Thena muttered.

Lyra glanced back once at the group's chatter but didn't intervene.

Valeria said nothing at all.

The morning path curved gently through the rise and fall of the wooded terrain, their boots crunched over dry brush and the occasional loose stone. Sunlight filtered through a high canopy of thin, copper leaves, which cast shifting patterns across the ground.

Ro sidled up next to Tito as they walked, practically bouncing with every step.

"I still can't believe we're actually getting to practice today."

Tito glanced over, amused.

"You've been talking about it since we left the anchor."

"Because it's finally happening," Ro said, slapping a hand lightly on Tito's shoulder. "Out here, in the wilds, no magus breathing down our necks, no overcooked ritual circles, no walls to accidentally destroy. Just pure, unfiltered, dramatic casting."

"You really think Valeria's going to let it get that dramatic?"

Ro smirked, "She can try to keep it tame. I'm just saying, if I happen to create a five story tall phantom hawk during our warmup drills, who's really to blame?"

"That something you've been practicing?"

Ro puffed up, chin lifted with mock pride.

"No phantom hawks yet, but I did pull off a full reflection loop through two opposing mirror illusions."

"Is that good?"

"Let's just say Thena watched me for once and didn't correct me."

Tito gave a soft whistle.

"Damn. You've really been going."

Ro shrugged, but the pride didn't leave their face.

"They've been pushing me hard. Magi love to play favorites when someone flashes potential, and I'm nothing if not flashy." Then they grew serious. "You'll get your turn, Maldito. I know it's been rough, all those drills and not even getting to test your magic."

Tito kicked a small rock from the path.

"Yeah. They're worried I'll lose control if my body can't handle it."

"They're probably right," Ro said without hesitation, "but that's exactly why you need this."

Tito looked over, half-laughing, "Comforting."

"I'm serious! You need to feel it again, see what's changed from your training."

Tito exhaled slowly.

"Yeah but burning trees and all those worries are true."

Ro grinned.

"We'll handle it together. I'll illusion the fire into a tasteful cloud of butterflies."

The group stopped in a shallow clearing where the perimeter trail brushed along a ridge of mossy rock. A dry stream bed ran through the center, its banks smooth from decades of runoff.

Valeria gave the order, and the moment it left her lips, everyone scattered like children loosed from their parent's arms. Gear was shrugged off, cloaks folded, boots flexed against soil.

Ro rolled their shoulders like they were warming up for a stage performance, and even Thena looked mildly energized as she began inspecting a set of focus runes carved into the edge of her staff.

But the first demonstration wasn't Ro's, it was Callyn's and Lyra's.

Valeria called it with sharp formality.

"One-on-one. Water and wind only. Controlled contact. Begin when ready."

It never occurred to Tito that Lyra had magic, she wore no beads, and her forearms were always covered.

Callyn stepped forward, her stance already grounded, fingers flexing at her sides. She flexed her bracer lined with water channel runes that shimmered faintly in the sun.

Lyra stood opposite her, cloak discarded, hair tied back tight. Her hands were already lifted in a fluid motion that stirred the grass at her feet. Wind kissed the edges of the clearing.

"First spell's yours," Lyra said.

Callyn didn't hesitate. She thrust one hand forward, starting at the canteen from her belt. The water within rushed upward, spiraling around her arm where it grew in size, seemingly from the air itself, before launching in a sleek ribbon across the space between them. It cracked like a whip. It was aimed low, intended to trip, not to harm.

Lyra shifted, stepping into the strike rather than away, and twisted with a sharp motion of her palm. The wind caught the ribbon and split it, turning the tail into vapor that spiraled harmlessly to the dirt.

Callyn was already moving, drawing more water seemingly from the stream bed as a damp patch beneath the surface responded to her pull.

Lyra responded with a gust, kicking dust and dry leaves into the air, obscuring her shape.

The two circled each other in the half haze, pressure building in delicate increments.

Callyn pressed her advantage, channeling a shield of water to her left arm while sending a spiral across the ground, a thin film that slicked the soil just ahead of Lyra's foot.

Lyra slid or so it seemed. She leaned into the slip and used the momentum, pivoting midair with a burst of wind that lifted her several feet off the ground. She landed hard, sending a slicing current that blew Callyn's shield back and caused a wave to ripple through the stream bed behind her.

The group had gone quiet, watching with rapt attention.

Tito stood near the back, breath caught in his chest. He wasn't sure which was more mesmerizing, the wind carving lines in the dust, or the water responding like it knew what the air would do next.

Callyn narrowed her eyes and raised both arms. Water rose in a sharp column, curved like a crescent blade.

Lyra met it with a low gust, counterforce angled, and the two spells collided in a crack of vapor and heatless pressure that forced Ro to shield their face with their cloak.

Silence.

Steam drifted upward in lazy spirals. Valeria stepped forward.

"That's enough."

Both women relaxed, breathing steady but sharp, magic fading with practiced control.

Callyn lowered her hands, brow damp but eyes bright.

Lyra gave her a nod, not exactly friendly, but not dismissive either.

"Are you sure you're not magi?" she asked.

"You're better with wind than I expected," Callyn replied evenly.

Ro turned to Tito, wide-eyed.

"Okay. That? That's what I want to follow."

As the steam curled upward from the fading clash between Lyra and Callyn, Ro was already halfway out into the open space, arms out, feet bouncing. Valeria didn't even look at them when she spoke.

"You'll get your turn," she reprimanded him, "but Thena has been under magi discipline longer. She goes next."

Ro threw their hands up with an exaggerated sigh but backed off.

Thena stepped forward, focus rod in hand.

Valeria watched her for a moment.

"Your wind studies recently have been rooted in flow, mapping, and residual tracking, yes?"

Thena dipped her head, "Correct."

"Good," Valeria said.

She then turned, pointing up the ridge to a cluster of half fallen trees, their limbs stripped by seasons of elemental exposure. At their base were patches of scattered leaves, dust, and brittle debris.

"You'll be given a scenario," Valeria said. "A squad of soldiers is moving through a fractured ravine in enemy territory. An enemy stone magus just released a rockslide to separate you from the group in an attempt to deter them. Visibility is low...dust in the air, no line of sight. You're two ridges above them, and your job is to guide them safely to the rest of the group thirty paces ahead."

She paused, then added, "You may not speak. You may not descend. Use wind alone."

Thena blinked, then glanced once toward the others. Ro's curiosity was piqued, Callyn narrowed her eyes with interest, and Tito stood motionless, focused.

"No lift. No pulses?" Thena asked.

Valeria shook her head, "No. Subtlety only. You do not want the enemy to know you're aiding."

For a long breath no one spoke, then Thena moved. She walked up the incline, past the trees and stones until she found her footing atop a rise just out of range. She stopped there, eyes scanning the layout like a general reviewing a map. Then she raised her rod and whispered to the wind.

There was no rush, but slowly, the leaves began to stir.

Thena directed them in flowing patterns, using tiny ripples in the air to simulate paths that could be followed. The dust along the ridge rolled in controlled ribbons, revealing safe gaps between the rocks, and guided an invisible force from point to point. No debris lifted. No wind lashed.

She shifted once, and a soft pressure blew upward through a hollow trunk, releasing a tone. A signal, a call without voice. Then she circled the final position, her hand rotated gently, spinning dust into a tight, slow-moving spiral exactly where a target might stand.

The entire group watched in silence. Then Valeria raised her hand.

"Done."

Thena let the wind fall still. Dust drifted and settled. Leaves fluttered one last time and dropped back into place.

"Clear and readable," Valeria said. "Minimal disruption and high strategic value."

When wind had come to Tito back during the evaluation with Valeria, it had come like a crash of waves. A reflex, born from desperation and instinct. It had saved him, maybe even impressed Valeria. But this? Tito let out a breath he hadn't realized he was holding. Callyn was an artist. There was no thrill like in Lyra's sparring. No danger, no clash. Yet, she had accomplished something more impressive. This was precision. Elegance. Tito felt he could watch it forever.

Thena came back to the group and set her traveling pack near Tito, no sweat or exhaustion bled into her frame. Valeria glanced over at Lyra and Callyn, who were still taking heavy breaths.

"Ro," she called.

Ro lit up like someone had just flung open the gates of a theater. "Yes?"

Valeria gave them a measured look.

"You've been building the skill you possess since we left the Citadel."

"That is an accurate assessment, Vice-Commander," Ro scoffed dramatically.

"You've also been training under magi supervision for only a week with no active field demonstration."

"I'm aware and creatively stifled."

Valeria's mouth twitched, just slightly.

"I'll admit, illusion magic isn't my expertise. I've seen tactical uses such as camouflage, decoys, and sound masking; but I won't pretend to grasp the nuance behind your particular non-militaristic skill."

Ro blinked.

Tito watched them shift slightly, their usual ritual of calming to focus.

"So," Valeria continued, "I'm not assigning you a task."

Ro stilled.

"You have five minutes," she said. "Impress us."

Ro bowed at the waist, low and graceful.

"Finally," they whispered, "an audience."

Ro walked to the center of the dry creek bed and stretched their arms slowly to each side, eyes closed. For a heartbeat, they simply breathed.

It didn't begin with light, or flash, or even movement.

It began with presence.

The air shifted.

Not like the magic from Lyra and Callyn, or even Thena. With them it was excitable and eager. Ro's was different, subtle, like gravity deciding to lean in closer.

Light bent, just slightly, as if curious. Many duplicates of Ro came into being. One split cleanly from their side, another from their back. A third, fourth, fifth, sixth, each illusion was them, but not quite. Different expressions, different stances.

One grinned like Ro, another stood solemn. One hunched low, twitching, while another carried themselves with quiet nobility.

They moved like dancers orbiting a star. And then they changed. Each Ro flickered and shimmered into someone else.

One became a robed magus, face glowing with rune-light.

Another cloaked in Queen's Guard crimson, Valeria's blade strapped tight to their back.

One became monstrous, limbs elongated, eyes full black.

Then one stood bloodied but proud, wearing half-burned armor, while another went quiet and serene, dressed in pure white, hands clasped over a glowing orb. And the last...

The last one looked like Tito.

Ro raised a hand, and the world around them shattered. Not in violence, not in sound, but like a dream breaking apart.

Illusion rose around them, reshaping the trees and ridge and sky. In seconds, the clearing became something else entirely...the Citadel courtyard...almost.

The sky above was a swirl of purple and gold. Close stars turned slowly in a rhythm not of this world. Cracked towers leaned in ways that defied balance and runes floated in the air like drifting fireflies. Even shadows passed across high balconies.

And in the center of this strange, beautiful ruin stood Ro. The illusions stepped back in, one bowed before the burning robed magus, another lifted a blade, saluting the version of Tito, now dressed in deep crimson and glowing with elemental power.

The monstrous Ro lunged at this Tito but shattered into a flock of silver butterflies spiraling into the sky.

Another Ro took a lantern from the ground and held it high, casting light that sent shadows fleeing, shrinking into the corners of the twisted courtyard.

Each action blended soundlessly.

Ro was weaving a story, giving a glimpse into their mind. Their fears, their hopes. Who they could become.

The illusions faded as the courtyard dissolved.

The strange sky peeled away, replaced once more by trees, dust, sun, and silence.

Ro exhaled and bowed, slower this time.

A long moment passed.

Then Valeria said softly, "That was definitely not what I expected."

Ro looked up, "But good?"

Valeria gave a single nod.

"Exceptionally. I wish I had a better word for it."

Ro turned to the others, Tito especially.

"So?" they said, not hiding their pride.

Tito was still trying to process it all. That had been Ro's magic. It had been a dream told in wind and light and shadow.

"It was...," he started, then shook his head with a half laugh. "Ro, that was incredible."

Ro grinned, "Told you I had something."

CHAPTER 28

The clearing felt different now. Too real. Too still.

Just moments ago, they'd been standing in a place that shouldn't have existed, in a dream spun from light and memory, summoned by someone who, until a week ago, had only ever used the magic of words to get out of being caught. And yet there Ro stood, brushing imaginary dust from their sleeves with a theatrical bow, grinning like it was nothing.

They had made a world.

For all of Lyra's deadly elegance, for all of Thena's conceptual brilliance, and even Callyn's raw elemental poise, Ro had created something almost alive, something moving; and it hadn't just been clever, it had been deeply honest.

Callyn watched the space where Ro's illusion had been, lips slightly parted. There was no jealousy in her eyes, just quiet surprise. And maybe, somewhere behind it, a flicker of respect that Tito had come to detect.

Even Thena, composed as always, seemed awestruck though she tried to hide it behind crossed arms.

Tito looked back to his sibling.

Ro gave him a quick wink, as if to say, "No pressure."

His stomach twisted. *How do I follow that?*

He had spent the week running drills, lifting weights, and sparring until his bones screamed. He'd been told, over and over again, that he needed to strengthen his body before channeling.

That the elements within him were too unstable to handle casually. That if he reached too deep, they might reach back. And yet, here he was called and expected.

The boy with Eryon's mark.

The *Shardborne*.

Valeria's command came clean through his spiraling thoughts.

"Tito."

He straightened on instinct, heart thudding.

"I've considered several approaches," she said. "Your magic is not simple. You carry the four elements inside of you, no mere affinities; and your attunement was violent. Uncontrolled. Enough to damage the stone that marked you. A gradual approach may be of no help here,"

Tito nodded once.

The others were quiet now, eyes turning to him.

Valeria continued, "We don't have a standard for you, honestly. There isn't anything to particularly compare you to."

Tito exhaled slowly.

"So, I'm improvising."

His brow lifted, "That's comforting."

She allowed the smallest twitch of a smile.

"The best approximation I can offer is a similar scenario I found in the records concerning Eryon, when he was around your age. Before he was immortalized in stories, when he was still something the magi didn't understand."

Everyone was still. Valeria stood in the center of the flattened ring of stone, her stance square, her tone even. She raised a hand and pointed to Ro.

"You're constructing the illusion."

Ro raised an eyebrow, but stepped forward, already rolling their shoulders.

"You'll be shaping a trial," Valeria continued, "not a performance, this isn't about wonder. This is about pressure. Eryon's magic didn't respond to clarity, it responded to conflict. Tito's seemed to mirror that during our evaluation and Cordef's report of finding him."

Ro tilted their head, "So... we give him conflict?"

"We show him what happens when everything he values demands his power at once."

Ro went quiet, then slowly nodded.

"I can come up with some, but I won't turn away from any input."

Valeria looked to the others.

"Then let's build it."

Ro stepped toward the center of the group, shaking out their fingers as they began to draw the first tethers of illusion magic, anchoring threads. The real substance would come from the prompts. Everyone except Valeria came up to Ro with hushed voices, each adding their own input to their illusion test for Tito.

Ro turned back toward the illusion field, fingers flexing, and began to work. The threads of light returned, but now they pulled tighter, sharper, living sigils that sliced through the space and began to form scenes.

The clearing grew heavier with each breath before Valeria stepped forward once more. From her belt, she drew two thin bracers, metal gleaming with faint purple script.

Tito stiffened.

"Wait, what are those?"

Valeria's voice was calm.

"Power dampeners lightly tuned. They are typically used for magi that are on the opposing side of wars."

"I thought you said..."

"I did," she said. "Right now, your elements have the chance of responding in a cacophony. These will quiet the noise."

She held them out, but Tito didn't move.

She stepped closer.

"You'll still feel them, all of them, this will just help you pick out their voices." She paused. "They'll also protect the others, if something goes wrong."

Tito looked at her. She wasn't afraid, but she wasn't pretending there wasn't danger, either. He lifted his arms out. Valeria wasted no time as the bracers clicked into place.

Ro turned back, eyes glowing faintly now from the effort.

"It's ready," they said.

Tito stepped forward before a thick veil, a curtain to the complete unknown.

"Hope you didn't go easy on me just because I'm your brother."

Tito stepped through the veil. It didn't ripple, or shimmer, or distort like he'd expected from the previous illusion Ro cast. There was no edge, no sensation of crossing through some magical membrane. One moment he was in the clearing with the others, and the next, he was somewhere else entirely.

He was on a shattered street. Above him, the sky was smeared with smoke and fading gold. Around him, broken buildings bowed inward around him, some half consumed by fire, others overtaken by creeping moss and shattered roots. The air was thick with heat and the unmistakable scent of ash. Somewhere distant, water roared. Voices cried out, overlapping.

It was real.

His breath caught as he spun in place, heart pounding. To his left, flames curled around the crumbling shell of what might have once been a barracks. The structure groaned with each new flare of fire. And inside, Ro's voice, shrill with panic, cracked through the smoke.

"Tito! Tito help! I...I can't...I'm trapped!"

To his right, down a slope, a rush of water surged between jagged banks. A child flailed in the current, slipping beneath the surface, then breaking free again with a wail of breathless desperation.

Tito's stomach turned.

Behind him he heard a low rumble.

He turned to see a pile of broken rock and blackened timber, and beneath it, a shifting figure with an outstretched hand... Callyn.

"Please...please, I am still alive. I don't want to die h... here."

Tito staggered backward, his chest tight. It was too much. Too many sounds, too much light. Too much pain. His arms twitched at his sides, the bracers felt like they were buzzing.

For a moment, he forgot the illusion.

He was moving forward before he even thought to question it, toward Ro. Toward the fire. The heat rolled off the collapsed building in pulses, waves that pushed against his skin and clawed down his throat. Smoke bit at his eyes as he approached, and for a moment, he swore he could hear Ro coughing between the timbers, their voice hoarse and cracked.

"Tito, th...there's a beam. My leg, I... I think it broke my leg."

Tito's throat tightened.

"I'm here!" he shouted. "I'm here, I'm gonna..."

He stopped. It was real, too real. He could smell Ro's sweat beneath the smoke. Hear the pain in their voice, not just panic, but fear. He knew that voice. Knew how Ro sounded when they were bluffing, laughing, scheming. This wasn't that.

His shaking hands worsened. This was an illusion, he knew it was; but his heart didn't believe it. His body certainly didn't.

That's when the pressure began. It started behind his eyes, a pulse. Not painful. Just...immense. Like the air around him had depth now, like there was a texture to it. The smoke swirled unnaturally, twisting in slow eddies around his arms. The heat stopped biting. It was waiting. It was listening.

Tito closed his eyes to focus, tuned out the crackling of the fir and the painful groans from Ro. He reached something just below breath.

And he felt it. A tug. A river of energy, no longer chaotic but threaded, pulled tight beneath the skin of the world. A whisper that came from the west.

His eyes burned and his skin flushed as his breath caught on the smoke. But the wind...the wind moved. Not rushed but curved. Guided, just like Thena had, as if he had spoken a command not with words, but with grief.

The smoke cleared in a spiral.

Tito raised one hand, slowly, unsure if he was commanding or receiving. Flames curled inward and chased along the walls and pulled away from Ro's shape. Ash parted, embers coiled harmlessly around stone. A powerful gust tore through a window, hit a beam, and slammed it upright, creating a gap in the wreckage.

Light poured in. Ro's face looked toward him through the smoke. Tears tracked through the soot, Tito could see the moment their expression changed from fear to hope. He stepped forward again, heart thundering, and embraced his sibling. For a split second, he forgot it was all fake until the body in front of him dissipated out the window like the wind called it.

Tito had done it. It was an element he had called before, but it answered. It answered how he needed it, and it didn't take the building down with it.

He stood for a moment in the crumbled shell of the burning structure, the phantom heat fading as the illusion pulsed around him like a heart adjusting to a slower rhythm. Embers curled harmlessly at his feet now, drawn back into cinders. The air was lighter, the wind quiet again.

But the trial was not over.

A breath, then a voice, "Please! Help, I can't..."

He turned sharply back out the door, his success fueling his stride.

Down the slope, past a broken wall and under a stretch of ruined stone, the sound of rushing water swelled. The river curved sharply into view, frothing and too full, as if recent rain had swollen it beyond its banks. The current churned, a foam crusted beast tearing at the edges of the world, with a child at its center. Barely visible between the surging waves, flailing. Slipping under.

Tito's breath caught.

The child's features weren't sharp, but there was a shape to them, a familiar cut to the jaw, a slant of the eyes, like a memory seen through tears.

It's me, Tito thought. It was odd, seeing himself, but he was already moving down the incline. Boots scraped against broken stone. The roar of the river grew louder with each step. When he reached the edge, spray hit his face, cold and sharp. It didn't feel like an illusion.

The child slipped beneath the surface again, and something in Tito's chest snapped. He raised both arms, instinctively, desperately, remembering his last day in Ethyrae and the cold terror that tore through him.

The water listened, but unlike wind, it didn't simply respond to his request. It glided along his feeling, the tug of his terror forming pulled the water with it.

Too much. Too fast. The river heaved, a wall of liquid rose all at once like a great serpent snapping skyward. Spray burst outward in a massive plume, drenching the nearby rocks and knocking trees askew. The current broke apart in midair, suspended as though gravity had faltered.

The child was flung free from the water but hurled toward the shore. Behind them, the river cracked its banks. The illusion faltered, trying to adjust, but the banks collapsed. Stones were pulled loose, and an illusory structure nearby, a small footbridge Tito hadn't even seen, buckled and split as the displaced current ripped beneath it, cracking supports and sending shards flying across the stream.

Tito dropped to one knee, eyes wide, arms still raised. The child was safe, lying in the mud beside the stone bank, coughing, but the landscape was wrecked.

Tito staggered up from the slope, heart hammering, breath ragged. The water shifted like a rampaging beast. The terror inside him was stifled by fear now. The bracers buzzed again. A warning. He looked at his hands.

I did that. I...

And then the third voice called out.

"Please. It's too heavy."

It was distorted, wrong. Where before was Callyn's crisp voice, now it sounded like an unsure mix.

Right, Tito thought. *Just an illusion.*

Tito stood at the base of the slope, soaked from the river, skin still hot from fire. His limbs ached, his thoughts felt half drowned, and yet, the world had never felt more still. Except for the hand rising from the broken stone. It reached skyward, trembling.

"I... I can't move."

Beneath the fractured beams and laced roots, a shape was pinned. It was Callyn, with blood on her temple, her face smeared with dust. Her eyes were open but dazed, blinking rapidly as though fighting sleep.

"I think... my ribs.... something's wrong! It hurts to breathe!"

Tito's stomach lurched.

"Callyn! I'm coming, just stay awake!"

He dropped to one knee at the rubble's edge, hands moving instinctively to brace the larger stones. Then something else shifted, the voice beneath the rock changed.

"Tito! You can't leave me!"

It was still Callyn's voice, but the inflection was wrong. Too soft, too needy.

When he blinked, her face changed. The lips repeated the words half a second after the sound.

"Don't let me die under this."

Tito's spine stiffened. The face below flickered. It was Ro, then Valeria, then a stranger with eyes too dark and lips not moving at all. Then Tito himself.

And the voice deepened, layers folding over each other, the distortion crackling like rocks sliding over a canyon wall.

"Help me, help yourself. I am buried beneath it."

This time, he didn't recoil. He took a breath, deep and slow.

It's not real, he reminded himself.

Tito exhaled once and lowered himself beside the rubble. His fingers brushed the edge of a moss covered slab. He didn't reach for his power the way he had with water or open the door for assistance as he did with wind.

He simply listened as the earth spoke through an ancient pressure that ran beneath everything. He felt the stones under the stream, the roots wound around broken wood, the beam barely holding on above the flickering figure. He could feel how the weight distributed, how a single misplaced shift could bring it all crashing inward.

Beneath that, he felt patience. Earth did not rush, it did not leap to serve. It waited to be known. So, he let it know him.

Tito placed his full palm flat against the warm slab of rock. His heartbeat quieted as his breath found its rhythm. He closed his eyes and leaned in.

The stone responded.

He could feel the stress fractures spidering out across the rubble. The weight of one beam pressing against another, the mud beneath the pile still soft from the runoff of his earlier surge. He could feel which root would need to slide free first, which piece of timber could bear a moment of suspension. Which stone wanted to shift, and which would resist.

He didn't command the earth, he worked with it.

One hand moved, and a stone slid free, guided by a creak in the roots. Another breath, and he rolled a thick slab with his shoulder, using its weight to pivot a larger mass off to the side. Soil gave, then settled again. Not a single movement was wasted, not a single crack echoed. The figure beneath the rubble was still now. Its face no longer shifted or flickered.

It was his own face, and it was calm as it slowly left with the world around it.

CHAPTER 29

Tito couldn't believe his eyes as the illusion broke like mist in the sun.

There was no flash or burst, just a slow unraveling. The shape of the crumbling world dissolved around him with fading colors, like a great weight lifting from the air. The sky bled back into blue, trees realigned, and the stone beneath him grew lighter. Less ancient. Less loaded.

Then his knees buckled.

Tito didn't realize how much expending the elements takes, even in imaginary states.

Ro's illusion had been perfect, terrifyingly perfect.

He staggered forward a step and caught himself against the nearest boulder, still breathing hard. The bracers around his wrists were glowing faintly now, overcharged runes pulsed like they'd taken the full strain of a failing dam.

Only then did Tito realize the earth was wrong.

The clearing had changed.

Trees along the outer perimeter had been shorn at the base, their trunks folded and twisted. Crushed. Some had been lifted entirely by roots and dropped yards away like discarded matchsticks.

Near the far slope, stone formations rose from the ground like fingers. Miniature mountain ridges that hadn't existed an hour ago curled and spiraled upward in arcs. One boulder cracked in half.

Water trickled from its center like the mountain itself had begun to weep.

Farther out, where the ground sloped gently away toward the trees, the dirt was torn like claw marks had dragged through it. In the middle, a new stream had carved its way across the trail.

It wasn't wide, but it was flowing. Fresh, clear water winded around a curve in the land that hadn't existed this morning.

Tito just stared. No words came.

The rest of the group was watching him from across the battered space, standing just outside the ripple of destruction.

Even Valeria had stepped back.

Thena's lips were parted slightly, eyes flicking between the newly formed creek and the mountain-like ridges of stone.

Callyn looked stunned.

Ro was the only one who looked like they might laugh, their hands still on their hips, breathing a little hard from the energy it had taken to keep the illusion stable as long as they had.

Lyra hadn't moved toward her sword, but her stance said she might, if something unexpected happened.

Valeria stepped forward saying nothing at first, only surveying the field, her eyes scanning the trees, the crushed undergrowth, the warped topography. Her gaze landed on the creek last and stayed there.

Tito felt the silence like pressure in his ears. He opened his mouth again, then closed it.

"I didn't...," he began finally. "I didn't mean to do that."

Ro stepped forward now, a slow grin spreading across their face.

"You created a landscape." They swept a hand toward the stream. "You made a whole creek."

"That wasn't supposed to happen."

"Neither were the ridges," Thena added quietly. "Or the crushed trees."

Valeria's voice came finally.

"The bracers held. That's the frightening part."

Tito looked down at them. They were dulling now, the light fading, the runes nearly burned out.

Ro stepped up beside him, bumping him gently with an elbow.

"You thought I did a lot in a week?" they said.

Tito turned to look at them.

"I built a world," Ro said, "but you *bent* the world."

"Thank you," Tito said quietly. "That illusion..."

Ro shrugged, "I know you better than most. I just put your heart in a maze and let you walk through it."

Tito nodded, still partially staring at the damage.

"I don't know how to control it."

"No," said Valeria. "You don't. Not entirely yet, but we understand better what is in you."

She surveyed the scene one last time, her boots scuffed the dry edge of the newly formed stream. Her eyes paused briefly on the splintered trees, the warped terrain, and the faint glow of Tito's bracers still cooling on his wrists.

"And," she said, "the world mostly survived."

Ro gave a short laugh, still catching their breath, "And so did Tito."

Callyn was quiet, but her head turned toward the crushed trees behind them.

Even Lyra, who had said nothing for the past few minutes, let out a low breath like she'd been holding it the entire time.

"That was a good exercise," Valeria continued. "Better than I expected. You handled yourselves well, Ro especially, for crafting something of that complexity. And Tito," she paused, her eyes flicked toward him with something like reluctant approval, "you made choices and felt elements independently. That was huge."

Tito said nothing, he wasn't entirely sure he could.

Valeria gave them all a moment longer before straightening.

"Starting tomorrow, we continue our real task of scouting the perimeter of the barrier."

Callyn shifted, attentive now.

"We'll be walking a wide arc along the outer edges of the magical boundary," Valeria continued. "It spans several miles and is designed to shield Atheron and its surrounding routes. The job is simple...observe, record, and verify the barrier's consistency."

"What are we looking for?" Thena asked.

"Distortion, thinning, flickers in rune work. Anything that suggests instability. We're not authorized to make modifications, only to log our findings."

"And if we do find something unsafe?" Ro asked.

Valeria nodded toward Lyra.

"That's what the blade is for."

Lyra finally spoke, voice quiet but certain.

"If something breached the barrier, it won't get far."

The silence that followed was respectful, but Tito barely heard it. Words simply flowed around him like wind through tall grass. He was still standing where the trial had ended, just outside the new stream. The bracers on his arms had gone still, but he could feel a faint echo of everything they had tried to suppress, the residual hum of what had slipped through anyway. The wind that had ripped trees from the ground, following his desperate reach. The water he had pulled from a river he couldn't even see, that now carved a new path through the land like it had always belonged there. And the earth that had lifted for him like it had been waiting for someone to listen.

His stomach twisted. The power within had powerfully shaped the world around him. Even with the bracers. Even while restrained. He swallowed hard.

What happens when I'm not restrained?

Ro bumped shoulders with him again as they passed, eyes bright with pride but softened with concern.

"You okay?" they whispered.

Tito nodded but didn't answer because more than anything, the thing that echoed loudest in his chest wasn't the magic, it was what Ro had done. A perfect illusion...a perfect mirror of him. His fears, his guilt, his choices.

In one week, Ro had stepped into the depths of his heart and turned it into a stage, and he still couldn't figure out how they'd done it without flinching.

How do you know me that well?

He glanced at Ro again, but they were already turning toward the others, making some joke about needing a full meal and two naps before the next hike.

Tito just stood there, quiet, watching the stream he had made curl through the grass.

The next two days passed under wide skies and longer shadows. They rose with the sun and walked the line of the invisible, unbroken magic boundary stretching across the hills and hollows like an ancient promise the land had agreed to, even if reluctantly. Ro had described it once as a curtain stitched with old light and buried sigils, but to the naked eye, it looked like nothing. Just air, still and unchanged.

The first day was easy.

The land outside Atheron still held signs of life with rolling grasslands rippling in the breeze, old fences half swallowed by ivy, and long abandoned way posts marking roads that once saw traffic. A few sporadic homes, crumbling and empty, stood silent as tombstones. At some point, they passed what used to be a village but now was only a moss eaten well and a stone threshold with no door.

The terrain was changing. By midafternoon of the second day, the air began to shift into something dryer, thinner, with a faint chalky taste clinging to their breath. The trees grew sparse, the soil lost its loam, cracks spidered beneath the surface, widening as they drew closer to the canyon that Lyra had mentioned in her report.

There were no more homes, just grass giving way to wild country, like the land had started pushing back against human settlement. This was why they were sent, to scout the spaces no longer mapped. To confirm the barrier was holding even where no one was left to benefit from it.

Each day followed a rhythm. Mornings were for walking in long stretches of quiet observation, checking the shimmering runes partially buried in carved stones, or listening for the low hum of barrier anchors beneath their boots.

Midday brought some informal training which was practiced enough to build muscle and memory.

Valeria had Callyn run formation drills with Tito and Ro, swapping sparring partners between rest breaks.

Thena drilled fine control techniques into Ro until their illusions no longer flickered under pressure.

Lyra stayed apart for most of it, watching more than joining.

Tito practiced earth only, under Valeria's orders.

He didn't argue, he was still excited for the chance to unravel what had coiled inside him. His affinity for wind seemed better suited in large bursts, and water was what drove him to attunement. He was told fire was too destructive to be tested while unsure. All the elements felt too destructive in his hands; but again, he did not argue.

He focused on feeling the way soil crumbled under certain pressure, on the give of rock when coaxed rather than cracked. By the end of the second day, he learned how to sense depth beneath a surface before moving it, to know how much strain the earth would put on him for assisting in moving something from it.

Nights, however, brought a new rhythm of tension rather than movement. It began subtly.

Valeria stopped standing with her arms folded and started standing with her hand on the hilt of her short blade.

Lyra, who had once lounged near the edge of camp, began pacing at dusk in small silent loops like a wolf testing the perimeter.

They spoke little of it, but everyone noticed.

Sleep came slower, watches grew longer, and though no one said it out loud, each pair of eyes searched the dark just a little longer than the night before.

The fire burned low the fourth night. Its embers glowed like old stars across the darkened camp. They had made it to the high ridges just a few hours before dusk, stopping short of the canyon itself. The land dipped ahead, folding into deep shadows, so Valeria called an early halt rather than risk navigating unknown ground in the dark.

They would reach the canyon tomorrow; but for now, the group had spread out into soft rings around the campfire.

Ro and Thena were still debating the possible weave work in the barrier runes they'd spotted along the southern stretch.

Lyra sat silent, sharpening her blade with slow, steady motions.

Valeria was already checking the morning route on her map by low light, her silhouette quiet but alert.

Tito and Callyn found themselves on the edge of camp.

She was seated across from him, tending to her boots. The silence between them wasn't new. It had stretched out over the last two days like a cord neither of them had the nerve to pull. Still, Tito tried.

"We're almost there," he said quietly. "The canyon that Lyra reported. The vault. Nobody has mentioned more about it, but it would be cool seeing something we weren't supposed to even read."

Callyn gave a short nod but didn't look up, "Yeah."

Another silence.

He frowned slightly.

"You've been quiet."

She shrugged, "So have you."

"Back in the chambers," he said after a pause, "it felt like we were..."

"We're not in the barracks or the chambers," she interrupted.

Her voice was too quick, too sharp.

Tito sat up straighter.

"I didn't say we were. I'm just trying to..."

"Why?" she snapped, finally looking at him. "Why are you trying anything, Tito? This isn't home. It's not sparring or shared rations or pretending like none of this matters. Out here, people die. You want to be friends, but we're soldiers, and right now, we're scouts. This is real now."

Her voice cracked at the end just slightly, and then she was up brushing past him in the dark.

"I need air," she muttered, disappearing into the quiet between the trees.

Tito sat in stunned silence, heat burning in his cheeks. He didn't understand.

She'd been warm before. She'd helped him learn to brace his stances, offered him insight on sparring techniques, even laughed at his jokes. They'd eaten together nearly every night in the barracks. Now it was like a wall had gone up between them. He stared at the fire, trying to figure out what he had said wrong. A moment later, a shadow approached.

Valeria.

He hadn't heard her coming, but she stopped beside him without speaking. After a breath, she crouched beside the fire and nudged a fallen branch into the flame.

"I saw that," she said softly.

Tito didn't respond.

"She's not angry at you," Valeria continued. "She's angry at herself, maybe even the world."

"She didn't have to..."

"She did," Valeria cut in gently, "because she doesn't know how else to carry it."

Tito looked at Valeria and she sighed.

"Her brother died out here," she said. "Two years ago, a scouting mission just like this one. They were checking a village past the second anchor out near the basin. No signs of threat before a Bonecaller emerged from the nearby hills. Where there's one, there's many. It ambushed them."

Tito stiffened.

Bonecallers were whispered about even in stories in Ethyrae. They were creatures of marrow and spirit, said to use the bones of the dead to fuel their strength. They were said to be endless when attacking.

"She watched it happen," Valeria continued. "Managed to help hold the line with her magic until her group could escape, but it was too late. Her brother was already gone."

He looked down.

"I didn't know."

"Neither do most people," Valeria said. "She doesn't talk about it. I only learned from reading reports. She was offered bereavement leave but she removed herself from magi training entirely. I thought she was completely done with duty until she reenlisted under the Queen's Guard."

"Why are you telling me?"

"Because you looked like you needed to hear it."

Valeria stood, brushing her gloves clean.

"She's still learning how to be out here," she said, "same as you, just for different reasons."

She turned and walked back toward the firelight, her figure tall against the flicker of gold and shadow.

Tito awoke with a start, chest tight, hands gripping the bedroll like it might anchor him to something real.

He had been walking through fog...endless, never-ending fog. Voices called out to him, but every time he turned, he saw only statues. Stone figures with their faces...Ro, Callyn, and Lyra, frozen in a scream, reaching toward him. One cracked apart when he touched it and beneath, it wasn't stone at all. It was glass. His reflection stared back from beneath it, silent and wide-eyed, trapped inside.

He rubbed his face with both hands, trying to slow the pounding in his head. The camp was still, only the soft crackle of dying coals and the hush of wind brushing through the trees kept him tethered to the waking world.

He looked around slowly.

A single silhouette sat near the fire, back lit by the warm glow, shoulders straight, long braid pulled over one shoulder, the curve of her cheek visible in the faint light.

Callyn.

After a few seconds of hesitation, Tito stood quietly, wrapped his cloak tighter and walked over. She didn't flinch when he approached, just looked up and gave a small nod.

"Couldn't sleep?" she asked softly.

"Bad dream," he admitted, settling down beside her.

They sat like that for a while, staring at the glowing coals.

Then she let out a slow breath.

"About earlier..."

"You don't have to..."

"I do," she interrupted, glancing at him. "I snapped and it wasn't fair."

Tito was quiet a moment, then said, "Valeria told me what happened."

Callyn stiffened slightly but didn't pull away.

"I'm sorry," he added, "not just for bringing it up unknowingly, but for not asking about your family...about you."

She shook her head, brushing a loose strand of hair back behind her ear.

"There's nothing to apologize for. Not like you had much of a chance, given your week."

Tito hesitated, then looked over at her.

"I'm glad you told me, or... I'm glad she did."

A small smile tugged at the edge of her mouth.

"You always stumble your way through heavy things like that?"

"Only with grace," he said.

She let out a soft laugh.

Silence returned, but it wasn't the same as before. Then, she shifted, leaning her head tentatively onto his shoulder. Tito's breath caught, but only for a second.

"You know," he said, "I was convinced for a while that you were some kind of genius."

Callyn lifted her head slightly, "Excuse me?"

He grinned, "I mean, the way you talked about magic theory and formation drills, the people in Atheron, I figured you'd been secretly training since you were five. Some prodigy plucked from a tower with a crystal crown or something."

She blinked at him, deadpan, "Crystal crown?"

"I imagined it had wind runed points. Maybe a glowing gemstone or..."

She slapped his shoulder lightly, letting her head fall back with a quiet laugh.

"You wore a metaphorical crown. It was beautiful."

"I wore borrowed boots and got kicked in the ribs my first day in the barracks."

"Majestic," Tito said. "Truly royal behavior."

Callyn shook her head lightly against his shoulder, a soft laugh warmed the space between them.

"Honestly," she murmured, "I probably looked about as pathetic as you did after fainting when you saw me naked."

Tito choked.

"I didn't faint...not exactly."

"Oh, you absolutely did," she said, sitting up just enough to glance at him, one eyebrow raised. "I turned around, and you were just laid out in the doorway like someone had smacked you with a staff right in your temple."

"I was exhausted!"

"Sure," she said, smiling, "from resisting temptation."

"Callyn..."

"I mean, don't get me wrong," she added with glinting eyes, "it was flattering but really, you couldn't have lasted two more seconds?"

Tito groaned, dragging a hand down his face.

"You said not to bring that up again."

She leaned back into him, voice softer now, but still carrying that mischievous edge.

"I changed my mind."

He blinked, caught off guard by the shift in tone.

"I'm not going to let you forget it," she said gently, "not until you find a way to make it up to me."

Tito glanced sideways, unsure whether to laugh or apologize again. "What would even count as making that up?"

"That's your problem to solve," she replied. Her smile was just barely visible in the firelight.

She didn't pull away again.

CHAPTER 30

The fire had burned low overnight, now reduced to ashen rings. The faint scent of smoke drifted through camp, but the tension that had clung to Tito like a second skin for the past two days was gone.

The morning sun rose into a sky scraped clean of clouds. There was a crispness to the air as the group stirred, Tito was impressed with how quickly the temperature could change just a few days' walk outside of Atheron.

He and Callyn moved together again with the kind of ease they'd shared back in the barracks. Once again, they fell into the silent rhythm of nudging elbows during breakfast and sharing glances that filled the space where words used to be. She bumped his arm when he passed her rations, he stole half her flatbread in revenge. When she slipped while tightening her boot strap, he caught her elbow without thinking.

Ro noticed within five minutes.

"Oh," they said, stretching with exaggerated slowness as they watched Tito and Callyn mess around near the packs. "*Oooohhh*, look who found his courage again."

Tito looked up.

"What?"

Ro smirked, "Nothing, just admiring the restoration of a battlefield alliance, strategic proximity, and mutual gear inspection. Excellent teamwork."

"I'm going to throw your sketchbook into the canyon," Tito muttered.

Callyn didn't even look up, "Only if I don't get to it first."

Ro's grin widened as they turned to Thena.

"Look at them, back to the banter before we left. The smoldering awkwardness has evolved into flirt until you faint levels."

"Someone did faint, I recall," Thena said dryly.

"Never proven," Tito called, already moving to help Valeria break camp.

Ro gave a triumphant little nod, "Case and point."

By the time they packed up and shouldered their supplies the group's rhythm had returned. They moved as a unit again. Tito swore they were more focused and cohesive than they had been since leaving the Citadel.

The land sloped steadily downward as they resumed their trek. By midday, the lack of trees had thinned even further to spindly tufts of dry brush. Grass became patchy or nonexistent. The ground crunched beneath their boots in a different way now with less spring and more breakage.

Valeria raised her hand near a jagged ledge.

"Canyon's just beyond the ridge," she said.

Lyra stepped forward, leading them to a stone partially buried in the slope.

"This is where I left the marker," she said, brushing aside a layer of windblown dust.

A thin line of chalk arced around a rune scratched into the surface, simple but clear.

Ro approached, crouching beside the mark.

"It's faint," they murmured. "You can tell it's been sitting for a few weeks. The wind has stripped some of the chalk away, but it's untouched."

"That's good," Valeria said.

"Means no one's crossed it since I made it," Lyra confirmed. "Nothing came out or went in, at least from this side."

The descent began with a narrow path cut into the side of the canyon wall. Loose stones skittered underfoot, and dry wind howled between rock faces like something alive, slipping through cracks that hadn't been disturbed in ages.

They moved in a single file line with Lyra leading this time.

Valeria, seemingly unbothered by the relinquishing of authority, followed close behind, though her hand hovered near the hilt of her sword.

Tito came next, with Callyn just behind him while Ro and Thena brought up the rear.

They exchanged whispered thoughts about the layout of the ridge, noting faults in the stone that looked too symmetrical to be natural.

The deeper they went, though, the less it felt like just a canyon.

At first, it was the narrowing of the path, how the walls pulled in like arms folding across a chest. Then the texture of the stone itself began to change, the color deepening to a matte gray. Dust became soot. Patches of dried moss clung in strange formations like circles, spirals and lines.

"They're runes," Ro muttered, trailing a hand just above one of the symbols etched faintly into the rock.

"Old ones," Thena added. "I can't read them, but they're not natural."

Valeria stopped suddenly.

Lyra stepped beside her, pointing downward along the slope.

"There," she said, "that's where I saw it."

The path widened near a cliffed landing where two massive rocks had split centuries ago, revealing a cleft in the canyon floor. Between them, shrouded in shadow, a structure emerged low and sloped, built into the earth itself. It wasn't tall or grand, but it was intentionally built, impressive in its own right.

The vault.

Tito couldn't feel his face. Even from here, he could feel the vault pressing outward with a kind of resistance. Like the stone didn't want to be found.

Ro stepped forward, eyes wide.

"That's not a shelter."

"No," Lyra said, "it's not."

"Doors?" Callyn asked.

"Sealed when I came before," Lyra replied. "Partially buried under that overhang there, but I didn't get closer. I wasn't sure what it was."

"And now?" Valeria asked.

Lyra exhaled, "Now the Magi say they're sure it's worth checking."

Valeria turned to the group.

"No one goes in yet," she said. "We approach slowly. Ro and Thena will check the runes first. Then we'll gauge for pressure, temperature, and light. I want to know if this place is warded, cursed, or breathing before we set foot inside."

The party was in agreement, but Tito didn't move right away. Something in the stone was humming. His brow furrowed, and he stepped forward slightly, eyes locked on the stone threshold of the vault.

"Do you hear that?" he asked.

Ro looked at him, "Hear what?"

"That sound. Like... a hum. Low. It's coming from inside." He pointed toward the cleft in the earth. "It's not loud but, it's there."

Thena turned slightly, brow creased.

"I don't hear anything."

Valeria's eyes narrowed, and she stepped toward him, slow and calculating.

"Describe it."

"It's like...," he listened closely, "like stone rubbing on stone, but it's constant. Like something shifting beneath the ground...but rhythmic. Almost like..."

"A voice?" Valeria asked, eyes locked on his face.

"No," he said slowly. "Not words. *Presence.* Like it knows we are here."

Valeria didn't move for a long moment. Then, something shifted. Not in the vault, but something behind them.

They heard a faint crunch of gravel higher up the slope, and everyone stilled.

Valeria's head snapped up, eyes cutting toward the narrowing ridge they'd descended earlier. Her hand moved to her blade in a fluid, practiced motion.

Lyra was already moving before the others even processed it, her posture snapping upright like a wolf catching blood on the wind.

Callyn drew closer to the edge, her body lowering instinctively.

Another sound, heavier this time. A scrape, then a thud. Footsteps.

Valeria's voice cut sharp and clean, "Initiates, into the rocks. *Now.*"

Tito barely had time to move before Ro grabbed his sleeve and pulled. They ducked behind the sloped edge of the boulder beside the vault's mouth, pressing into the shadows where the sun hadn't yet reached.

Thena followed close behind, silent, her breath low.

Callyn stayed frozen in her spot a moment longer before tucking herself behind Thena, hand on the dagger at her belt.

Valeria nodded once, and Lyra moved.

She ascended the slope at an angle, using the broken path and narrow switchbacks to climb without exposing herself directly. Her blade wasn't drawn, but her stance was ready, shoulders low, knees coiled, eyes scanning every ridge above.

Tito crouched lower. His heart pounded in his ears. Beneath the rush of adrenaline, the hum remained, gentle and insistent, like a voice underwater, whispering only to him. He pressed his back to the stone and waited.

Lyra moved like a shadow drawn thin across the canyon wall with silent boots and low shoulders, one hand trailing the edge of the stone for balance as she slipped through a gap in the rock and disappeared from view.

A few moments passed and Ro leaned closer, breath barely a whisper. "Should we...?"

Valeria's hand snapped up, two fingers raised, palm out.

Silence.

Ro swallowed whatever words had been forming, they all held still. Even the canyon seemed to pause.

Then came a rush of wind, sharp and sudden, curling down the path above them. Tito tensed, eyes darting up toward the cliff edge.

No one moved as the wind died. A few more heartbeats passed, each stretched long enough to feel like rope unwinding. Then, footsteps again.

Lyra reappeared at the ridge upon the edge of the path. She didn't speak until she reached Valeria, her voice low and tight.

"It's not nothing."

Valeria stepped forward, "Report."

"My scout rune," Lyra said, "was intact when we arrived. I placed it right where the ridge curves, just above the descent." She paused, then added, "I just checked it again. It's been disturbed."

Callyn frowned.

"So, something followed us down?"

Lyra's grim countenance said it all.

Ro shifted closer.

"But you didn't see anything?"

Lyra's jaw flexed.

"No. I backtracked, climbed the ridge. Nothing on the slope. I didn't see any footprints, but that isn't saying much out here."

Valeria's expression darkened.

Lyra looked toward the vault.

"There's more."

She pointed toward the sloping path that disappeared into the canyon floor.

"I saw something further ahead. A shape. Just a glimpse of a form."

"What kind of shape?" Valeria asked.

"The wrong kind," Lyra said flatly. "Tall. Too tall. It moved like it wasn't part of this world. And it wasn't hiding, it was just... waiting."

Ro's voice came soft, "So, we've got maybe something behind us and for sure something ahead. A lot of somethings going on here."

Lyra didn't turn.

"I think the thing I saw ahead is worse."

Tito's heart sank into a cold pit.

"What is it?" he asked.

Lyra turned back to answer, but the air cracked open.

The sound of splintered bone under pressure, shrill and guttural, a rising crescendo of agony that had no throat behind it.

Tito flinched, his instincts flooding with pressure and memory and fire.

The others turned in unison.

At the ridge above, less than twenty feet up the path they had descended, something stepped into view, rising from a shadow like it had been carved from the stone itself.

It moved with grace, but its shape was anything but graceful. Its limbs were too long, uneven and knotted in places where no joints should exist. Its arms hung low, ending in gnarled, bony claws, pale and chipped like old ivory. From the elbows down, strips of dark flesh were wrapped in sinew and bark, and bones were braided into its skin like decorations. Its torso was twisted, a corkscrewed mockery of human anatomy. Ribs protruded through stretched skin, not from inside, but stitched on, lashed across its chest like armor.

The bones weren't its own. They were worn.

The head was the worst of all, for there was no face. Only a bleached skull, smooth and expressionless, affixed like a mask. It didn't sit cleanly atop the neck and twitched now and then as if adjusting to an invisible weight.

Where eyes should have been, there was only hollow emptiness. And from those hollows, a low keening began to echo a sound that vibrated in the bones, in the teeth...in the soul.

Around its feet, the wind spun with not dust or leaves, but bones. Tiny, clicking bones.

Ro exhaled sharply beside Tito, "That's..."

"Bonecaller!" Valeria's voice rang out, sword already in hand. "Form up!"

The Bonecaller didn't charge. Two steps forward, and its body shifted like a marionette dragged by unseen strings, head twitching, shoulders crackling, claws curling inward like it was savoring the moment before the cut.

It shrieked again, a sound like the sky fracturing down the middle.

Lyra surged forward already in motion, one hand drawing her blade, the other flaring an invitation to the wind. Her boots kicked up a spray of dust as she launched herself across the slope, closing the distance between her and the creature with terrifying speed.

The Bonecaller didn't recoil. It seemed like it welcomed her.

She met the strike before it could finish its arc, ducking beneath its reaching claws and slamming her blade into its side, driving through brittle bone plating and the slack ropes of meat and bark that twisted across its ribs. A wet sound rang through the canyon. The blade should've sliced through, but instead, it tore. Lyra skidded out of range and pivoted. The creature twisted toward her, that suspended skull tracking her with jerking, birdlike movements. Beneath the mask, its body shuddered, the flesh slithered.

Where her blade had struck, strands of sinew and ligament began to pull back together, winding like muscle over cracked bone, knitting through animated threads of gristle.

"Gods," Ro whispered behind Tito.

The Bonecaller reached toward Lyra again, claws dragging through the stone wall like chalk. The wind hissed around its feet, the swirling tide of loose bones clicking louder now, orbiting faster.

"Behind me!" Valeria's voice cracked through the growing panic. "Get behind me, now! Back up the slope!"

The group began to move, but only two steps into the retreat, Callyn gasped, staring up the ridge.

Tito turned.

There were more. At the slope's summit, three new figures stood, staring as if they'd been waiting.

"We're boxed in," Thena whispered.

Ro's voice shook, "They waited. They were watching us the whole time."

"Fall back to the vault!" Valeria shouted, voice fierce and low, pulling in magic now as she raised her sword.

Callyn hadn't moved. She stared up at the ridge, eyes wide. Her weapon hung at her side, fingers white-knuckled.

"Callyn..." Tito started.

The Bonecallers above began to descend.

Tito made his choice. He tore from the group and rushed to her, grabbing her shoulder, pulling her back just in time as a chunk of stone exploded beside them from a stray blast of force.

"Move!" he shouted. "Callyn, we have to move!"

She blinked once, her breath catching, and finally began to step back. They ducked behind the ridge, stumbling toward the vault wall. Tito turned toward the structure, and something immediately flared. A symbol, carved into the face of the vault. At first, it was just an etching, weathered, easy to miss. Then it pulsed, ever so lightly.

Tito's heart stopped.

It was the same mark that burned along his forearm, the same pattern the Runestone etched into him.

CHAPTER 31

The ridge exploded into motion.

Valeria surged toward the slope, feet barely touching the ground, her blade flashing with etched runes as she leapt upward. The edge of her cloak snapped like a banner, her sword caught the sun as she moved faster than Tito had ever seen her, not like a soldier, but like a force of will.

The Bonecallers atop the ridge hissed in unison, the sound less a breath than a chorus of scraping stone. One stepped to meet her, but Valeria was already there, blade arcing in a brutal crescent that caught it beneath the ribs. The creature staggered, and the others shifted in response.

Below, the first Bonecaller lunged.

Lyra caught it mid-motion, steel met sinew in a thunderclap of magic and bone. She twisted under its reaching claws, slamming her shoulder into its chest as she drove her enchanted dagger into a gap between the plates across its twisted neck. A gout of dark fluid sprayed sideways, but the creature didn't fall. It convulsed, muscle writhing like rope, and snapped its jaws in her direction.

It was all happening too fast. Tito stood frozen beside the vault, breath fogging as the symbol pulsed once more, glowing faintly. Another voice pulled him out of the trance.

"Tito!"

He turned immediately. It was Callyn. She was crouched behind a rock just feet away, Ro beside her, and Thena beside him. Tito ran to them, heart hammering.

"You okay?" he said, dropping to his knees.

Callyn nodded, still shaking, her face pale. "I'm...yes. I just didn't expect to see them again."

Tito reached out, steadying her shoulder.

"You're not alone this time."

Then a shout cracked through the chaos.

"Ro! Thena!" Valeria's voice rang out, sharp and commanding from up the slope.

They looked toward her.

One Bonecaller lay in ruin at her feet; the rest circled her, keeping their distance. They turned toward her as she stood partway up the incline, a streak of blood across her bracer. One Bonecaller lay crumpled and twitching at her feet, while two more circled like vultures just beyond her.

"Assist me! Use your distance, keep them distracted!"

Ro didn't hesitate. They spun on their heels, hands already crackling with violet light.

"Let's go!" they roared.

Thena was right behind them, wind lacing around her limbs as she launched up the slope.

Together they flanked wide, Ro darting up a lower path while Thena arced left, climbing with smooth steps like she'd trained for this exact terrain.

From below, Tito could see Ro lift one hand high. With a twist of their fingers, a shimmer rippled outward. Illusions danced forward, flickering copies of Valeria herself, charging toward the Bonecallers with blades drawn. It wasn't enough to fool them for long, but it was enough.

One Bonecaller lunged for a phantom, leaving its back exposed. Valeria didn't waste the moment. She turned into it, blade arcing in a vicious downward slash, and drove it into the thing's spine, where flesh gave way with a wet, snapping crunch. The creature shrieked, limbs spasming, and Valeria tore the blade free with a short exhale.

Above her, Thena reached the ridge and released a torrent of wind, blasting the other Bonecaller back just as it reached for Valeria's side. Tito watched all of it as the others held the line, the battle churning around the rim of this cursed canyon.

The Bonecaller Lyra wounded was still fighting with unholy speed, lashing at her with claws that extended midswing, sinew stretching like wet rope. She ducked one blow, but another grazed her side, her padded armor taking the worst of it, but not all. Then, two more Bonecallers emerged from the canyon's far end, dragging themselves up the stone.

No.

They rose behind Lyra like shadows given flesh, bone fragments swirling at their feet. Tito stood before he realized it.

"Let me help!" he shouted, already stepping away from the vault.

Valeria didn't turn, but her voice cracked out like a lash across stone.

"No! Hold position!"

"I can...!"

"You'll die, or get one of us hurt," she snapped, slicing through another Bonecaller that collapsed twitching at her feet, only for another to crash down from the slope above, catching her sword arm as it landed.

She grunted, twisted her body to absorb the hit, but her stance broke. Her knee buckled, the blow knocked her down to one elbow, her blade clattering nearby.

Tito took a step forward then turned to Callyn.

She was still against the rock, eyes wide. Her breath was sharp and uneven, her sword in her hand but unmoving.

Tito had never seen her not in control.

"Callyn," he breathed, "I need you."

Her eyes locked on his. There was fear there, real fear. Not of the Bonecallers. Of failing again. Of seeing someone else die while she couldn't save them.

"Please!"

A scream echoed from above. One of the Bonecallers struck Valeria hard across the ribs, and she hit the ground with a thud that shook the slope. Her sword skidded out of reach.

"Valeria!" Ro cried from the ledge above.

Tito turned back to the chaos.

Ro was losing illusions faster than they could cast them.

Thena's wind faltered for half a heartbeat before rising again, and Lyra was alone, now fending off three Bonecallers at once with only grit and footwork keeping her alive.

Tito's fists clenched. He didn't think...didn't ask.

He reached down, pressed his hand flat to the canyon floor, and pulled.

The earth answered.

The ground cracked beneath the Bonecallers, a jagged spike of stone ripping upward in a violent eruption that sent two of them reeling back from Valeria in a spray of bone fragments and dust. They screeched in fury, their skeletal masks twisting in unnatural angles, but the hit had landed hard.

Valeria rolled, gasping, reaching for her blade.

"Tito!" she roared, her voice more pain than command. "I told you to hold! You don't break command in the field, especially now!"

She tried to stand, but another Bonecaller lashed out, claws raking across her pauldron. She cried out and dropped to one knee again.

Ro saw it from the ridge and immediately slid down the slope, casting illusion decoys as they descended.

"Valeria!"

They reached her side in seconds, arms up, shielding her with flickers of light that danced like flame, pulling attention as Valeria gritted her teeth and forced herself upright.

At the canyon's base, Callyn flinched at the scream. Her eyes flicked from Valeria who was bleeding, to Tito standing with his arm still half-glowing from the stone's response. And something broke inside her, Tito saw the moment it did.

She surged forward, blade drawn, sprinting toward the slope. The Bonecallers hadn't descended further yet, blocked by the fragments of earth Tito called, but they stood like pale sentinels above, blocking any chance of retreat.

"Ro's with her!" Tito shouted, but she didn't slow.

"That's not enough!" she yelled back.

Then she was gone, charging up to help Valeria as Ro held the line, illusions flashing, wind kicking up dust behind them.

Tito turned and noticed Lyra.

She was staggering now, her cloak torn, blood darkening one shoulder. One Bonecaller swung too close, carving through the air with a shriek. She blocked it with the flat of her blade...just barely.

Tito raised his hand, calling again to the earth, but he hesitated. The symbol on the vault behind him blazed, brighter than before. Not loud, not violent. Insistent. Like a thread pulled tight in his chest. Calling...

Calling.

Tito's fingers trembled where they hovered above the earth, still humming from the last strike. He looked toward Valeria struggling to her feet as Callyn reached her side. Then he noticed the spike he'd summoned had been too close. He could've hit her. One breath off, and it wouldn't have been bone that cracked, it would've been armor.

He looked to Lyra, still dueling three Bonecallers, her footing staggered, her shoulder slick with blood. He wanted to help, he ached to help; but his power...he didn't know how to form it perfectly to what he needed. Not here, not in this chaos. Not without risking everything. Behind him the rune burned like an ember in the vault's stone face, pulsing with familiarity.

Tito turned. His boots scraped against the rock as he stepped to the face of the vault. The air around it was still and unnatural. The battle faded behind him into a muffle, like sound had thickened, slowed, drawn inward.

His hand rose on instinct as he placed his palm to the rune...and the world exploded. Not outward...inward. A flood of raw, ancient power surged into him, blinding and absolute. Not like fire. Not like earth or water or wind. Like the land itself had memory, and he had touched it.

His body arched, as his breath left him in a ragged gasp. He couldn't see the canyon anymore, couldn't feel the stone beneath his feet. Only the weight of history was felt, of magic layered in stone and sealed behind time. Runes blazed across his mind's eye shifting, curling, reshaping themselves into pieces that fit into him, like keys into a lock long rusted.

He remembered things he had never known before. A vault buried by Magi long before he was born, sealed against what it contained. Or protected. Or preserved. And through it all, the mark on his arm seared with radiant light. Not with pain or fury, but recognition.

And then silence.

CHAPTER 32

Tito hit the ground hard.

Or at least, he thought he did. The stone beneath him was gone. The canyon, the screaming, the Bonecallers. The blood. Gone.

He opened his eyes to a sky cracked with light. Long, glowing veins stretched across a horizon of shifting color, like the world itself had been split open, and the marrow inside was burning with memory.

He lay on a field of stone that pulsed with life. The ground was breathing. And beneath his palms, he felt it not as warmth, but as remembrance. It was old, echoing through layers of time, earth and ash.

Ahead, mountains rose and fell in slow, impossible motion, like they too were caught in a long exhale. Rivers reversed and unraveled. Trees grew upward in seconds and crumbled to dust just as fast. Everything was unfolding and folding again, a world unstuck.

Then came the voice, low and deep. It sounded like stone breaking open underwater, smooth and ancient.

"The earth remembers."

The world rippled at the sound.

Tito tried to stand, but his body sank into the stone, like he was being welcomed.

"And so, now, will you."

The sky shifted above him not into stars, but into runes. Massive, brilliant, living runes etched into the very fabric of the sky. They drifted like constellations but moved with intention. They spun slowly, orbiting each other like moons, lines curling and intersecting, forming new shapes, new meanings, before folding back into the void like the language of gods being spoken in slow motion.

They were watching him.

Each one radiated heat, cold, and memory.

One passed overhead and filled him with the feeling of being buried under centuries, another with the sensation of a heart breaking, another like the wind holding its breath before a storm. He didn't understand them with his mind, he understood them with something older than thought.

Each shape spoke a single truth.

Protection.

Sealing.

Burden.

And then a fourth, bleeding rune rotated into place. Its lines dripped with molten light, curling like iron being bent against its will as it locked into place among the others.

The firmament above fractured.

A long, jagged, glowing red crack split the horizon, as if the sky was only a lid on a fire.

Through the crack came a surge of that fire, crawling across the land like a sickness. It consumed with deliberate hunger, devouring rivers until they boiled into mist, turning trees into ash before their leaves hit the ground. Mountains cracked and melted in its path.

And still it came closer and closer, until it reached the edge of the stone where Tito stood. Then it stopped because of a single rune that burned across the ground like a scar.

His rune. The mark on his arm.

The seal on the vault.

The fire reeled back, like a snake hissing.

Tito stepped forward, transfixed, his breath catching as the rune before him flared, echoing the lines etched into his skin.

And then came the voice again, woven into the bones of the world itself. It didn't echo, it settled, like an anchor against the ground.

"You were not born for war..."

The fire beyond the line pulsed.

"...you were born after it. Made of its ash."

Tito's hands clenched. The earth at his feet rose and fell in slow rhythm, like it was breathing, helping the voice speak.

"This place remembers what others have chosen to forget."

Around him, stone figures began to rise from the ground, but in movement. A woman weeping beside a vault door. A child with a burned arm, carried by a magus wearing a broken crown. A soldier running toward the flame, knowing he would not return. All of them made from sand and ash, their faces etched in suffering; and one by one, they turned to look at him.

"The seal. The sacrifice. The price."

The fire beyond the rune twisted, rising like a storm caught in slow motion. It coiled into a flickering, shifting figure. Not man, not an elemental, but something in between. It stepped forward from the fire, skin blazing, body haloed in wind and ember. Its face took form. Tito's face, only older, tired and torn, burned by everything he had not yet lived through.

And then the voice spoke one last time.

"The vaults were never meant to be opened. But you..."

The figure raised its hand, his hand, and pointed.

"You were always meant to try."

The sky fractured again as the earth cracked beneath his feet. The runes spun into chaos. The fire surged forward and the world... shattered.

L ight came back in blinks.
 Not warm or kind.

It was cold, raw, flickering through Tito's lashes as he drifted up from whatever place he had fallen into. A hand gripped his shoulder.

"Come on," someone whispered. "Come on, Tito. You're back. Stay with me, please. It can't be you too."

Ro.

Tito's vision swam, the canyon above like torn parchment in the sky. His body felt wrong, like his limbs weren't his, like something inside him had been cracked open and filled with fire and stone and too much memory.

His head lolled. To his left, he saw Thena.

She was dragging a limp figure across the dirt, a woman with a single braid sliding out behind her, blood across the side of her face.

Tito tried to call out, but no sound came. His anguish threw his head right.

He saw a woman kneeling in the dust. Their thick armor was shattered, shoulders hunched as if the weight of the sky had broken across her spine. Blood soaked her side, more than anyone should be able to lose. Her gauntlet clawed at the dirt, but her other hand...

Her other *arm* was gone. She was weeping. Someone lay across her lap, shadowed.

Ro gripped Tito harder, trying to lift him.

"Don't look," they murmured. "Just stay awake. Help's here, you're okay. You're okay."

And then...

A figure moved between the Bonecallers. Not running. Fighting.

A man, tall and cloaked in dust and rune worn armor, sliced through the enemy with a staff carved in white stone, its edge ringing like crystal and thunder combined. His hair, white and unkempt, whipped as he moved. His face was carved from grief and fury.

The Bonecallers flinched from him.

He turned toward Tito and Ro not with panic, but command.

"Inside!" he barked, his voice like stone grinding open.

Ro pulled harder.

The armored woman didn't move, not until the man stepped between her and the next Bonecaller and hurled a storm of arcane fire that shattered the creature into smoking shards.

Then he looked at Tito with a deep, ancient familiarity, and Tito met his gaze, catching his eyes even from here. Mismatched, one a burning orange and one an icy white. The man who wept beside Eryon as he died.

Uldris.

And then, Tito's strength broke as the air tunneled around him. His vision folded inward, black, as the ground met him.

ABOUT THE AUTHOR

URRIAH WRIGHT

Urriah Wright is an imaginative storyteller from North Carolina, where he shares a vibrant life with his wife, Stephany Gutierrez, and their lively green-wing macaw, Aolani, who often adds a dash of inspiration to his writing sessions.

Urriah is currently crafting the second book in the *Shattered Bloodline* series, an epic tale that sets the stage for many more stories to come. With a passion for building intricate worlds and unforgettable characters, Urriah is just getting started on his journey as an author.